ZORBA'S TAVERNA

THE TROUBLE & WITH GOATS MAYORS

PETER BARBER

SCAN THE QR CODE FOR MORE
INFORMATION ABOUT
PETER BARBER AND HIS BOOKS.

BOOKS BY PETER BARBER

THE ZORBA'S TAVERNA SERIES:

Zorba's Parthenon: A Taverna by the Sea

THE PARTHENON SERIES:

A Parthenon on our Roof

A Parthenon in Pefki

The Parthenon Paradox

THE MUSINGS SERIES:

Musings from a Greek Village

Musings from a Pandemic

CONTENTS

ZORBA'S TAVERNA

THE TROUBLE & WITH GOATS MAYORS

PETER BARBER

INTRODUCTION

Dramatis Personae (and One Goat)

Arefresher for new readers, and a tribute for old ones. As the sun sets over Telios and the whispers of the lemon grove curl into the night, much has changed at our little taverna by the sea since we first pulled up a wobbly chair in *Zorba's Parthenon*. We've reopened shuttered doors, hosted more crises than weddings, burned things both intentional and unintentional, and, somehow, served lunch.

What follows is a completely accurate, utterly subjective list of the usual suspects who populate this village of well-meaning madness. They are poised (whether they know it or not) for new adventures in *Zorba's Taverna: The Trouble with Goats and Mayors.*

Alex – The undisputed queen of chaos and the solar system around which all village drama orbits. When Alex enters the taverna, conversations stop, wine glasses pause mid-air, and even the goat takes a respectful step back. Armed with charm, sunglasses that double as weapons, and a rolling pin that is only occasionally metaphorical, she is the spark behind every rebellion, reconciliation, and emergency menu redesign. Alex doesn't only believe anything is possible; she announces it like a royal decree, repeats it until it becomes prophecy, and then adds oregano until it tastes like destiny.

Peter (me) – Narrator, husband, reluctant participant, and note-taker of nonsense. Goal: to observe the village from a safe distance with a glass of wine in hand. Instead, he finds himself stuck in philosophical debates with fishermen, chased down the road by goats with a grudge, press-ganged into hauling chairs for weddings, and forced to rewrite the menu at midnight because someone decided "fish of the day" wasn't actually a fish. He writes it all down so nobody can later claim it was exaggerated. (It wasn't. If anything, he leaves out the worst bits.)

Mary – The taverna's front-of-house hurricane. As beautiful as she is blunt, she once turned down a marriage proposal that came with a penthouse apartment because it clashed with her Thursday shift. She moves like a woman who owns the ground she walks on, knows every order before it's spoken, and can deliver a tray of *saganaki* while dismantling a man's ego with a single eyebrow.

Theodora – Mary's mother, and culinary high priestess of the kitchen. She doesn't shout – she *radiates expectation*. Her food is divine, her standards terrifying, and her opinions on parsley non-negotiable. Soft only for George, and only if he brings her cheese and keeps quiet.

George – Theodora's husband, cheesemaker, and the human embodiment of "it'll be fine". He speaks rarely, but when he does, entire conversations pause to listen. He moves at a pace that makes glaciers look rushed, yet somehow always gets things done, usually before anyone notices. He creates dairy miracles in a shed that smells faintly of eternity and oregano, and he knows where everything is: the spare keys, the missing corkscrew, the goat's dignity after last week's incident… George is never confused. He's waiting for the rest of us to stop panicking and catch up.

Spiros – Philosopher-bench-dweller. Nobody re-members what Spiros did before retiring, including Spiros. He holds court from his bench like a sceptical oracle, offering wisdom disguised as insult and commentary steeped in cigarette smoke. Occasionally confused for being in charge, which he discourages by remaining absolutely still.

Zorba – The taverna's founder; retired; forever lurking. He returned for one dramatic week of kitchen warfare that became legend, a week in which no tourist dared ask for ketchup twice. His presence is still felt in the menu, in the walls, and in the occasional scent of grilled octopus and fear.

Claude – Artist, idealist, and professional hazard to logistics. Claude believes in beauty, truth, and creative expression, especially during peak service. His ideas are always "only one detail away from brilliance", which is how we ended up with an indoor kite festival during lunch. We still haven't recovered the *spanakopita*.

Maria – The village's walking newspaper. She knows everything, even things that haven't happened yet. Her gossip sheets – *The Telios Tribune* – are read religiously by locals, tourists, and the occasional tax inspector. She sees all, hears all, and reports most.

Dimitri – Fisherman, philosopher, and unintentional agent of chaos. He supplies the fish, brews the *tsipouro*, and frequently causes existential confusion. He once accidentally invented a new religion while trying to explain how octopus works. Will cook if left unsupervised, which we've learned to avoid.

Eleni – Bureaucracy-tamer, form-wrangler, and keeper of the sacred stamp. She understands the system, fears no office, and has reduced grown men to tears with her mastery of paperwork. If it needs approval, Eleni already has it – and a backup.

Father Evangelos – Village priest and part-time therapist. He blesses livestock, pastries, and occasionally the internet. Known for his compassion, confusion, and gentle attempts to shepherd his flock away from metaphysical cliff edges.

Vassiliki – Baker of dreams and bringer of peace. Her *koulourakia* can solve family feuds. Her honey puffs once silenced a visiting politician. She is the village's pastry-based conflict-resolution service, and no one argues with her – at least not with a full mouth.

Stamos – Builder, fixer, breaker. Stamos believes everything can be improved with either concrete or fire. He is almost always wrong. His innovations include the wine fridge sauna, the self-dimming toilet, and the world's only collapsible pergola.

Katerina (the goat) – Terrorist. Mascot. Orphan rescuer. Serial menu-eater. Katerina is the only creature in the village with complete immunity. She has chewed through three extension cords, one health inspector's shoe, and a highly sensitive EU funding application. Also, she recently adopted five kittens.

These are our people. Our chaos. Our village.
Let the madness begin – again.

CHAPTER ONE

Zorba's Taverna, Take Two

We didn't mean to take over the taverna.

Honestly.

We just wanted a bit of peace. A view of the sea. Maybe the odd grilled sardine and a decent sunset.

But in Greece, things rarely go to plan. And even when they do, it's never *your* plan.

My wife Alex and I arrived in Telios looking for calm. Serenity. Possibly early retirement. What we found was a fishing village clinging to the edge of Evia with more stories than street names (street names didn't actually exist) and more opinions than road signs (they didn't exist either).

We were outsiders. Briefly. Then we met Zorba. Then we joined a village meeting.

Then we accidentally adopted a goat, survived a flood, and found ourselves in the centre of a whirlpool of bureaucracy, olive oil, the wrong kind of feta, and unsolicited advice.

And then, when Zorba finally closed his taverna – not for lack of customers, but because someone in Athens decided tables near the sea were now "a threat to coastal harmony" – the whole village mourned.

The chairs were stacked. The octopus line came down. The *tsipouro* stopped flowing.

The soul of Telios went quiet. Zorba never spoke about it. He didn't need to.

The morning after the closure, he sat by the empty grill, coffee in hand, watching the sea with the kind of quiet that it hurts to interrupt.

He didn't swear. He didn't rage.

He looked at the place where the tables used to be, where they had been for decades, and shook his head once, like he'd heard an old joke retold badly.

"I built this so people could sit, eat, and listen to the sea," he said eventually. "Now they say the sea is dangerous."

Then he turned his chair away from the view. And for a while, that was worse than any argument.

The rule, in theory, was simple. No more beach bars. No

more beachfront discos with neon signs offering "Mykonos Mojitos" and basslines that could be heard from space. It was meant to save the Aegean from becoming one long, sunburnt playlist with overpriced cocktails.

But the thing about bureaucracy, especially the Greek kind, soaked in paperwork and sealed with stamps that haven't changed since the Ottoman Empire, is that it rarely stops where it should. Once the rule left the ministry office in Athens, it took on a life of its own. Somewhere between the third signature and the fourth coffee break, it transformed from a sensible regulation into an indiscriminate purge.

Suddenly, it wasn't only the thumping monstrosities of Mykonos under threat, the beach clubs with foam cannons and sunbeds more expensive than rent.

No.

Now it applied *everywhere.*

Even here. In Telios. Where the loudest thing on the beach was the goat. Where the closest thing to a beach party was Dimitri falling asleep next to a lantern and a plate of sardines.

Zorba's Taverna had existed in quiet defiance of modernity for decades. Same tables. Same recipes. Same view. On the beach, close enough to taste the salt in your wine glass. Nobody raved. Nobody played house music.

But the rule was blind. It cared not that Zorba had fed three generations of villagers. Or that people came not for noise, but for peace. The file said *no seaside operations.* Full stop.

And so, a man in a shirt too clean for local life arrived with a measuring tape and an attitude, declaring Zorba's chairs illegal by precisely four and a half metres.

"This is to protect the coastline," he explained.

Zorba, to his credit, didn't throw him into the sea. He just looked at the tape measure, then at the waves, then back at the man and said, "The coastline has been fine protecting itself for the last thousand years."

But reason doesn't fill out forms. And so, the taverna, the heart of the village was closed.

Not because of music. Not because of crowds. But because someone, somewhere, couldn't tell the difference between a disco and a dream.

But if there's one thing you should know about Greeks, especially the rural kind, the sun-baked, olive-fed, thoroughly-suspicious-of-authority kind, it's this: they do not accept silence for long.

Which is why we, a strange mix of locals, misfits, and one particularly persuasive Athenian (Alex) decided to do the impossible:

Reopen Zorba's Taverna.

Not as a business, but as a cooperative. Which, in Greek, roughly translates to: "an agreement to argue loudly, ignore structure, and feed everyone anyway."

So we did. We reopened the taverna. Together. As a village. As a family. As a half-legal experiment in how many people can run a restaurant while refusing to follow the same recipe.

We have no formal hierarchy at Zorba's. We have no titles. No uniforms. No real rules, unless you count "Don't let the goat near the kitchen," and "Don't argue with Theodora about the menu unless you've lost the will to live."

But if we did have a chain of command, Alex would be in charge. She simply is. She orbits the taverna like a moon goddess with caffeine for blood. She runs on instinct, volume, and a psychic sense for trouble. Alex is a storm disguised as a woman. Fire-hearted, razor-eyed, and powered by sheer will. She doesn't enter rooms so much as take control of them. The wind changes when she's annoyed. Fruit ripens faster when she laughs. If the homemade *tsipouro* stops flowing, she kicks the still, and if that doesn't work, she looks at it with a disapproving look. That always works. Her temper is legendary. It arrives like lightning, sets fire to everything in its path, and is gone before you've finished your coffee. Then she brings you a pastry and tells you she loves you. And you do. You always love her back. Fiercely loyal and allergic to stupidity, she's why anything works around here. And heaven help the man who tells her otherwise.

The kitchen is Theodora's realm. Part chef, part oracle, part 12-bore shotgun, she doesn't need recipes – she is the recipe. Her eyebrows alone have more culinary authority than most food critics. Parsley in *moussaka*? Blasphemy.

Her daughter Mary, meanwhile, serves like someone born in a perfume ad and raised in a thunderstorm. Where Alex commands, Mary suggests. Alex demands order; Mary creates chaos that somehow functions. She doesn't carry plates; she dances with them. One moment she's balancing two overflowing trays, the next she's flirting, translating, and dodging Dimitri, all without spilling a drop. She once fixed the lights, rewrote the specials board, danced with a tourist named Gary, and called a plumber with one hand while garnishing the *moussaka* with the other.

Alex is the fire.

Mary is the smoke.

Together, they're unstoppable.

Then there's Vassiliki, baker of miracles, whisperer of dough, and unofficial Minister for Peacekeeping via Pastry.

It was the morning the Great Menu War broke out: Theodora wanted to serve lamb, Maria insisted it was a fish day, and Claude had rewritten the entire menu in French with a quill although no one had asked him to.

The shouting started in the kitchen, migrated to the terrace, and by midday, half the village had taken sides. Tourists were hiding behind wine lists. The cat had left in protest.

And then… Vassiliki arrived.

She didn't say a word. She just walked in, placed a tray of still-warm *tiropitas* on the table like a holy offering, and smiled.

Theodora, mid-rant, took a bite. Maria took two. Claude ate four. Silence descended. It was broken only by chewing and one quiet sob from Dimitri, who claimed he tasted his childhood.

"I brought extra," she said, placing a second tray down, "because someone always wants more cheese when they're losing an argument."

She left before anyone could thank her, the smell of buttery pastry lingering like a promise you'd never break.

Nobody remembers who won the argument. But the fish was delicious. And the lamb lived to see another day.

If you need advice, go to Alex.

If you want truth, ask Theodora.

If you need your soul stitched back together with sugar and warmth, find Vassiliki.

And of course, there's Dimitri. Fisherman. Philosopher. Liability.

He brings fish, chaos, and unsolicited wisdom in equal measure. He often delivers something hissing in a bucket, says it's "probably legal", and dares anyone to disagree. He hates dolphins. He claims they're "smiling assassins".

Dimitri talks like a man who was hit by lightning and considered it a spiritual upgrade. Because he was.

It had been bound to happen sooner or later. You can't spend years waving a trident at the sea during thunderstorms, shirtless, barefoot, and shouting at Poseidon, without eventually attracting the attention of both the gods and the weather.

He claims it was only once. Maria insists it was twice. Father Evangelos says the lightning struck him, paused, and then went back in for a second go, just in case it missed a limb.

Whatever happened, Dimitri now carries himself with the unshakeable certainty of someone who believes he's already died once and now answers only to Poseidon, *tsipouro*, the tides, and occasionally Alex when she gives him, "one of her looks".

And to this day, when storms roll over the bay and the air smells like metal, he lights a cigarette, raises his chin to the sky, and murmurs, "Try me again, I dare you."

He and Alex argue like weaponised siblings. Then they drink coffee and unite in their hatred of the fridge, which only works if you threaten it.

Once, during a health inspection, he presented a raw octopus, stared into the inspector's soul, and said, "This is your reflection." The inspector left without further questions.

And the rest?

Maria handles the gossip like fine art, seasoning it just enough to make it worth repeating.

Claude handles the wine and whatever he decides counts as "culture" that week, usually involving candles, poetry, and baffled tourists.

Stamos breaks things, occasionally by accident, often for emphasis, and once because he mistook a fuse box for a wasp nest.

Spiros sits on his bench like a retired oracle, sipping *tsipouro* and growling out pronouncements that somehow always turn out to be right.

Eleni does the paperwork none of us understand. Entire bureaucracies tremble at her approach. She once silenced an inspector mid-sentence with nothing but a frown.

Father Evangelos floats gently through it all, blessing tables, calming storms, and quietly sipping shots of *tsipouro* when no one's looking. He doesn't gossip, but somehow he knows everything.

And me? I write things down. I listen. I watch. I hold the odd spanner and the occasional grudge. I translate gossip into written words, and fish deliveries into philosophy. I once brokered peace between two fishermen over the ownership of a bucket. I am the village scribe, the unofficial chronicler, and the last line of defence between Stamos and his plan to install a wood-fired pizza oven where the sink used to be. He still insists it would "elevate the brand."

This isn't just a sequel. It's a continuation of the madness. Of our absurd little revolution. Set in a Parthenon, not of marble, but of chairs, goats, arguments, and joy.

Pull up a seat. The table wobbles. The fridge needs kicking. But the sea is close. The company's warm.

And the story is just beginning.

CHAPTER TWO

A View, a Goat, and a Hint of Trouble

We had our place.

Our people.

Our tables.

Our goat.

And that, we believed, was enough.

Telios isn't so much a fishing village as it is a bundle of contradictions wrapped in sunshine. It's a place that shouldn't quite work, and yet, it does. Beautifully.

Perched on the northernmost tip of Evia, Telios peers wistfully across the gulf at the mainland, like a daydreaming poet reluctant to pack up and go home. The village stretches along the coast in a gentle sprawl, part fishing harbour, part farmland, and part open-air theatre where the drama is usually small, but the opinions are spectacular. It is a place where time moves sideways. Deadlines are negotiable, clocks are ornamental, and "tomorrow" is a promise as flexible as when the fish will bite, or when the cucumbers will be ready in the field.

A five-minute walk to buy milk might take an hour, because you'll stop seventeen times, to greet, to gossip, to argue gently about nothing in particular. Telios runs not on schedules, but on who is out at the same time as you.

The sea is a mood: sometimes calm and twinkling like a lazy saint; other times stormy and loud, as though Poseidon himself is trying to clear his throat.

Goats have authority. They climb anything, eat everything, and occasionally become godparents to kittens. No one questions them.

Disputes are dramatic, loud, and often solved over coffee, ouzo and a pastry. Or ignored entirely until they evolve into legend.

Over the years I've lived in Greece, married to Alex, embedded like an olive pit in the soft bread of village life, I've been slowly, irreversibly absorbed into the culture. It's not assimilation so much as marination. You don't realise it's happened until you catch yourself arguing about the correct texture of a fava bean or developing strong feelings about the best *tsipouro* – the kind that only blinds you in one eye.

Greek life wraps around you like a familiar wool blanket. It's warm, comforting, and smells faintly of lemon and woodsmoke. But occasionally, yes, the ants get in. Nothing is ever entirely comfortable for long. A rooftop may be for drying tomatoes and storing fishing nets, but it can as easily become a stage, a wedding venue, or, as in our case, the location of an entirely unnecessary, small-scale Parthenon. Not a metaphorical one. We actually built it. Out of bits of marble, idealism, and enthusiasm.

And that's when I began to understand that in Greece, place and purpose have a looser relationship than in other parts of the world.

Telios isn't only a village. It's a working theory. A cheerful argument against order. A kind of living proof that logic and Greek village life are rarely on speaking terms. Problems here are solved not with policy but with wine, whispered negotiations, and occasionally, a goat who's been given full symbolic authority over local decision-making.

Slowly, I learned the rhythms. The shutters that creak open just before dawn, the hour when everything smells faintly of salt and bread. The quiet wisdom of Spiros, anchored permanently to his bench like a warning buoy for bad ideas. I discovered that even Father Evangelos, robed and righteous, will accept a midday shot of *tsipouro* if the sun's warm and the olives are brined just right.

And now, with Zorba's Taverna reopened – less a business,

more a loosely choreographed circus with cutlery – Telios has deepened into its delightful contradictions. The lemon grove behind the kitchen has become a battleground of romance, rumour, and unspoken territorial claims by the goat. The taverna itself is Greece in miniature: glorious, infuriating, stitched together with shouted advice and unlabelled jars of something homemade.

It's not perfect. But then again, nothing sacred ever is. It is, in fact, gloriously imperfect. But it's alive. It hums. It bickers. It feeds. And it welcomes, in its own odd, unpredictable way, anyone who's willing to sit down, pour a glass, and surrender to the chaos.

Telios is the kind of place that hugs you while yelling in your ear. Where beauty hides in the cracks. Where every single thing, from the hum of a fridge to the flaring of tempers at the *kafenio*, becomes a story.

It's more than a setting. It's *home*.

The taverna, once shuttered under the weight of regulations and one man's weary soul, now stood again, crooked and beautiful. The sign still hung at a slight angle. The fridge still had to be kicked twice before it agreed to chill anything. But the tables were full. The stove was hot. The sea was close.

Mary, meanwhile, had evolved into something far beyond a waitress.

She was no longer just a woman. She was a legend. A story told to overconfident sons as a warning: *"Mind yourself, or Mary will hand you your ego on a plate."*

She was the kind of beautiful that caused mid-sentence stumbles, wine-glass spills, and the occasional poetry attempt from grown men who had no business near metaphors. And every day, like clockwork, she was proposed to. Sometimes with flowers. Sometimes with fish.

She'd turned them all down.

One particularly persistent offer came with a yacht, a villa in Melbourne, and a life of colour-coded towel sets and frozen calamari. Mary took one look at the brochure and said, "No."

Not with cruelty. Just honesty.

And in doing so, she didn't only reject a man. She rejected the script. She chose the village, the chaos, and sea.

She said no, and somehow, that became the loudest yes any of us had ever heard.

Now she moved through the taverna like grace in heels. Even Katerina the goat had learned not to block her path.

And so the days flowed. A typical afternoon might include:

Two tables of happy, sun-pink tourists leaning back in their chairs, murmuring to each other in soft, reverent voices about how authentic everything felt, as if authenticity were something we had printed on the napkins. We often ran out of napkins. We had bits of paper towel, and a general agreement to wipe your hands on your own legs.

A few tables over, three old men would be deep into their fifth round of *tsipouro* and their third decade of the same argument: who, exactly, had planted the first vineyard on Evia.

"My grandfather did it," one would declare, slamming his glass down. "Nonsense," another would say, "it was old man Giannis, and he only used one eye." The third would say nothing, but point at the sky and then at his shoes, as if that settled it.

Maria would be wandering between them all with a notebook and the expression of someone conducting vital sociological research, despite having absolutely no qualifications. The truth was simpler: she was gathering material for her gossip sheet, *The Telios Tribune* – a kind of unofficial village newspaper, published irregularly and entirely without consent.

"I'm archiving the soul of the island," she would declare, scribbling without looking. "How did you feel when the goat stared directly into your heart?"

The notebook itself was infamous. Half diary, half tabloid, and entirely unreliable. Once, she ran a headline that read: "Local Priest Blesses Coffee Machine, Miracles Imminent". Father Evangelos still denies it, though he never quite meets your eye when he does.

Claude would emerge from the shadows holding a bottle of something red and faintly glowing. "It's deeply misunderstood," he would say proudly, which usually meant it was illegal in most EU countries. "The monks made it to forget things." He would then pour it into three glasses and refuse to tell us what needed forgetting.

Eleni would slip out of the back room carrying a thick stack of paperwork and the face of a woman who had once stared down a tax auditor, a police inspector, and an EU compliance officer, and emerged victorious. She would walk past like a war general surveying a battlefield she secretly controlled.

And at the edge of it all would be Spiros, sitting on his bench, his throne. Smoking. Squinting. Watching the world with the expression of a man who had lived long enough to find it all funny.

Someone once asked him whether he would be voting in the mayoral elections this year.

"Life," he replied, exhaling slowly, "is like borrowing tools from your cousin. You never get what you asked for, but somehow you still end up fixing something."

No one quite knew what that meant, but it sounded right.

The food would come. The wine would flow. Laughter would rise, dip, and dance between tables. We would spill, refill, and clear plates and stories in equal measure. And at some point, each evening, when the sun started to drop behind the fishing boats and the world turned golden for ten glorious minutes, we all, staff and guests alike, would stop to look.

Just for a moment. At the sea. At the light. At each other. It was messy. It was imperfect. But we had built it ourselves.

But lately… something had shifted. Nothing dramatic. Not yet. But the air was different. The breeze had teeth. The mayoral elections were approaching.

And in most places, this would be a time for posters. Pamphlets. Debates. Speeches.

But not in Telios. Here, politics was a group activity held around a table with olives and three different versions of history. There were no parties, only personalities. No manifestos, only grudges. We weren't a political people, not in the usual sense. We held votes the way others held toasts: often, emotionally, and always with a fish involved.

But this time, it felt different.

There were whispers. That Stavros might not stand again. That someone new was waiting. Younger. Hungrier. With ideas that sounded neat in Athens, but sharp-edged here.

And that was dangerous.

Because in Telios, the law isn't what holds us together. The story is.

CHAPTER THREE

The Invasion of the Spoon-Wielding Matriarchs

ere in Telios, we don't point at laminated menus or glossy photos of food that never quite look like the real thing. We certainly don't argue about who ordered what or demand separate bills with military precision. This is not that kind of place.

Running a taverna in a Greek village is like conducting an orchestra where every musician has a strong opinion and three of them brought goats. In winter, the customers are locals, bundled in layers, seeking warmth, gossip, and familiarity. They come not for a culinary experience, but for comfort. A seat. A story.

A place to be.

Come summer, everything shifts. The tourists arrive. Sunburnt and slightly dazed, clutching guidebooks, sunscreen, and expectations. But here's the magic: we all share. The villagers don't mind. In fact, they enjoy it. Everyone ends up mixing: locals, visitors, old friends, strangers who become regulars. Conversation flows like wine. Someone always translates. Someone always laughs.

In Greek village tavernas, food is never simply food. It's emotion. It's memory. It's a full-body, full-table experience.

We don't order individually here. You don't get your own plate of grilled meat while the person next to you eats their salad in isolation. That's not how this works. In the villages, a meal is a team sport.

Fish is ordered by the kilo. Salad comes in a bowl that could double as a birdbath. Dishes of potatoes, wild greens, grilled vegetables, and beans appear and settle in the middle of the table like old friends. Everyone reaches in. Everyone shares. There's no ceremony. No politeness required. If you want something, reach for it. Or point. Or ask loudly across the table.

It took time, and no small amount of intervention, to get our visitors to understand this. Especially early on, when we'd get orders like "two pork chops with fries" and "a small plate of spaghetti for the child". The kitchen would sigh. Theodora would raise an eyebrow so sharp it could slice aubergine. And eventually, someone (usually Alex) would gently explain, "No, my darling. You don't order for yourself. You order for the table."

At first, they resisted. We saw the panic in their eyes. The need for control. The fear of a rogue anchovy. But then, slowly, gloriously, they adjusted. They dipped their bread into communal *tzatziki*. They passed the octopus. They tried the mysterious green thing and liked it more than they expected.

They relaxed.

Because this isn't only about efficiency. It's about trust. About being part of something, even if just for one meal. You learn that food, when shared, tastes better. Jokes land harder. Wine lasts longer. Strangers feel familiar.

We still have to gently re-educate the occasional stubborn tourist, the one who wants a gluten-free burger with no onion, no burger and no bun. But most? Most get it eventually. And when they do, they don't just eat.

They belong.

That's the Greek village way. Messy. Generous. Loud. And absolutely perfect.

***

But sometimes, we're tested to the very edge, and beyond.

Because not all tourists are wide-eyed and curious, ready to try something new. No. Occasionally, we get the *others*. The ones who already know *exactly* how Greek food should be. Because, according to them, their family *invented* it. Somewhere between the invention of democracy and baklava.

And when that tourist comes not alone, but in numbers – say, an entire *busload* of Greek grandmothers – well, that's not a visit. That's an inspection. A culinary inquisition. A cross-generational ambush with handbags and rolling pins.

They descend like a benevolent yet terrifying thunder cloud, armed with opinions, embroidered handkerchiefs, and enough cooking expertise to host a twelve-part documentary on the History Channel. And they don't just eat.

They *judge*.

It crept up on us like all disasters do in Greece: quietly. With sunshine, good intentions, and a phone call that should have been a warning.

"A quick stop," the man said.

"Only a bite," he promised.

"A group of pilgrims," he added.

"They've been visiting Saint John the Russian."

Which, in retrospect, was the first red flag. Because anyone holy enough to survive a pilgrimage to Prokopi, and devout enough to schedule thermal baths after, wasn't coming here for a light lunch. They were coming for answers. And possibly vengeance.

What he did not say was that the "group" consisted of 42 Athenian *yiayiades*. Each one with arthritis in the knees, righteousness in the bones, and at least three generations of culinary superiority flowing through their veins.

Zorba's Taverna was about to receive the ultimate test.

The bus arrived with the energy of a Trojan horse. Doors hissed open. Feet descended. Umbrellas were unsheathed like bayonets. They came in floral prints, orthopaedic sandals, and expressions that could cause milk to curdle.

Alex appeared at the gate. "No," she said. Only that. Then she turned to Theodora. "Battle stations."

Inside, George calmly refilled the cheese drawer. Mary tied her hair back with the air of a woman about to charm or kill. Dimitri hid the octopus, not because it wasn't fresh, but because he feared for its soul.

Claude ran off to hang bunting. Eleni reached for her strongest stamp. I, naturally, grabbed a pen. Useless in a fight, but excellent for recording the casualties.

The first *yiayia* entered. Marched past the tables. Walked straight into the kitchen.

No hellos. Just a sniff and a narrowed eye.

"Where is the ladle?" she asked.

Theodora, already seething, pointed. "In my hand."

Another arrived. "Why is the grill cold?"

"It's not," said George, turning it up.

The floodgates opened. One by one, they entered the sacred kitchen space. Theodora's realm. Our temple. Within minutes it had become a battleground of conflicting wisdom and passive-aggressive expertise.

"This oregano is tired."

"Who taught you to salt beans like that?"

"My cousin's daughter's neighbour is a chef in Piraeus, and even she wouldn't dare boil this cabbage."

One leaned into a pot, sniffed deeply, and said, "Too much onion."

Another leaned into the same pot two minutes later: "Not enough onion."

Theodora flinched – inwardly – then turned to George with the calm of a woman announcing the weather. "I'm going to jail today," she said matter-of-factly, reaching for her apron like it might double as legal defence. Meanwhile, Mary tried to steer the rest toward the tables with her usual weapon of choice: grace.

"Would you like to sit, *kyria*?" she offered sweetly.

"I'll sit when I see the fish," came the reply.

Dimitri burst into the taverna with the theatrical flair of a man delivering a national treasure, lugging a crate of the day's catch as though he'd heroically plucked it straight from Poseidon's beard. He was glistening with seawater, sweat, and misplaced confidence.

The Athens *yiayias*, all forty-three of them, armed with handbags, prayer beads, and weaponised opinions, immediately swarmed around him like piranhas in floral cardigans.

He set the crate down with a grunt. "Fresh from the rocks," he declared. "Still dreaming of the sea."

One *yiayia* leaned in. "That one's cloudy-eyed."

"Cloudy? It's soulful!" Dimitri insisted.

Another poked a silver specimen with a crucifix. "Looks like it died of embarrassment."

A third *yiayia*, whose earrings could pick up satellite channels, sniffed loudly. "You call this a red mullet? I've seen redder faces at funerals."

Dimitri's grin faltered.

One particularly fierce granny, wielding a lace fan like a judge's gavel, pointed to a bream. "This one's bloated. You leave it too long in the sun?"

"No! It's just… robust," Dimitri offered weakly.

"They smell wrong," someone suggested.

"Smells fine to me," said Dimitri, sniffing a sea bass defensively.

"Are you sure they're fresh, *koumparé*?" came the reply.

"They were swimming this morning!"

"Towards what? A sewer?"

"Back in my day," one *yiayia* announced, arms crossed like a general, "you'd never serve this in a house with dignity. We'd have thrown it to the cat."

The cat wandered past, sniffed the crate, and left silently. It was devastating.

They picked through the crate like forensic inspectors at a crime scene. Tails were lifted, gills examined, tiny fish interrogated for their culinary intentions.

One pulled out what might have been a sardine. "What's this one even trying to be?"

"A lesson," said her friend.

And then, with a communal sigh of dismay and the solemnity of a church committee about to reject a bake sale, they turned to Dimitri.

"Young man," said the eldest, adjusting her orthopaedic sandals, "go back to the sea. Apologise to it."

By the time they moved on to critiquing the kitchen knives, Dimitri was complaining to himself in the corner, nursing a bruised ego and possibly a *tsipouro*.

Most of the fish were quietly sent to the back of the kitchen, their fate postponed.

And the *yiayias*? They made their way behind the counter, sleeves rolled, opinions sharpened.

One brought out a lemon and held it up dramatically. "Did you pick this in anger?"

Claude arrived with a jug of wine and said something poetic about Dionysus. One of them slapped his hand away from the olives and told him not to waste time talking when the *tzatziki* still needed straining.

Zorba didn't move. He sat by the door, arms folded, one eyebrow arched in a way that suggested he'd seen wars with fewer casualties.

Father Evangelos was summoned to "bless the kitchen before someone swears".

He arrived, saw the chaos, and promptly blessed himself.

The kitchen now had nine active cooks, three arguing over

whether lentils needed mint, one restocking the fridge, and two demanding access to the storeroom to see the potatoes. Theodora defended the pans like a lioness defending her cubs. George guarded the feta.

Alex tried to restore order.

"Theodora runs this kitchen!" she shouted.

"No, she *organises* it," a *yiayia* corrected. "Running requires soul."

And then, from somewhere near the sink: "The spirit of your moussaka is willing. But your béchamel is weak."

Outside, the tables groaned under the weight of unsolicited wisdom. *Yiayiades* were shouting across the terrace in the universal language of culinary judgment:

"Did you see the rice?"

"It was trembling."

"Too much salt. Or too little. Depends how much you care about your arteries."

"I had a dream once where the *pastitsio* was perfect. This is not that dream."

And yet, they ate.

Every bite came with commentary. Every swallow with a side of advice. And every glance towards the kitchen with the expectation of repentance.

But then came dessert.

Vassiliki, quiet until now, emerged with her tray of *galaktoboureko* like an ancient priestess revealing the oracle. She said nothing, but placed it gently on the table.

One *yiayia* spooned a bite into her mouth. Paused.

"My grandmother made it like this," she said softly.

The others stopped. Tasted. Remembered.

"I was a child again," someone whispered. "In Kalamata. Before the war."

Silence descended.

Then: "You used semolina?"

"Yes," said Vassiliki.

"Good," the woman said. "Otherwise, I'd have to kill you."

They left as they came – loud, opinionated, floral – but somehow healed. Whether it was the food, the laughter, or the brief skirmish over the olive oil, no one could say. But as the bus disappeared in a cloud of dust and eucalyptus rub, the taverna exhaled.

Theodora leaned on the counter. "If I ever see another floral handbag in my kitchen–"

George handed her a biscuit.

Alex flopped into a chair.

"They stormed us," she growled.

"And we fed them," I said.

"Barely."

Zorba stood, stretched, and said simply, "Now you're ready."

"For what?" asked Mary.

"For everything," he replied.

And we believed him.

Because if you can survive a bus full of grandmothers, you can survive anything. Even the tourism board.

After the Storm

The kitchen, once a battlefield, now smelled of thyme and liniment.

Chairs were crooked. Plates were empty. George had gone to lie down somewhere cool. Theodora was polishing a ladle like it had been through combat, which, to be fair, it had. And the rest of us were still counting spoons to make sure none had been taken as souvenirs or weapons.

That's when Alex found it.

Tucked beside the napkin holder, half-hidden under a stray crumb of *koulourakia*: a rosary. Wooden. Worn smooth by decades of faith and fingers. The kind your grandmother would use in church, in traffic, and during long conversations about your life choices.

No note. No name. Simply the gentle presence of something sacred left behind.

"It was deliberate," said Father Evangelos, who had appeared as if summoned by the scent of spiritual residue. "They leave things sometimes. When they've been moved."

"Or when they're plotting something," said Alex.

He shrugged. "Same thing, really."

Mary picked it up reverently, set it on the shelf behind the counter, next to the olive oil and the emergency *raki*. A quiet shrine to chaos, holiness, and elderly ferocity.

But the rosary wasn't the only thing left behind.

Later that night, when we were wiping down the tables and pretending the fridge didn't sound like it was dying in Morse code, Theodora found something else.

A folded piece of paper.

Slipped into the cutlery drawer, carefully tucked between the forks and wisdom.

It was a recipe. Handwritten. In perfect, spidery script.

"Dolmadakia tou Theou" – vine leaves of the Lord.

Instructions. Ingredients. Warnings. A final note: "Only make these when you truly forgive someone. Otherwise, they'll be bitter."

Theodora stared at it.

"Well?" I asked.

She didn't answer. Instead, she folded it back up, slipped it into her apron pocket, and went back to stirring the soup.

We never found out who left it. No one returned to claim the rosary. No yiayia phoned to check on the missing beads. And no one mentioned the incident again.

But the next time *dolmadakia* appeared on the menu, they were softer. Richer. Forgiving.

And Theodora, for once, smiled while cooking.

We didn't ask why.

Because in Telios, you learn not to ask too many questions about the divine, the dead, or grandmothers with unfinished business.

You just eat the food.

And say thank you.

Even if no one's there to hear it.

CHAPTER FOUR

THE FIVE-METRE MENACE

Telios had a mayor. Technically.

His name was Stavros. He lived two villages away and appeared twice a year, as reliable as a tax demand and almost as welcome. He would roll into town in a cloud of exhaust and self-importance, armed with a clipboard and the unique gift of turning happiness into a violation.

Stavros was no leader, no visionary. He was a man who could spot joy from fifty paces, something homemade, sunlit, vaguely salty, and promptly declare it illegal.

You liked your olive oil fresh from the village press? Cloudy, golden, singing of the hillside? Sorry. Needs a barcode.

You fancied calamari by the shore, your toes flirting with the tide? Dangerous. Environmentally suspect. Potentially criminal.

You enjoyed a chair wobbling companionably outside a *kafenio*, the kind that came with a view of the sea and unsolicited life advice? Too close to the edge. A hazard. Stavros struck.

This was the Five-Metre Rule, a law that arrived from Athens like a rumour wrapped in official notices, declaring that no table, no chair, no shred of joy should stray within five metres of the sea.

It was meant to stop beach discos, neon cocktail bars, and Mykonos basslines you could hear from space. The result? Chairs dragged inland, patios bulldozed, terraces uprooted by honest-to-goodness JCBs, diggers rumbling like mechanised grief, tearing up stones laid by grandfathers who knew nothing of planning permission but everything about love. It was like being told that sunsets were now available only via approved slideshow.

The new rule sent shockwaves. Tables retreated away from the sea. Some tavernas folded. Others lied. Ours sulked. Zorba, in defiance, folded his arms and declared that if he couldn't hear the waves, he wasn't serving the sardines, and promptly closed.

Where we saw heritage, Stavros saw hazard tape. Where we saw charm, he saw non-compliance. And when he finally turned back towards his own village, trailing bureaucracy like a bad smell, we were left blinking in the sun, wondering why spontaneity required such thorough policing.

Because in Telios, joy is handmade. Unruly. Served with bread and shouted across the road. It doesn't fit into forms. It pours too much wine and insists on sitting by the sea.

Strangely, two villages down, the tables are still there, lined up along the beach, stubborn as old fishermen, clinging to the sand like gossip to a *yiayia*. The Five-Metre Rule, it seems, is highly location-sensitive.

But we remembered how it used to be. And we weren't quite ready to let go of the sea, the salt, or the simple, glorious crime of eating octopus with a view.

All this, in Greece. A country where entire meals are conducted with your feet in the sand, your elbows on the table, and your chair half-buried in a dune. A country where octopus drying on a washing line counts as advertising. Where the sea isn't scenery, it's seasoning.

Ah yes, but there was another rule to be obeyed too. The Smoking Ban.

Now, of course, most reasonable people will agree smoking is unsociable, filthy, and a proven health hazard. It stains your teeth, your fingers, and occasionally, the lace curtains. Brussels, in its infinite wisdom, decided it was time to save us from ourselves. A well-meaning decree: no cigarettes in enclosed public spaces. Logical. Civilised. Sensible.

But logic doesn't always get invited to dinner in Greece.

You see, in our village, smoking wasn't a habit, it was a punctuation mark. Conversations never ended without it. Arguments never began without it. A *kafenio* without the soft haze of cigarette smoke was like a church without icons: cleaner, perhaps, but strangely hollow.

This wasn't about nicotine. It was about ritual. Identity. A generation that lit up not for rebellion, but because their father did, and his father before him. Usually after building a house with his bare hands or surviving a minor dictatorship.

So when the regulation arrived, delivered in bureaucratic blue envelopes, with warnings and fines and polite threats of EU disapproval, the villagers nodded. Smiled. Lit another cigarette. And opened a window.

Because here, change doesn't come by force. It comes slowly. On the wind. Through conversation. Through the stubborn belief that even if something's bad for us, we'd rather arrive at that conclusion ourselves, ideally over coffee, with someone grumbling about Brussels and passing the ashtray.

We'll get there. Eventually. But on our own terms. Preferably with a match.

It was a noble effort. A grand gesture. A bold, deeply theoretical attempt to align Greece with European norms, the kind of law that looks excellent printed in Helvetica on glossy paper, and utterly delusional once it crosses the Adriatic heading for us.

Posters arrived. Big ones. Bold red. Slightly aggressive, like they'd been designed by someone who'd never been loved.

"NO SMOKING," they screamed. In six languages, to make sure no one could claim ignorance. They were handed out by a nervous man from the regional office who wore a tie despite the heat and insisted on saying "health and safety" like it was a spell.

In Zorba's, the sign was given the respect it deserved. Laminated. Gently wiped. Then ceremoniously placed beside the ashtray, as a coaster. It held up remarkably well under the weight of ouzo glasses.

Of course, everyone in the village smoked. From teenagers to priests. Katerina the goat had been seen nosing around a half-lit roll-up, and no one ruled out second-hand addiction. So naturally, everyone in the village completely ignored the ban. Not rudely. Just… completely.

They smoked in the taverna. They smoked outside the taverna. They smoked in the post office, the bakery, and during weddings. During the annual Easter vigil, there were more Marlboros than candles.

I'll always remember one of my earliest, most educational introductions to Greece.

Long ago, in another life, I was still English. Alex fixed that fairly quickly. I had toothache, a wisdom tooth. Proof that the body occasionally tries to grow something useful, only to have it painfully removed later. Mine had decided to erupt. It was somewhere near August. Alex, in her usual, terrifyingly efficient way, said, "I have a friend."

Her friend was a dentist. We were booked in for "a quick coffee and a small extraction", which seemed to be presented as a sort of social double-feature. At that time, we both smoked. Alex with her Rothmans, me with something called Embassy, chosen largely because it was on sale and came with a free lighter shaped like a horseshoe.

We arrived late, on purpose. This was not only accepted; it was expected. Any earlier would have been rude.

The surgery was, at first glance, familiar. Chair. Sink. That faint, metallic smell of disinfectant and fear. But there was no bib. That was the first surprise. The second was the ashtray. It was placed squarely on my chest. Alex settled into a chair beside me. The dentist took her position on the other side. They both lit up.

"Don't mind us," Alex said, waving smoke from my face. "We're just catching up."

And they did. Coffee arrived at some point. My tooth disappeared shortly after. It was the only time I've had dental work performed while my healthcare team casually discussed holidays in Syros over espressos and ash.

"It wasn't exactly clinical," I said, still spitting a bit of cotton into a paper cup.

Alex shrugged.

"Or efficient."

"That too. But you got your tooth out, didn't you?"

"I did. Somehow."

"And the coffee?"

"Strong enough to resuscitate a goat."

She smiled. "And she only charged us for one."

I looked at Alex. "The coffee or the tooth?"

She lit another Rothmans. "Does it matter?"

***

So, the smoking ban failed. The whole village agreed with the ban in principle, but decided it would only apply between bites. Or when the anti-smoking police were sniffing around. Or on alternate Mondays. Or maybe not at all.

Maria wrote an article titled "Smoke Signals: The True Voice of a Nation".

Zorba's coaster remained in place. Still laminated. Still unread. But now it had a little burn mark in the corner where people had stubbed their cigarettes out, which somehow made it feel more authentic.

Then came the Olive Oil Decree. It arrived not with a bang, but with a sealed envelope, and the kind of logic only a civil servant could admire.

All tavernas, according to the new regulation, were to cease the dangerous, uncivilised practice of serving olive oil in communal glass bottles. No more topping up from the vat in the back room. No more seasoned bottles passed down like heirlooms, cloudy with character and history and maybe an ant floating around. No. From now on, olive oil had to come in sealed, tamper-proof, factory-labelled bottles.

These bottles were to be placed, unopened, on every table, as if they were precious artefacts or offerings to a health-and-safety-obsessed deity. Certainly not near the ashtray. And never, under any circumstances, should they contain *actual flavour*.

The reaction in Telios was immediate and dramatic. George the cheesemaker, husband to Theodora, was the first casualty. He was fined for what the inspector called "unauthorised drizzling". The term caused such scandal that Maria dedicated an entire day's gossip to it.

Theodora, naturally, refused to sacrifice her olive oil. She had picked the olives herself, pressed them with her own press, bottled them in jars that still smelled faintly of last year's harvest.

"If there isn't the chance of sediment, a sprig of thyme, or a stray bee wing," she declared, slamming a pot onto the stove, "then it isn't olive oil. It's water pretending to be Greek."

She held out a spoonful of the good stuff. The inspector declined, whispering something about hygiene.

She raised an eyebrow, tilted the spoon towards his shoes, and suggested a "demonstration drizzle". Then, as he backed away, she added, "Or perhaps your car engine? It runs better with proper olive oil."

He left in a hurry.

Zorba's reaction was perhaps the most elegant of all. When the inspector came by, clipboard trembling with overregulation, Zorba presented an unlabelled glass bottle with great ceremony and announced: "It's hand sanitiser."

The inspector looked at it. Zorba poured a little on his hands, sniffed, nodded solemnly, and went back to the grill. The inspector backed away slowly, and left.

By the end of the week, the new, official olive oil bottles had been quietly retired across the village. Most were now used to store buttons, hold flowers, or prop open windows. Some ended up back in circulation, refilled with the "approved" oil, which, if you asked Eleni, was simply the local stuff decanted behind a curtain.

The rule, like many before it, was not so much broken as… gently ignored until it faded into irrelevance. Which is, to be fair, the most traditional way of dealing with any law in Greece that threatens the sacred right to dip your bread without paperwork.

Then came the Helmet Law: another regulation sent with the best of intentions, presumably by someone in Brussels who's never attempted a left turn in a Greek village while balancing a watermelon and a grandmother. The problem was, in Telios, everyone had a moped. They were not for speed. They were for practicality. For carrying sacks of flour, crates of lemons, small children, two aunts, and in one case, a chicken coop that needed returning to Spiros's cousin in Ellinika.

Helmets, as a concept, were seen as optional at best, and actively rude at worst.

In theory, of course, it made sense. Helmets save lives. Nobody's arguing that. But try telling that to an eighty-three-year-old named Kostas, who's been riding the same sputtering moped since the junta.

To him, a helmet wasn't protection; it was an insult.

You see, in our village, the morning ride through town isn't just transport. It's ceremony. It's theatre. The moped is less of a vehicle and more of a mobile personality unit. You putter past the *kafenio*, give a regal nod to Spiros, maybe honk twice for Maria, who'll pretend she didn't hear you but smile anyway. You cruise past the bakery, perhaps stop to wave at your cousin, who might beckon you in for a glass of lukewarm *retsina* and an unsolicited medical update.

But now, now they wanted full-face helmets. Visors. Chin straps. Buckles. At forty degrees in the shade, wrapped in what essentially amounts to a padded oven for your skull.

And here lies the true cultural crime: how on earth are people supposed to know it's you?

Without your moustache blowing freely in the wind, your eyebrows arching at the priest, your toothpick bouncing with every bump in the road, who are you, really?

Recognition is half the journey. That quick glance, that wave, that silent invitation to stop and complain about the state of the olives. With a helmet, you may as well be a stranger. And what kind of village waves at strangers?

So yes, the law was sensible. Sensible like boiling your shoes because they might be dirty. But sensibleness has never been our strong suit.

It was announced with all the urgency of a national emergency. A full directive, dispatched from Athens, declaring that *all* scooter drivers, regardless of age, speed, or number of chickens being transported, must wear certified, EU-approved, full-face helmets at all times.

This included:

- People driving to the next street to check on a cousin.

- Anyone transporting a chair, a plank of wood, or a live goat.

- And, most controversially, anyone wearing a hat. Which, in this village, was practically everyone. Men here are born with their favourite hat, live in it, argue in it, and, according to rumour, some even sleep in it. Asking them to remove it just to wear a helmet was like asking them to remove their dignity. Or worse, their identity.

The mayor, looking particularly pleased with himself that day, called it a "critical step towards road safety and European alignment". This was met with total silence.

Spiros, never one to shy away from confrontation (unless it involved paying a bill), decided he would lead by example.

He re-emerged the next day wearing what might once have been a helmet, but was possibly a war relic, or possibly something that fell off a tractor. It was cracked, sun-bleached, and appeared to be held together by olive oil stains and electrical tape.

He declared himself "invincible", revved his wheezing scooter with the confidence of a man who believes rules are a foreign problem, and promptly drove straight into the village fig tree. There weren't any injuries, save for the tree's pride.

The helmet rolled off. So did Spiros's glasses. Zorba offered him a chair and a glass of wine. The mayor, watching from a distance, pretended to receive a phone call and left the scene.

The village took this as a sign. The law was, from that moment on, considered *advisory at best.*

People went back to riding as they always had: bareheaded, breezy, and gloriously impractical.

When asked about enforcement, the local police officer, who mostly served as an occasional referee, said, "If I arrest one person, I'll have to arrest everyone. Including my aunt. And she's faster than me."

So the helmet law, like many foreign ideas, was absorbed into the Greek system of interpretation. Which is to say, it was laughed at politely, set aside, and left to gather dust in a drawer full of expired licenses, unpaid parking fines, and one unused breathalyser.

Eventually, the police stopped checking. Not because the law changed. But because, like most things in our village, enforcement wore out before the people did.

Because here, a helmet may protect your head, but it risks obscuring your soul.

The mayor never brought it up again.

And neither did Spiros, though he did gift the helmet to Katerina, who now uses it as a feeding bowl.

Safety, in Telios, is defined more by convenience than legislation, and that seems to work just fine. And what's the point of safety, if no one knows it's you whizzing past their vine-wrapped gate?

So no, we didn't like the mayor. That much was clear.

But, and this is important, we *understood* him. In the way you understand a recurring rash. You know when it's coming. You know it itches. And you've made peace with the fact that, short of divine intervention or bribing someone in Athens, it's probably not going away anytime soon.

Stavros, the clipboard crusader, was, at the very least, familiar. Predictable. But we knew his weaknesses. His patterns. We knew he could be distracted by a decent *spanakopita* and that he feared Theodora's wrath more than European law.

But that's when the whispers started. Stavros might not be running again. And worse, far worse, he might be replaced. By someone new. Someone with a spreadsheet for a soul. Someone who saw chaos where we saw charm. Someone who used words like "standardisation" and "compliance potential" without blinking. The sort of person who followed rules so faithfully they lived by them. Someone who might care more about digital solutions than legends. Who arrived not with a crumpled folder and a hangover, but with charts and rollout plans. The kind of person who would look at our hand-built patio and say, "This could be a designated waiting area."

That's when the village began to stir. Not dramatically, at first. We're not a dramatic people. (Unless it's about food, fishing or honour. Or parking. Or anything else that upsets us.)

But quietly. A tremor in the olive grove. A twitch in the *kafenio*. Raised eyebrows over backgammon boards. Nods exchanged over *retsina*. People began speaking in lower tones. Cooks stirred a little more aggressively. Old men stared out to sea, muttering vague threats to no one in particular.

No one said it out loud.

But everyone was thinking the same thing:

Better the idiot you know than the genius who wants to install recycling bins.

We needed a different mayor. But who?

CHAPTER FIVE

THE MAN WHO WOULD GOVERN BY ACCIDENT

It all started the way most dangerous ideas do in our village: late at night, too much food, and someone with access to *tsipouro.*

We'd cleared away the last plates. The moon was up, the cats were prowling, and the only sound was the clinking of cutlery and the distant rustle of Katerina the goat, trying to eat a tablecloth.

Alex nursed a hot tea with the suspicious expression of a woman who knew someone was about to say something stupid. I sat beside her, bravely avoiding a glass of Dimitri's *tsipouro,* which sat in front of me like a dare. Mary and Maria joined us at the corner table. Claude drifted over from the wine store with a bottle of something "aromatic and possibly French", clutching a copy of *Le Monde Diplomatique*.

Spiros was exactly where he always was: on his bench, one leg over the other, a glass in one hand, a cigarette in the other, and an expression of philosophical resignation that suggested he'd already lived this evening in a previous life.

Zorba sat where he always sat, too: under the tin roof extension beside the kitchen, perfectly framed by a sagging bougainvillaea and the soft glow of a string of slightly broken fairy lights.

The conversation turned, as it often did, to politics. Not national, of course. We leave that to people with shouting problems. This was serious. This was about Stavros.

"He's leaving," said Alex, blowing on her tea.

"Running off to Athens," Maria added, arms folded, as if he'd abandoned his own grandmother during Lent and taken the church raffle basket with him.

"Apparently," chimed in Claude, "there's a suburb desperate for his particular brand of chaos."

"Yes," I said, nodding gravely. "The kind of leadership where nothing gets done unless it requires three forms, a blue ink signature, a commemorative stamp collection, and a complete misreading of both the law and the situation."

The true scandal, of course, involved the outgoing mayor

of that Athens suburb, who had, in a truly Greek act of bureaucratic generosity, left a convenient vacancy for Stavros. The official story was that he was retiring to focus on "heritage conservation". The unofficial story was that he'd been caught using municipal funds to build a three-storey shed listed as "Cultural Heritage Storage".

This so-called "shed" turned out to be less a shed and more a Bond villain's hideout. It had five en-suite bedrooms, a marble kitchen, and a wine cellar cunningly disguised as a plumbing archive. The windows offered a panoramic sea view, perfectly positioned to catch the sunset.

Beneath the ornamental herb garden (which contained three types of thyme but served no actual purpose) was an underground garage, hidden below the swimming pool. Inside sat his mother-in-law's Fiat 500, two electric scooters, and over six thousand pristinely catalogued issues of *Modern Bureaucrat Weekly*. Issue 438 had a scratch-and-sniff page that smelled faintly of filing cabinets.

And so, Stavros, our very own champion of unnecessarily complex bin permits, could not resist the siren call of urban dysfunction on a larger scale. He packed up his rubber stamps, his framed certificates of ambiguity, and what I can only assume was a filing cabinet filled with strongly worded letters addressed to him, and left Telios for the capital.

At this point Alex looked up from her wine, gesturing at me with the bottle.

"Wasn't it Eleni who told us that bit?" she said.

"It was," I nodded. "She said she saw him boarding the bus with three clipboards and a look of destiny."

Maria, who had been scribbling in her notebook the whole time, didn't even look up.

"Destiny or not, that's how we ended up with Nichos running as his replacement."

And the conversation, reluctantly, turned to him.

No one quite knew who nominated Nichos. Some swore it was a clerical accident, the result of a community form-filling workshop gone rogue. Others insisted it was Claude, halfway through a rant about streetlight symmetry, who drunkenly scrawled Nichos's name under "Suggested Improvements" in a moment of municipal mischief.

Either way, the paperwork was submitted, the ink dried, and by the time anyone realised what had happened, the nomination was both legally binding and ethically regrettable.

"Nichos," said Alex, with the tone one usually reserves for invasive species, "is the kind of man who alphabetises his socks and cross-references them with a seasonal wardrobe spreadsheet."

Mary rolled her eyes. "He once tried to ban whistling. Said it was 'acoustic pollution' and could 'undermine village serenity.'"

Claude, never one to be outdone, added, "He also petitioned to have the church bell silenced after nine p.m. because it disturbed his digestion."

Spiros blew smoke thoughtfully. "He tried to measure my bench once. Said it might not be regulation width."

Theodora brought over a plate of sardines and snorted. "He once reported my oregano plant for being too close to the pavement. Who even *notices* oregano?"

Even the goat, sensing the general mood, ambled past and headbutted a chair.

"So he's a local?" I asked, trying to picture him.

"Oh, he's local," Alex said. "Born here. Lived here. Never left. Which is the problem. He thinks he *is* the village."

"And now," Maria said, scribbling furiously, "he might actually get the chance to run it."

The table went silent for a moment, the way it does when the punchline is a little too close to reality.

Claude topped up everyone's glasses with *tsipouro*, the bottle already half-empty from the "discussion" that had been going on since morning.

"Well, of course," he said, raising his glass like a man toasting the end of civilisation, "this is the man who lodged a *formal complaint* about the irregular chirping of the sparrows."

Mary snorted. "He also once tried to get the rooster moved to another village because it crowed off-schedule."

"He once proposed a one-way walking system for the square," Claude said. "To 'improve pedestrian flow.' Can you imagine?"

Maria, slumped at the bar like a woman staring down the

barrel of a future filled with fines, added, "And he wants to introduce parking permits for mopeds. Ones with serial numbers."

Claude refilled his own glass. "Exactly. Nichos doesn't want serenity. He wants *order*. Which is far more dangerous."

"Well," I said, raising my glass, "if Telios is going to burn, we may as well have front-row seats."

Now, Nichos wasn't evil. He wasn't even particularly ambitious. He simply believed in rules. Not justice, not fairness – just rules. He collected them. Filed them. Treated bylaws like bedtime stories. His idea of governance was a colour-coded folder system and a town hall meeting about font consistency.

He had once floated the idea of compulsory early-morning fitness classes for pensioners – a bold proposal, considering most of the village's pensioners were perfectly content spending their mornings in the *kafenio*, sipping thick coffee, arguing about football, and easing gently into their second glass of *tsipouro* by 10:30 a.m. The rebellion was swift. One man threw a worry bead. Another threatened to power-walk in protest – to the bakery and back, very slowly. By lunchtime, the entire suggestion had been buried under a pile of backgammon boards and righteous indignation.

Nichos wasn't born fussy. He was forged.

Long before his campaign to regulate mopeds, before he threatened to alphabetise the fig trees, Nichos was a child of contrast. He remembered the early days, when Telios was wilder – not dirty, not neglected, simply… untamed.

The square was a place where fishing nets dried across the paving stones, where cats lounged like little emperors in the sun, and where you could hear three different radios at once playing three different kinds of music. The air was full of oregano, laughter, and arguments that were always solved with coffee.

Cars were parked wherever they fit, under olive trees, half on the road, half off, as though placement was more suggestion than science. People sat on doorsteps, traded fish for wine, waved to strangers, and shouted greetings across the street just to check if they'd been heard.

Sheds turned into homes, homes into goat shelters, and nobody thought to stop it because it somehow worked. If a pergola appeared on your land by mistake, it stayed. It became part of the scenery, the way grapevines do, until one day you found yourself sitting under it, drinking *retsina* and calling it fate.

It was beautiful. It was unplanned. It was the kind of place where you could still see the stars at night, where the church bell told you the time better than any watch, and where nothing, absolutely nothing, was identical, symmetrical, or regulated.

And Nichos worried about it.

He didn't see a living, breathing village; only a place one step away from disaster. He worried that charm was another word for risk, that the looseness everyone else loved might one day break.

So he studied bylaws. Learned building codes.

He dreamed of a Telios with smooth pavements and fresh-ly painted curbs, where signs matched in a single approved font and where there was an official noticeboard instead of news be-ing shouted over the *bouzouki* player.

He wanted safety. Predictability. Modernity.

In his mind's eye, Telios could be something better, a mod-el village, a shining example of European alignment. A place with tourist-friendly QR codes and colour-coded recycling bins, where visitors would marvel at the clean lines of its regulated seating areas and the uniformity of its signage.

What he never realised was that the very irregularity he wanted to smooth away was the village's heartbeat.

Yes, the paths were uneven. But they led to kitchens that smelled of thyme and lemon. Yes, the balconies didn't match. But they overflowed with geraniums and gossip. You couldn't straighten one without flattening the other.

And the more the mayors tried to impose order, the more the village resisted, not out of stubbornness, but because it knew what it was.

"Nichos doesn't understand," Maria said, pencil poised over her gossip sheet as Claude refilled everyone's *tsipouro*. "He thinks rules will make us happier."

There was a long pause. Even the goat stopped chewing.

And now, Telios would have to decide: did it want to be orderly, or alive?

There was a long silence. One of those thick, thyme-scented silences that only occur in small villages when the future begins to smell faintly of disaster.

Someone coughed.

In the corner, Spiros stirred his coffee like a man contemplating revolution.

We needed a plan. Fast.

Or at the very least, someone with less enthusiasm for symmetrical hedge trimming.

"We need someone else," I said.

"Someone who won't change anything," said Alex.

"Someone who understands the village," said Claude.

"Someone who's so deeply rooted here, he practically photosynthesises," said Maria.

We all looked in the same direction… at Spiros.

The wine did a little tap dance in my brain.

Alex giggled. Mary smiled. Maria looked like she might protest but then paused.

"He doesn't do anything," she said.

"Exactly," we all replied in unison.

Even Zorba's notoriously stoic expression softened into a rare, almost imperceptible smile. In Zorba-speak, this meant tremendous approval.

At that moment, Spiros flicked some ash onto the ground, sipped his drink, and stared into the night as if he was considering the weight of the stars, or wondering if someone had stolen his lighter again.

"Spiro!" Alex called across the patio.

He grunted.

"Do you want to be the next mayor?"

There was a pause. A long one. Spiros blinked slowly.

"No," he said.

"Perfect!" Maria clapped. "Any man who actually wants to be a politician should be banned for life anyway."

***

And so, a decision was made. Quietly. With that specific Greek nod – the one that means yes, *but never in writing.*

Spiros was the one.

Not because he was capable. Or because he was inspiring. But because he was gloriously, stubbornly inert.

In a world of men who want to do too much, we found comfort in a man who wanted nothing at all.

We didn't tell him.

This was important. We weren't about to mention that his name would soon be halfway onto the mayoral ballot, ink still wet, paperwork "borrowed" from the municipal office, and Claude rehearsing a victory speech that involved a goat and a smoke machine.

We all went very still, as if silence could hide our collective guilt. If Spiros had heard us, he'd have stubbed out his cigarette, given us that slow, withering look, and reminded us, in no uncertain terms, that democracy was overrated.

Instead, we called it Definitely Not A Campaign.

Step One: Rebrand the Ordinary

Maria began peppering his name into conversations with the subtlety of oregano in a salad:

"Spiros would never pave over history with concrete. He's seen concrete. Didn't like it."

"Spiros understands the rhythm of the village. When to speak. When to sip. When to grunt meaningfully."

"Spiros has no opinions about digital signage. That's leadership."

Step Two: Emotional Manipulation Via Baked Goods

Vassiliki began making biscuits shaped like tiny benches, with little icing cigarettes.

"They're commemorative," she said.

"But if you mention his name," added Alex, "you get extra cinnamon."

It became known as the Cinnamon Code.

Step Three: Infrastructure

Eleni, saint of stamped forms, quietly pre-filled the nomination papers "just in case he accidentally agreed". When asked what would happen if he didn't, she replied, "I'll just leave them there. Or pretend Claude signed them, but in any case, it could have been signed by the goat with a hoof print. Nobody ever checks."

Claude, who once accidentally declared himself a notary, raised no objection.

Then came The Soft Rally – a long communal lunch "just because", which somehow included a banner that read, "Let the Silence Continue".

The menu included dishes called "Policy-Free Lamb" and "Administrative Abstention Salad".

No one said the word *election*.

But Spiros, arriving late, sniffed the mood and said, "Feels like treachery." Then he ate two plates of fava and stayed anyway.

The real turning point, the moment things went from theoretical coup to full-blown conspiracy, was the Microphone Incident.

Technically, it was bingo night. But Claude "accidentally" set up a sound system. Maria "accidentally" read out a list of "essential traits of a good mayor". And Dimitri, already three ouzos deep, shouted, "Let Spiros speak!"

A microphone was passed. Spiros waved it away like it had offered him decaffeinated coffee.

"Leave me alone," he said.

Which, of course, was the most powerful thing he could've said.

The next morning, someone chalked a message on the taverna wall:

Spiros for Mayor: Because He Won't Bother You

No one claimed credit. But the goat had chalk on her nose, and Claude smelled faintly of conspiracy.

And now? We're almost at the deadline for mayoral nominations. The papers have just been filed (unbeknown to Spiros). The whispers are louder. Claude's drawing campaign posters in charcoal. And Spiros? He still sits. Still smokes. Still complains about "people who wear lanyards like they invented democracy". He has no idea. Which is exactly the point.

Because in Telios, the best leader is one who doesn't move. One who holds the centre of gravity for the rest of us to spin around.

And when future generations ask how we overthrew the system and elected a man without his knowledge… We'll nod toward the bench and say, "He was already there."

CHAPTER SIX

The Hour of the Olive Shadow

There's a moment in Telios, somewhere between the late lunch rush and the early evening drinks, when time doesn't stop (this is Greece, not a fairy tale), but it does something quieter.

It exhales.

The cicadas hush. The sea grows contemplative. The sun softens its glare, as if it too is tired of shouting and would like a sip of something cold.

We call it the hour of the olive shadow.

Zorba insists it's the best time of day. Not because of beauty or meaning or any of that foolishness. But because it's the one hour when no one expects anything from anyone. The hour when ambition itself dozes off with a half-finished frappe and one shoe off.

At the taverna, the chairs sit empty. The grill is cold. Claude isn't experimenting with bunting. Dimitri has wandered off in search of an olive tree that grants wishes. Alex leans on the kitchen counter with her arms crossed and a coffee in hand, silently judging the fridge.

Mary sits beneath the fig tree with her notebook and a pen that doesn't work but still travels with her everywhere. Sometimes she draws – "Maria's Last Argument", "Claude's Existential Corner", and "Spiros's Bench of Reluctant Wisdom".

As for me, I wedge myself between two flowerpots and a cat, scribbling half-thoughts into a notebook that claims to be for receipts. Notes like:

- "Don't trust a man who uses a fork for olives."

- "Lemon and truth: both sting a little."

- "Never argue with someone who owns a goat and a chainsaw."

And Spiros sits exactly where you'd expect: on his bench, cigarette in one hand, silence in the other. No one talks to him during the olive shadow. It's understood. It's sacred.

This is the time when everything softens. Before Claude catches fire again. Before Alex discovers the new health inspector form has a third appendix. Before Dimitri tries to convince us that *tsipouro* improves with age.

It's also the time when, if you're quiet enough, you begin to understand why Spiros is the right choice.

He won't say yes. He'll grumble. He'll deny. He'll flick ash in the general direction of enthusiasm. But that's exactly why he's perfect.

Because sometimes what a village needs isn't a mayor with ideas.

It's a mayor with memory.

Someone who knows what happens when too many rules arrive too quickly, when the bins are suddenly numbered, the olives are taxed, and the cats need vaccination records to sit under a table.

Someone who remembers what it was like before the mayor tried to mandate matching shutters.

Someone who can tell you, over a bitter coffee, exactly where the last overachiever cracked.

Spiros doesn't want change. He wants the hour of the olive shadow to stay exactly as it is, slow, quietly alive.

And maybe, just maybe, that's not laziness.

Maybe it's loyalty.

And if you're lucky, you'll hear Spiros say something that sounds like annoyance but is actually a kind of blessing:

"Let things be."

CHAPTER SEVEN

ALEX: THE RELUCTANT CO-CONSPIRATOR

Somehow, a whisper turned into a movement.

And Alex, on reflection, was furious.

She had played along at first, asking Spiros if he wanted to be mayor, adding her sharp little quip about the Cinnamon Code, even laughing when Claude suggested bunting. But the more it grew, the more it began to smell like politics. And Alex hated politics.

"This is politics," she said now, folding napkins with the kind of intensity usually reserved for interrogations. "You know how I feel about politics."

It wasn't that she hadn't seen the humour in the idea at the start. She had. Everyone had. But somewhere between a joke, a poster, and Spiros's unhelpful silence, things had stopped being funny. And Alex, with her fierce instinct for when the line had been crossed, was the first to call it.

Alex never cared for politics. Not the official kind, with suits and slogans and campaign songs sung by people who've never unclogged a drain. What she had wasn't political at all. It was something older, purer, and far more terrifying: she had justice running through her veins instead of blood.

Before she became the woman who could silence a room with a single look and convince an electrician to rewire the kitchen using only a pencil sketch and a shared bottle of *tsipouro*, Alex was only a small girl with scraped knees and stubbornness in her spine. She also had a moral compass so finely tuned it once got her barred from lunchtime duties for quietly re-packing every child's food so that the ones with nothing found *koulouri* in their bag, while the ones with extra mysteriously ended up with a little less. No one saw her do it. Except Yiayia, who gave her an extra olive and whispered, "You've got your grandfather's heart."

She grew up in old Glyfada. Not the polished version with boutiques and rooftop sushi bars pretending to be inspired by Cycladic seaweed. No, hers was the real Glyfada. Laundry on balconies. Fish bits on the pavement. Arguments louder than the evening church bell. Her house had cracks, possibly due to the tremors of history, but more likely thanks to the sheer gravitational pull of her grandfather's opinions.

Captain Manolis. Retired sea captain, reluctant hero, occasional storm cloud. He lived nearby and haunted the house like a particularly principled ghost. During the war, the real one, he had been captured by the Nazis and escaped. Twice. Once freed by a German sea captain, who knew Manolis from before the war, and once by impersonating a Swedish priest. The stories changed slightly each time, but the moral never did: "Sometimes the law must be ignored to save what's worth keeping."

He taught Alex how to tie knots, how to listen to silence, and how to detect dishonesty from the way someone stirred their coffee. He also taught her that speaking up wasn't a choice; it was a duty. Even if your voice cracked. Even if no one listened. Especially if no one listened.

She absorbed it all. Like sea salt into skin.

By six, she'd started collecting bottle tops and string for the village school's craft table, redistributing them to the younger children like a benevolent supply smuggler. By seven, she'd convinced the headmistress to stop burning old notebooks and instead let the children use the blank pages at the back. By eight, she was leading an informal morning inspection of the school courtyard, tutting at cracked steps and sweeping it with a broom twice her size. And by nine, she'd marched barefoot to the town hall with a handwritten note demanding to know why the school had no proper toilet doors and why the only swing in the square had been tied up "for maintenance" since before she was born.

Her kindness ran as deep as her fury. She wept at the stories of her grandfather's wartime friends, some lost, some scarred, all remembered. She would rescue injured pigeons, and hug anyone who looked like they hadn't been hugged in a while.

But if you crossed a line, any line, she'd draw a bigger one around you in chalk and make you answer for it.

As Glyfada modernised, Alex felt each change like a paper cut. First came the boutiques. Then the neighbours who didn't greet anyone. Then the cafés charging extra for ice. The fig tree behind her house was chopped down for a parking space. The street signs changed to English. Then came the sushi bar with no fish. It stopped feeling like home.

She missed it all – the fig trees, the old women shouting across balconies, the smell of wet ropes and thyme, folded into her chest like a secret map of what the world could still be.

So when we arrived in Telios, our sunburnt, cat-drenched, gloriously inefficient corner of coastal chaos, she didn't hesitate. She embraced it.

When we reopened Zorba's Taverna, she looked at the half-crumbling wall, the seaweed drying on the railing, and the electrical wiring that hummed and sparked, and she said, with terrifying calm, "Perfect."

She brought with her a moral code that predated most forms of government. She said no when no one else would.

She said yes when it mattered. She didn't wait to be asked. She fixed things. Argued. Pacified. Rallied. Rebuilt. She hung her grandfather's compass above the taverna sink and claimed the fridge.

She moves through the village like she'd been born knowing where the broken things were. She settles arguments without choosing sides. She calms storms by appearing in the doorway, hair tied back, tea towel in hand, daring anyone to continue shouting in her presence.

No job is beneath her. No nonsense goes unchallenged.

She has a way of listening that makes you forget you'd meant to lie. A way of looking into your soul that makes you remember the lie anyway. She handles bureaucracy like it was a personal insult.

But she is kind, too. Fiercely kind.

She remembers names. She remembers who hates parsley. She visits the cemetery to tidy the graves no one else did. She slips *koulourakia* into the hands of crying children and the pockets of men too proud to ask for help.

She laughs loudly and doesn't apologise. She cries in public and doesn't explain. She yells at Dimitri, then feeds him. She calls Theodora terrifying and means it lovingly.

Some evenings, after the rush of plates and politics and people needing things they didn't quite know how to ask for, she would walk out to the lemon grove behind the taverna, where the goat slept like an empress and the stars hung low enough to scold.

She'd stand there, quiet at last. Arms folded. Breath steady. And I swear, for a moment, she'd close her eyes and breathe in so deeply you'd think she was filling her lungs with Greece itself. Not the glossy postcard Greece, but the real one, the Greece built from grief and gossip, garlic and goats, the Greece that smells of sea salt and bureaucracy and never quite dries in the sun.

She held that Greece tight, fiercely protective of its unruly soul and deeply suspicious of anything with a stamp, a slogan, or a municipal budget.

So when we whispered our idea, just a little campaign, a gentle nudge to get Spiros to run, she slammed her glass onto the table, growled something unprintable in Greek, and announced that if we'd finally lost our minds, we could lose them somewhere else.

Then she stood, marched to the shoreline, and glared at the Aegean until even the waves seemed to hesitate.

No one spoke while she was gone. Claude stopped mid-gesture with his wine glass. Maria froze with her pen over her notebook. Even Katerina, who had been chewing on a chair leg, paused and looked nervously towards the sea.

When she returned, sand clinging to her heels and the sea still muttering behind her, she stopped at the edge of the square. She looked at the old men playing cards, the women trading herbs and opinions, the kids drawing hopscotch lines in the dust.

And then she sighed, the deep, theatrical sigh of someone who knows she's about to say yes to something she'll regret.

"If we must fight to stay real," she said, "then fine. I'll stand with you. But no posters. No slogans. And if anyone says the word 'manifesto', I'm flipping a table."

CHAPTER EIGHT

The Proposal (and the Goat's Approval)

The prospect of the new mayor being elected hung in the background like the smell of overcooked cabbage: unpleasant, lingering, and not quite serious enough to act on just yet. Spiros's nomination papers, quietly filed by Eleni weeks ago, ensured his unwitting candidacy was already in motion. For now, the village cooperative had done all they could do; the elections were still a couple of months away. That particular headache could wait.

For now, we had other things to worry about.

Mary received proposals daily. It had become as routine as the wine order or Alex swearing at the fridge. Tourists left their numbers scribbled on napkins. Locals offered goats, fishing boats, and, once, a karaoke machine. She accepted none of it. She smiled, handed over the bill, and moved on. Gracefully. Uninterested. Unshakeable.

But this time… something was different.

This time, the proposal hadn't come to Mary directly.

It had come through the weakest link: Theodora. Her mother.

Theodora, whose maternal instincts had gone fully weaponised since Mary turned thirty, saw every eligible man as a potential future son-in-law. She viewed every child in the village as a missed opportunity to have one of her own to spoil rotten, leaving them sugar-high and gloriously defiant.

She wanted Mary married. Not eventually: soon. Yesterday would have been ideal.

She wanted grandchildren to chase around the lemon grove, small enough to sit on the counter and big enough to complain about the olives. She wanted someone to teach her *moussaka* recipe to, someone who wouldn't even attempt to pronounce *béchamel*, just eat it, wipe their face with their sleeve, and call her Yaya.

Preferably a girl. With wild curls and strong opinions, who'd sneak spoonfuls of the sauce, track muddy footprints through the kitchen, and still somehow get away with murder.

She wanted a future that smelled like cinnamon and roasted lamb. A future with someone to roll out filo pastry with, to argue with about salt, to feed until they couldn't move. Greece doesn't do arranged marriages. Not officially. No, Greece has *introductions. Encounters.* The kind of romantic ambush your family insists is fate but feels more like a hostage situation with *spanakopita.* This is typically how it begins, the way all great conspiracies do in Greece: with a coffee and a whisper. Not a dramatic whisper. Not even a juicy one. Just a mild, conspiratorial murmur that rides on the steam from burnt sugar and inherited opinion.

"She'd be good for him," someone says, stirring her coffee clockwise for good luck.

"He's a good boy," another agrees, folding her newspaper with the finality of a judge declaring a sentence.

"She's the right age," adds a third, which is not a compliment so much as administrative approval.

And just like that, with no votes, no formal introductions, no official paperwork, no announcements, and absolutely no input from the people involved, a romantic union is quietly launched into orbit. An invisible shift in the atmosphere, like the change in pressure before a summer storm. And suddenly, everyone except the couple in question knows that they are, in fact, now on a collision course with marriage.

Because this is not democracy. Not even close.

This is *yiayia*-cracy – a form of government that predates

the Parthenon, ignores the Constitution, and has absolutely no tolerance for delay, hesitation, or personal autonomy.

Forget ballots and forums. This is decision by collective intuition, hammered out across hair salons, *kafenia*, basil-trimmed balconies, and the slightly aggressive silence of Sunday communion.

Then they begin the sightings.

The couple is not allowed to know they're being observed, of course. But somehow, every encounter is reported.

"They walked past each other by the olive press."

"He helped her carry tomatoes."

"She let him off without yelling when he dropped the tomatoes."

Proof, obviously, that love is blooming.

The young man, oblivious, probably trying to remember if he paid his electricity bill, becomes a marked man.

The young woman, possibly just looking for the cat, is now "spoken for" in whispers and winks.

And from there, it escalates.

Menus are adjusted. Seating arrangements are manipulated. Plates of food "accidentally" arrive in pairs. *Bouzouki* music, which had taken a seasonal break, returns mysteriously to the playlist.

Yiayias begin to send plates of pastries to the boy "just in case he's hungry", using the opportunity to watch his reaction. He eats. He compliments the cinnamon. One *yiayia* faints with satisfaction. The others call it fate.

He does not know that accepting a *koulouri* from the wrong old woman can be legally binding.

He doesn't stand a chance.

The girl, meanwhile, has noticed nothing. Or pretends not to. Or maybe – just maybe – smiles slightly when his name comes up. This, of course, is interpreted as a vow.

"She smiled," someone says, peering from behind a hydrangea.

"It's done," replies the other. "The banns can be mentally posted."

By this stage, the couple has achieved pre-married status.

Unofficially married. Officially clueless.

Every room they enter together goes silent.

People stare with the smiling intensity of those who believe they're witnessing destiny and are wondering what to wear to the wedding.

The couple stands awkwardly beside each other, holding glasses, talking about cheese prices, while the crowd practically hums with anticipation.

And then it happens.

Some well-meaning aunt – there's always one – leans in and says, "You know, you'd make a beautiful couple."

And just like that – *snap* – the spell is broken.

They look at each other.

He raises an eyebrow.

She laughs.

There is a pause.

The kind of pause that makes you wonder if the ancient *yiayia* magic worked after all.

And if it didn't?

No matter.

The village will try again next summer.

After all, they have infinite time, unlimited coffee, and a list of eligible candidates longer than the electricity bills.

The *yiayias* are not simply matchmakers. They're architects of destiny. Armed with lace shawls and lethal instincts.

And if you ask them how they know it's meant to be, they'll sip their coffee, glance over their glasses, and say, "I just know."

Which is, of course, the most terrifying kind of certainty.

And then one day, a man arrives. No fanfare. A man like any other, inexplicably appearing in your home at the exact time you're wearing yesterday's shirt and holding a toilet brush. He'll be described as "a friend of the family" or "your cousin's neighbour's godson from Melbourne". You've never met him. He smiles too much. He speaks Greek like he learned it from apps and romantic comedies. And yet, suddenly, everyone is acting like you've been dating for years.

"Sit with him," your aunt says, already dragging a chair.

"Talk. You're both young. He eats cheese! You eat cheese! That's a foundation!"

And you sit. You chat. Because in Greece, you don't cause a scene unless it's at a baptism. You're polite. You smile. You mentally plot your escape route.

Meanwhile, the campaign accelerates. Aunties begin ironing tablecloths for no reason. Your mother dusts the good plates, the ones she once said she'd only use for your engagement party, and mysteriously appears to be using… now. The goat is given a bath. Something is happening. Something *ominous*.

And meanwhile, you're still wondering how this man knows your name and why there's a new jar of imported olives in the fridge. You try to confront someone, anyone, but they just smile too broadly and say, "He's a good man." As if that settles it. As if *you* are the one being unreasonable.

The final straw usually arrives with a shrug. Maybe it's the man himself who casually refers to "our future". Maybe it's a toast you didn't realise was about you. Maybe it's your great-aunt pulling you aside and whispering, "We've booked the band, *koukla*, just in case."

And you realise, with a clarity that's both comedic and terrifying:

You are betrothed. By committee. Without consent, contract, or basic conversational forewarning.

This is not coercion; it's tradition. It's not pressure; it's love.

And if you object, someone will hand you a pastry and say, "Give him a chance. He's got a good heart. And he has his own teeth."

Because in Greece, arranged marriages technically don't happen. But if they did, this is *exactly* how they'd happen.

***

So when the message came, via email, via WhatsApp, via whatever device had the strongest signal and the weakest filter, Theodora opened it with the gravity of a woman about to read a prophecy.

She printed it. She underlined it. She read it out loud while making *dolmades*.

"It's from your cousin's cousin in America," she announced. "His name is Andonis. He has a good job. He wears shoes in every photo. He's serious."

Mary looked worried.

"He sent you a proposal," Theodora said, eyes gleaming. "A real one."

"I get real ones every couple of days," Mary said, not looking up from her coffee.

"This one is *through me*," Theodora said triumphantly, as if this granted the whole thing divine legitimacy. "It's a family connection. Which means he's not a stranger; he's just someone you haven't met."

"Perfect," Mary replied. "Exactly the kind of modern romance I've been waiting for."

But it was too late. Theodora was already humming. Planning. Visualising a wedding with lamb, lace, lemon biscuits and *koufeta.* She had waited years for this moment. And this time, she wasn't backing down.

Mary, meanwhile, took a long, slow sip of her coffee, and began plotting her defence.

Because this wasn't just a proposal. It was an ambush. And the enemy had gone through her mother. Or possibly through an uncle's cousin's friend who still uses fax. The exact method was unclear, because Theodora presented it as if it had arrived on parchment carried by a dove wearing a tiny engagement ring.

"Is this a marriage proposal or a livestock auction?" Alex asked.

"He owns a car that parks itself!" Theodora added, triumphant.

"Does *he* park himself?" Mary asked, dryly.

So, no, in Greece, marriages aren't officially arranged any more, but the system has simply evolved, into something subtler, slipperier, and far more dangerous.

The boy, Andonis, though he now called himself Andy, was twenty-eight, clean-shaven, well-spoken, and, judging by the deeply untrustworthy photograph Maria forwarded, devoted to two things: protein shakes and his own reflection.

He claimed he wanted to reconnect with his roots.

He claimed he wanted to find a nice Greek girl.

He claimed he wanted to get married on the island and "give back to the culture".

What he *really* wanted, we suspected, was a beautiful wife

who could dance, cook, and produce photogenic children while never asking too many questions about where, exactly, his "cryptocurrency consultancy" was based or why it had a Cayman Islands PO box.

Theodora was thrilled, the kind of thrilled that could power the village lights if you wired her up.

Mary was not.

"Absolutely not," she said, wiping her hands on her apron and reaching for her coffee like she was about to deliver a punch but wanted to be properly caffeinated first.

"He's family," Theodora insisted, as though that settled everything.

"He's a stranger."

"He owns three properties!"

"I own one goat," Mary snapped, "and I trust it more."

At that precise moment, Katerina the goat bleated softly, then wandered over and nudged Mary's elbow with what could only be described as moral support.

"See?" Mary said, pointing to the goat like a star witness. "Even she agrees."

Theodora glared at the goat, then at Mary, then patted Mary's hand once, firmly, like a judge bringing down a gavel, and turned back to her *dolmades*.

Maria, sensing this was better than television, took out her notebook and began taking minutes, presumably for her next gossip sheet.

Claude, lounging in the corner, poured himself more wine and announced to no one in particular, "If there is to be a wedding, I demand an open bar, and I'm in charge of the playlist."

Spiros muttered something about dowries and cigarettes, then returned to his coffee as though he had seen it all before and found it slightly disappointing.

Dimitri, who had been listening quietly, finally spoke up. "If there's going to be a wedding feast, I'll need to double my catch. And find someone to keep the dolphins away – they're scaring away the fish again."

Even Eleni, who never missed an opportunity to produce paperwork, appeared with a blank marriage application, "just in case".

It was the closest thing to a blessing we had ever seen: a silent, multi-generational agreement that this match was now officially a village project.

Mary groaned.

Katerina bleated.

And somewhere, far away, Andy posted another gym selfie with the caption *#IslandVibes*.

By midday, the news had spread. Eleni offered to draft a wedding budget template. Claude offered to officiate, "unofficially, but with flair". Dimitri offered to test the groom's commitment by locking him in a shed with a wild boar and a broken chair.

Maria began preparing a "Love Across Borders" feature for her next column, despite having zero quotes and no consent.

Tourists overheard and began asking if they could attend the wedding. There was no wedding. There was no engagement. There wasn't even a conversation. There was only a hopeful grandmother elect, a photograph, an overeager goat, and the full weight of village momentum.

And Mary? She went back to work.

She delivered the *moussaka*. She extinguished a kitchen fire. She corrected a tourist's pronunciation of "*souvlaki*" with a smile that melted feta. But every now and then, she'd pause. For a second. And we all knew: this story wasn't over.

Not yet.

CHAPTER NINE

WHEN THE GRILL WENT QUIET

Zorba still arrives every morning. Just after the bins have been wheeled out and before Claude starts fussing with bunting no one asked for. Not to work. Those days are behind him, though you'd never know it from the way he grumbles into his moustache and examines the *moussaka* with the quiet despair of a man who had once seen perfection, briefly, in 1983, and now considers everything else a disappointing sequel.

He doesn't speak much. He doesn't have to. His eyebrows communicate louder than any voice. A single twitch could mean "needs salt". Two twitches and a sigh mean "burn it and start again". A full raise? You'd better run.

Zorba always sits beneath the rusted tin awning at the side of the taverna, in his usual spot, where the breeze hits just right and the view includes the grill, the kitchen, and the sea – all the things that used to answer to him. He quietly nurses a thick coffee and stares at the sea like it has offended him. Observes. Grunts occasionally. Sometimes raises an eyebrow in a way that makes George quietly re-check the seasoning. Like a grizzled oracle, judging portion sizes, and casting silent shade on anyone who dares put parsley where it does not belong. We let him. He has earned it. (And also, he still owns it.)

We pretend he isn't still in charge. He pretends he doesn't care. It's a good arrangement.

But that morning, something was off.

He was late.

Only by a few minutes – and this is Telios, where time flows sideways. But we still noticed.

And when he arrived, he walked slower. Sat down harder. Didn't grunt at the salad. Didn't even complain when the goat briefly chewed the corner of a napkin and then walked off, un-impressed.

Alex was the first to notice when he suddenly went pale.

"He's gone white," she said, eyes narrowing.

"He's always pale," I replied. "It's part of his aesthetic."

"Pale like yoghurt," she said. "Not like Zorba."

And then he slumped forward.

It wasn't dramatic. There was no gasp, no collapse. Only a slow, silent folding. Like a man who forgot how to sit upright.

Mary dropped her tray. Claude shouted something in French. Eleni called for someone to get ice, then clarified, "Clean ice, not from the fish bucket, please."

Alex was already beside him, barking orders, checking his pulse, snapping at George to shut off the music and at Dimitri to stop shouting "IS HE DEAD?" quite so loudly.

He wasn't. But in that moment – still, slumped, silent – the whole village held its breath. The air itself seemed to hesitate. We carried him into the back room and laid him on the cool tile floor. The old fan was ticking overhead like a metronome of concern. Someone fetched a damp towel.

Someone else ran for the doctor, who, as usual, was not at home. Last time we needed him he was halfway up an olive tree "supervising" a harvest. Before that, he was in the kafenio refereeing an argument about whether *retsina* counts as medicine. Today, he was found at the harbour, trying to find something for lunch which didn't have tentacles. He asked if we had "tried water".

We hadn't. Yet.

Zorba was conscious, but barely. His eyes fluttered open briefly. He moaned something about the octopus being overcooked – which, given that there was no octopus that day, wasn't a great sign.

Claude offered brandy. Maria offered prayer. Dimitri offered to carry him to the sea for "restorative immersion", which was vetoed instantly by everyone, including the goat.

When the doctor finally arrived, he smelled like a fishing net left in the sun on a hot day, with a few suspicious scales still clinging to his sleeve and a plastic bag dripping steadily onto the tiles. He took one look at Zorba and said, "Mild dehydration. Bit of heatstroke. You people don't listen, do you?"

"He's Zorba," said Alex. "He doesn't do water."

"Well, he does now," said the doctor, and handed him a glass.

Zorba took it, sipped it, and made a face like someone had handed him a cup of betrayal. Then he drained it.

The diagnosis was simple. Not serious. But we had all been warned.

That night, the taverna was quieter than usual. The tables were full, but the laughter took longer to arrive. The chairs creaked a little louder. The fridge's hum felt mournful. No one dared complain about the wine.

Zorba sat in his usual chair, wrapped in a light blanket, sipping a small coffee. He looked… mortal.

It was strange.

We'd all built something around him. A rhythm. A myth. A sense that he was the anchor: unchanging, unshifting, immune to time and bureaucracy and whatever nonsense the mayor tried to impose.

But now we'd seen the truth.

He wasn't stone. He was skin. He was breath. He could fall.

And if he could fall, what else might tip?

Alex, uncharacteristically quiet, brought him a bowl of soup. She didn't ask if he wanted it. She didn't lecture. She simply placed it in front of him, tucked the napkin under his chin like a mother preparing a toddler, and sat beside him. No words. Just soup.

Mary brought bread – the soft one she makes for children and heartbreaks, rather than the crusty usual kind.

Even the goat sat quietly nearby, like a concerned niece.

Later, I found Zorba watching the sea again.

"Not today," I said, sitting beside him.

"No," he said. Then he added, after a pause, "But one day."

I nodded.

"Not before dessert," he assured me.

I smiled.

The sea shimmered. The chairs tilted. Somewhere in the kitchen, Theodora shouted about someone using the wrong oregano and the world felt if not fixed, at least familiar again.

And Zorba?

He sipped his coffee.

He watched the sea.

And he stayed upright.

CHAPTER TEN

ZORBA'S FOUNDATIONS
A MEMORY OF MARBLE AND MUD

Zorba was not a man for speeches.

When he sat, he sat in silence. When he smoked, he smoked as though the cigarette was telling him secrets.

But every so often, when the night was quiet enough and the sea was breathing slowly, Zorba would speak.

Not loudly, and not for long.

Just enough for you to remember that before any of us came along, before printed menus, before wine lists, before someone thought to write the words *taverna experience*, this place was his.

It was one of those evenings when the horizon glowed faintly, like an ember refusing to go out.

Alex had gone inside to stack glasses. Mary was sweeping. I was doing what I always do when I have nothing else to say: staring at the sea, waiting for it to answer questions I haven't yet asked.

Zorba sat under the tin roof, one boot hooked over the other, a glass of *tsipouro* balanced on his knee.

He didn't look at me when he started.

"There was nothing here," he said, quietly. "Not a floor. Not a roof. Only mud. And the sea."

I moved my chair to his table, knowing better than to interrupt.

"I built the first wall by hand," he went on. "Stone by stone. The good ones I carried from the beach. The flat ones I stole from the old quarry. Took me all winter. My hands split open before New Year."

He turned his palm over, as if he could still see the scars.

"I poured the first floor myself. No mixer. No help. Mixed the cement in an old fishing boat because that's what I had. My neighbour said it would never set. It did. Hard as marble. Hard enough that if you fall on it, it remembers."

He took a slow drink, his eyes somewhere far off.

"The first roof?" Zorba said, leaning back as though seeing it again. "I made it from driftwood and lies. Who knows where those planks came from – maybe the four corners of the world, maybe just the next village over. But somehow, they all found their way here.

I dragged them off the beach one by one, still smelling of salt and storms, nailed them into place with rusty nails and curses. Every gust of wind tried to take it. But I told it to stay. And it stayed."

He smiled at the memory.

"Some nights, lying here on the bare floor, I could feel the roof creak like it was alive, as if it was still deciding whether it wanted to stay or go back to the sea. But it stayed. Because I stayed. And when the first rain came, it barely leaked."

He gave a small shrug.

"By then I had already decided that if it did leak, I'd just sit here and get wet. Because this place was mine, and I wasn't going anywhere."

He looked up at the beams above us, and for a moment they seemed to stand a little straighter under his gaze. I felt it. That quiet, immovable certainty. The kind of stubbornness that builds tavernas and holds villages together. For a moment, I almost wished it would rain, just to see him keep his word.

"The first night I slept here," he said, "there was no furniture. Only me, the sea, and one pan. I made beans over a fire outside and ate them with my fingers. The moon was so bright it turned the sea white. I thought, 'If no one comes, this will still be enough.'"

He smiled then, not a warm smile, but one of recognition.

"They came," he said simply. "Fishermen first. Then shepherds. Then strangers. And little by little, it became something. Not just a place to eat. A place to sit. To argue. To forgive. To remember that you are alive."

He ran a thumb around the rim of his empty glass.

"When I handed it to you," he said, "I thought it would be easy."

He glanced at me, the faintest flicker of amusement in his eyes.

"Easy for me," he clarified. "Not for you."

And there it was, the thing beneath all his gruffness, all the sighs and criticisms.

He had bled for this place.

And then one day, he had let it go.

But he hadn't left. Not really.

He still sat here, still watched, still judged from his chair like some reluctant guardian saint. And maybe he still wasn't sure if handing it over had been the right thing to do.

The sea gave a long, slow sigh, as though agreeing.

Zorba reached for his cigarette case, and found it empty.

"Don't make it pretty," he said, standing. "Pretty makes people stupid. Make it honest. Honest lasts longer."

He paused, one hand on the doorframe, and added, almost to himself, "And don't make it easy. Things that are easy don't stay."

Then he left, leaving me with the stars, the taverna, and the weight of what he'd said.

I sat there until the glasses were stacked, the broom had stopped sweeping, and the moon had claimed the courtyard for itself.

I looked at the floor, the one he had mixed in a fishing boat. At the beams, the ones he'd convinced to stay. At the sea, the one that still brought strangers, still threatened to take it all back.

Alex and I had never really stopped to think about Zorba's legacy, not properly. We told ourselves we were keeping the taverna alive for the village. A place to sit, to eat, to gather.

We hadn't thought about what it meant to Zorba to hand it over.

The trust he had shown us was staggering.

It was, if we were honest, probably the highest honour we would ever be given.

And that night, sitting under the same roof he had built with his own hands, I finally understood.

What Zorba had given us wasn't just a business, or a set of keys, or a pile of tables and chairs. He had given us something he had wrestled out of the mud and the wind and the waves. Something he had fought for with his back and his hands and his stubbornness until it stood on its own.

He had given us a piece of himself. And it would outlast him, provided we managed not to ruin it.

That was the real weight of it.

And in that moment, I made the only promise that mattered:

We wouldn't let him down.

CHAPTER ELEVEN

A Wedding and a Scandal

It looked like a wedding was on the horizon.

We had never hosted a wedding reception before. The closest we'd come was last year, when we put on A Name Day to Remember for Father Evangelos. That celebration had reached what Maria called "biblical proportions".

The name day was supposed to host 150 people but somehow attracted exactly 150 plus everyone's cousin, neighbour, ex-boyfriend, and that one woman who once bought a jar of olives and now thinks she owns shares in the taverna.

Father Evangelos had invited "a few friends from the mainland", which translated to two boatloads and one distant cousin who turned up with a sound system and a box of fireworks.

The taverna and the lemon grove had been fully utilised for seating, along with the road, the beach, and, for a short but memorable spell, Dimitri's fishing boat.

Preparations had been heroic. Three lambs were spit-roasted. Eleni produced 187 *dolmades*, each measured to regulation size. Theodora and Vassiliki baked with such fury that flour was still turning up in unexpected places a month later. The kitchen teetered somewhere between divine inspiration and full-blown emergency, with cooks shouting, arguments breaking out, and feta flying through the air like confetti.

By the end of the night we'd run out of plates, Dimitri's *tsipouro* had been used as dishwashing currency, and Spiros was found asleep in the old bread oven, snoring softly like a man who had seen paradise and was unimpressed.

And yet it had been perfect. Chaotic, loud, glorious – a triumph.

But a wedding was different. Weddings had protocols. They had traditions older than the hills and more complicated than Greek tax law. With the possibility of a miracle occurring and Mary being so inspired by it that she agreed to marry Andonis. (Unlikely, but we had learned never to rule out divine intervention in this village.)

So, one day, we got lucky.

Someone else was getting married, and they wanted Zorba's for the reception.

It was Maria who broke the news, of course. She burst into the taverna like a one-woman news agency, waving her notebook as though it had been blessed by the Oracle of Delphi.

"Manolis and Irini are engaged!" she shouted, loud enough to make the cats scatter and Katerina stop mid-chew.

The room froze.

Not because anyone was shocked that Manolis was getting married – though that was miracle enough – but because he was marrying Irini.

Manolis had been the village's resident free spirit for as long as anyone could remember. Broad-shouldered, sun-browned, with his own boat and a way of talking that made even the fish lean closer. He'd never married, never been pinned down, and was widely assumed to have sampled most of the village's metaphorical fruit basket.

And then there were the rumours.

The ones nobody said out loud, not in daylight, anyway, but everyone somehow knew.

Whispers that Manolis had once pursued Irini's mother, back when both of them were still young enough to do reckless things and blame it on the moon.

Claude was the first to recover. He poured wine for everyone, including himself, and said, "Well. This will make for an interesting seating plan."

"At least we know he'll keep her in fish."

"Or in trouble," Mary said.

"Both," said Claude cheerfully, as though offering a toast, and topped up his own glass.

Dimitri leaned back in his chair, a slow grin spreading across his face.

"Good," he said. "A wedding with rumours is always a better wedding. Keeps the speeches short and the dancing long."

By morning, the news had gone feral.

Maria's *Telios Tribune* was out before breakfast – handwritten, photocopied, and already pinned to the wall of the *kafenio* by the time we arrived: "Engagement Rocks Telios: Fisherman Finally Nets His Catch."

Beneath the headline was a sketch of Manolis's boat with little hearts puffing out of the chimney and what might have been Irini dancing on the bow.

Maria had underlined the word *finally* three times in red.

By the second coffee, more theories had sprung up.

"They say she proposed," whispered old Kyria Sofia, clutching her worry beads like she was holding back the wrath of Zeus.

"No, no," her cousin interrupted, leaning so far forward his chair creaked, "he proposed at sea. Romantic. He spelled her name in sardines."

"That would take a lot of sardines," Dimitri said, walking past with a basket of bread.

Claude, who had come early purely for the drama, leaned back and smiled.

"Telios has been boring lately. Now we have a wedding and a scandal. Perfect."

Spiros lit a cigarette, blew smoke over the page, and asked the question on everyone's mind.

"What I want to know is whether someone's inviting her mother. Because that will be a party."

Theodora, already mentally arranging tables, said, "If her mother comes, she sits near the kitchen. That way we can keep an eye on her."

Maria was halfway through suggesting that they keep the kitchen door locked when Irini walked in, head high, curls bouncing. Irini was in her late twenties, glowing like a lantern, eyes flashing, looking like a woman who had personally orchestrated this outcome and dared anyone to question it.

"He proposed!" she announced, practically vibrating with triumph. "Well, he proposed six months ago," she added, rolling her eyes. "He's only just worked up the courage to let you all find out."

Theodora crossed her arms, her expression the human equivalent of a church bell warning of bad weather.

"He's nearly sixty! He could have been your father."

"He wasn't," Irini said quickly, before anyone could start doing the maths and ruin the moment.

Spiros exhaled smoke like a warning flare.

Maria scribbled faster, already composing the next issue of *The Telios Tribune*.

"Yes, I know," Irini said before anyone could scramble for an excuse. "Yes, he's older. Yes, people talk. And yes, I love him. Now, someone give me a coffee before I have to dance on this table to shut you all up."

Claude, caught mid-whisper, slid a coffee towards her with exaggerated innocence. "No one was saying anything," he said far too quickly.

Maria scribbled "Irini threatens table dance" in her notebook and everyone started talking again, louder than before.

Then Katerina wandered over, nudged Irini's knee, and bleated softly as if to say, *Well, if you're happy, we're happy.*

Claude raised his glass.

"To Manolis and Irini," he declared. "May your marriage last longer than his reputation – and may the past stay politely outside the church."

Everyone drank to that. Even Spiros.

By lunchtime, the village was divided neatly into three camps:

1. **The Romantics** – who thought it was a love story for the ages and were already planning what to wear.

2. **The Cynics** – who predicted disaster, scandal, or a fishing-boat-based divorce.

3. The Practical – who didn't care as long as there was lamb at the feast and enough chairs.

And somewhere in the middle of it all, Manolis stood grinning as though he had caught the biggest fish of his life – and was quietly hoping it wouldn't wriggle off the hook before the wedding day.

CHAPTER TWELVE

THE DRY RUN
(AND HOW WE ALMOST DIDN'T SURVIVE IT)

It began, as most Greek weddings do, with mild heatstroke, a crowd already whispering, and the distinct feeling that half the guests were only there to see if someone would slap someone else.

The service was held in the village church, which was whitewashed, sun-baked, and radiating the same energy as an annoyed aunt who had been dragged out of her house on the hottest day of the year.

It was 36 degrees before noon. Father Evangelos began his prayers with a small, heartfelt plea for air-conditioning, which, he assured us, was definitely in the Psalms somewhere if you knew where to look.

Inside, the icons glistened, the candles sagged like tired tourists, and the guests fanned themselves with service sheets while trying not to stare at the front pew, where she sat.

Irini's mother.

She had come.

And she was magnificent.

Perfectly coiffed, perfectly pressed, radiating the kind of calm that says, *Yes, I once dated the groom, and no, I am not apologising.*

The village tried not to look at her, which of course meant everyone was looking at her. Maria's pencil was moving so fast it nearly caught fire. Claude was already composing what he called "a discreet mural". Spiros smoked with the air of someone who had seen this coming since 1987.

Irini looked radiant, though whether from happiness or heatstroke was anyone's guess. Manolis looked like he had remembered all the details of his youth at once.

The Dance of Isaiah went sideways almost immediately. The couple were meant to circle the altar three times, led by the priest. Instead, Irini tripped over the groom's cousin, Manolis stepped on a prayer book, and Father Evangelos said something un-priest-like under his breath. "This is why I prefer funerals.

At least the guests sit still."

By the time the rings were exchanged, with a brief scuffle and a whispered "Left hand, LEFT!" from the front row, everyone had stopped pretending they weren't watching Irini's mother.

She smiled serenely through the entire ceremony, as if she was enjoying her own private encore.

And then we headed for the reception.

Zorba's Taverna had been transformed. Or at least, redecorated with a lot of fairy lights and blind optimism.

Theodora called it a "dry run".

Mary called it "an early warning from God".

Claude had been put in charge of "aesthetic atmosphere". He had hung olive branches from the ceiling fan, scattered flowers over every surface, and painted a six-foot banner reading:

Love is Like a Goat: Loud, Stubborn, and Occasionally on the Roof

He said it was romantic. Zorba said it was a cry for help.

Eleni ran logistics with the steely calm of a woman who had seen battle, or at least a school bake sale in Volos. She marched around with colour-coded seating plans, blowing a whistle, moving chairs as though re-arranging bureaucrats for maximum efficiency.

The real question, though, was where to seat Irini's mother.

"Not near the groom," Mary hissed.

"Not near the bride either," Theodora said, "or she'll start giving opinions."

Maria suggested putting her next to Father Evangelos so she'd have to behave.

Claude suggested putting her under the olive tree "for drama".

In the end she was placed at the far end of the table, close enough to watch, far enough not to comment, which felt like a victory until she began blowing kisses at Manolis every time the *bouzouki* hit a particularly emotional note.

The music started. The plates began breaking, deliberately at first, then accidentally. By the third smash, Claude had started a movement called "Smash for Love."

Spiros remained in his usual spot, claiming he was "supervising from afar" while refusing to move closer than six metres to the dance floor. "Too much risk to the furniture," he said.

The food arrived in waves: lamb, meatballs, trays of *dolmades* that could have fed a small island nation, and slowly, even the most dedicated gossipers forgot to whisper.

Then came Alex.

She arrived at the taverna like a godsent whirlwind of trouble and energy, scattering conversation and common sense in equal measure.

Her dress was red enough to alarm the icons, her earrings swinging like punctuation marks.

A child ran past with a sparkler. Alex grabbed it, produced one twice the size, lit it, handed it back, and said, "If you're going to cause chaos, at least make it spectacular."

She swept into the centre of the terrace, twirled once, and shouted "OPA!" so loudly that the goat jumped onto a chair, which everyone took as a blessing.

And that was it. The dancing started, the gossip stopped, and the taverna turned into something halfway between a festival and a controlled riot.

Even Irini's mother was on her feet by the third song, clapping along and looking pleased with herself. At one point she and Manolis ended up opposite each other in the dance circle. Maria nearly fainted from the sheer journalistic opportunity of it all.

By the time dessert arrived, most of the village had stopped whispering. By the time the last plate broke, they were laughing.

And by the end of the night, everyone, even the mother, even Mary, even Spiros, admitted it had been a good wedding.

No one was arrested, which is always the mark of a successful reception. Only one person fainted (for dramatic effect) and the only casualty was a chair that Katerina had claimed as her throne and eaten the armrests of.

The pergola now leaned at a hopeful new angle. The banner sagged slightly. A few glasses had vanished, possibly into the sea.

But the taverna had survived.

The marriage had happened.

Even the scandal had survived, now softened into a story that would be retold every summer, growing slightly more dramatic with each retelling.

"This," Zorba said, refilling Mary's glass as she watched the last guests drift into the night, "is what love looks like. Messy. Loud. Full of ghosts. And worth it."

Mary smiled, a small smile. "Still terrifying."

"Good," Zorba said. "Otherwise you wouldn't remember it."

CHAPTER THIRTEEN

COURTING AND CAMPAIGNS

Mary was still serving lunch like nothing had happened. As if a digital proposal from across the Atlantic hadn't detonated between the lemon trees. As if Theodora hadn't announced it to three tables and the vegetable delivery man. As if the taverna wasn't now being used as a staging ground for a wedding that, technically speaking, only existed in one auntie's WhatsApp group.

"We might be having a wedding!" Theodora beamed, with the confidence of someone who'd already picked out a dress and secured a discount on the bunting.

The tourists were delighted. Mary was not.

She moved with her usual composure – calm, elegant, unstoppable – but now with a slight tightness behind the eyes, like a pressure cooker ready to blow. Her tray was steady. Her smile convincing. Her mood? Homicidal.

Theodora, meanwhile, had entered campaign mode. If love was an election, she was handing out flyers. Printed photos of Andonis, or "Andy", were distributed like religious pamphlets.

"This is him near his apartment."

"This is him with a kombucha."

"This is him doing yoga. Very flexible. Still Greek in the heart."

Claude asked if flexibility was now a marital requirement.

"Only if you're serious," Theodora replied, solemnly.

Wherever Mary went, someone was "just wondering".

"Is it true?"

"Will it be a summer wedding?"

"Do we need to clean the goat?"

"Can I be in charge of sugared almonds?"

Mary's replies ranged from dry sarcasm to disappearing mid-conversation. At one point she left a table so fast that the olives were spinning.

By Wednesday, Katerina the goat had been fitted with a floral garland, and someone (probably Claude, definitely wine-fuelled) had made a "Just Engaged!" banner out of napkins. Theodora called it a divine sign. Katerina ate it.

Things escalated.

A package arrived from America. It was a handwritten note in calligraphy (we assume he paid someone) with the phrase: "I see your soul, and I honour its journey." Mary read it, frowned, and filed it directly into the bin. Andonis hadn't shown up yet, but his campaign certainly had. He was an idea now, more than a man. A concept. A lifestyle brand. Greekness rebranded. Still, Theodora adored him – or rather, the *idea* of him. To her, any man would do, as long as it resulted in grandchildren.

But Mary wouldn't fight it, not openly. That would've meant giving it power. Instead, she served. She smiled. The sort of smile that makes strong men check their insurance policies. She polished glasses, cleaned tables, and waited. I watched it unfold from my usual table: a tangle of family, fantasy, and unwanted futures being woven between sips of wine and the smell of grilled sardines.

There hadn't been a campaign for marriage this intense since Eleni's cousin tried to marry off his son to a Cypriot belly dancer with an allergy to goats.

But here we were again. Only this time, the bride wasn't budging.

Still, the wedding machine rolled on. The village had spoken. And though the vote was informal and mostly comprised old ladies and people with opinions on curtains, the result was clear: Mary must marry, and Andonis must arrive. And nothing would ever be the same again.

Except, of course, it probably would. Because that's the magic of the village. It builds catastrophes out of breadcrumbs, dances around them with wine and folklore, and somehow, always somehow, ends up back where it started. Slightly confused. Mildly intoxicated. Utterly itself.

But something was shifting. Not loudly. But certainly. The storm hadn't broken. Yet.

CHAPTER FOURTEEN

THE BATTLE OVER SEA-FACING CHAIRS

We don't mind change.

Let's get that clear up front.

We're not some grumpy archipelago of hermits clinging to a rock because we can't bear to leave behind our chamber pots and dial-up. We understand that some changes are good. Penicillin? Wonderful. Roads that don't collapse every February? Helpful. And, under very specific circumstances, we'll even accept traffic lights, provided they're ignored with precision.

But here's the thing: when something's already perfect, why change it?

That was the question on everyone's lips, usually between bites of grilled sardine or while arguing over who left the fishing net in the *kafenio* again.

Telios was, is, perfect. Not in a shiny, brochure way. But in a slightly-cracked-tile, lopsided-table, goat-on-a-bench kind of way. The kind of perfect that doesn't need fixing. The kind where the sea is close, the wine is nearer, and the only form of punctuality is sunrise.

It came from Athens. A notice printed in official Athenian grey. Folded by someone who had never sat outdoors with grilled sardines. And posted, naturally, on the side of the *kafenio* where no one ever looked unless they'd lost a cat.

It read, "New regulation: no chairs may face the sea, to ensure unimpeded pedestrian flow."

This, combined with the rule that started off the trouble in the first place, was beginning to get really silly.

It caused a ripple. Then a wave. Then a full-blown village tsunami. Because here, chairs don't face walls. Chairs face the sea. They always have. Since before the Persians decided to take a detour, since before the Turkish occupation. Since before the road was paved. Since before Dimitri stopped hunting boar and started brewing his own *tsipouro* (which, frankly, was far more dangerous).

Chairs face the sea because that's the point. You come to the taverna, you order something you didn't mean to order, and you stare at the water until the sun tells you it's time to go home.

This wasn't just tradition. It was a right. A spiritual necessity.

And now, they wanted us to sit with our chairs turned away from the sea, or worse, at an awkward angle along the shore. Like naughty children in a corner.

The cooperative was baffled. Then amused. Then furious. Alex, to her credit, tried to understand the reasoning. Something about visibility, something about traffic flow, something about "urban harmony". None of which applied to a village with no actual pavements.

Maria immediately declared it "a cultural assassination". Claude wept into a napkin. Theodora baked skull-shaped *koulourakia* "for morale". And Eleni started drafting letters so scathing they had footnotes.

But the one who took it hardest was Spiros.

Spiros didn't have a chair.

He had a bench.

His bench. His throne. Positioned perfectly in the shade, beside the outermost table of the taverna, angled like a philosopher's perch with a full panoramic view of the sea, the boats, and whoever happened to be trying to park near the bins.

He had sat there since before we took over the taverna. Since before they had electricity in the kitchen that didn't require two kicks and a prayer to Dionysus. And now they wanted him to turn his back on the water.

"They'll have to pry the view from my cold, *tsipouro*-soaked hands," he said, lighting a cigarette as if he was preparing for siege.

It was a quiet Thursday.

Which, in Telios, meant that only *three* things were on fire, Theodora was making *pastitsio* big enough to feed a battalion, and the cats had agreed to a temporary ceasefire.

But peace never lasts long here, especially when someone brings out a clipboard.

The mayor had sent an "observer".

Clean shoes. Eyes like photocopiers. The kind of man who had never eaten a proper tomato, or if he had, he'd filed a report afterwards.

He arrived with a measuring wheel, a notepad, and a faint but detectable dislike of joy. His job: to check their two favourite rules, that no tables were within five metres of the sea, and that all chairs were obediently pointing away from it.

He began pacing the taverna patio like a surveyor of dreams, tutting softly and drawing little diagrams that would almost certainly be used later to justify tearing something up. Then, as though called by an invisible tape measure, he veered off towards the lemon grove, talking to himself about "unregulated trellises" and "possible encroachment".

It was in that pause, with the inspector's voice still faintly audible from the grove, that the plan was hatched, quietly, decisively, and with just enough mischief to qualify as civil disobedience.

Maria lowered her sunglasses and watched him disappear.

"He's measuring happiness," she said darkly. "To see how much to remove."

Claude poured wine with the gravity of a priest at communion.

"He will need a very long ruler."

Theodora sharpened her ladle with such focus it was unclear whether she was preparing for lunch service or for battle.

Claude leaned on the bar. "How long do you think we have before he comes back?"

"Ten minutes," Maria guessed. "Fifteen if he stops to measure the goat shed."

"Then we'd better think of something quick," Alex said, eyes narrowing, as if sheer glare might summon a solution out of thin air.

Eleni arrived mid-conspiracy, clutching a printed copy of the new directive, laminated to within an inch of its life. She stood at the edge of the patio and cleared her throat like a woman about to deliver a verdict.

"For reasons of public safety, spatial uniformity, and pedestrian access integrity," she read with all the drama of a courtroom climax, "no persons may sit, dine, or otherwise remain seated for the purposes of eating, drinking, or social congregation within five (5) linear metres of the sea's edge at any point deemed a coastal access point, scenic promenade, or tidal-adjacent eating establishment."

She lowered the paper. The silence that followed was

broken only by the faint sound of the measuring wheel clicking in the grove. There was a pause.

Maria narrowed her eyes. "No *persons*?"

"Correct," Eleni confirmed, smug.

Claude raised a brow. "What about goats?"

Eleni smiled, the terrifying smile of someone who's found a loophole and intends to sprint through it in heels. "It doesn't say anything about goats."

At that moment, Father Evangelos leaned in and murmured, "Then may I suggest we set a table… for one particularly non-person guest?"

Then Spiros spoke. Or rather, growled. "One table, one chair, one guest. Put it in the five-metre zone."

That's when Father Evangelos leaned forward, eyes twinkling. "And we seat Katerina."

It made perfect sense. To us.

Ten minutes later, Katerina, our unofficial village mascot, mother of kittens and occasional menace, was seated at a perfectly dressed table, her chair facing the sea. She wore a sunhat. She had a glass of water, a menu in her hoof.

The inspector returned from measuring something tragic and stopped dead.

"What is *that*?" he asked.

"That," said Father Evangelos with saintly calm, "is our honoured guest."

"She's… a goat."

Claude gasped. "Sir! That is species profiling."

Maria stood. "She identifies as a diner."

The man blinked. Took notes. Blinked again.

Katerina bleated politely.

And for the first time in Telios's long war with rules, we watched as bureaucracy hesitated. Truly *hesitated*.

He flipped through his notes. No mention of goats. Nothing about animals with a preference for seating. And as for the Five-Metre Rule with Sea-Facing Chairs, it had clearly never been tested against a determined goat with a taste for tablecloths.

He took a photo, muttered something about "unusual compliance", and walked away.

We exhaled.

Katerina exhaled.

Then she ate the menu.

Father Evangelos raised his glass. "To resistance, in all its unexpected forms."

And we toasted the goat who saved the sea view.

The next morning, every chair at Zorba's was not only facing the sea, it was leaning into it. A rogue wave could've taken half the tables, but no one cared. Claude brought paint and turned each chair into a tribute: tiny waves, little suns, the words "Freedom Faces Forward" scrawled in Greek, French, and, unintentionally, something that looked like Aramaic.

The regional official sent another letter. Eleni sent him back a recipe for lemon cake and a list of famous Greek uprisings.

Spiros remained on his bench. Facing the sea. He added a small umbrella, and a sign that read, "Minister of Perspective".

We kept the chairs facing forwards not because we're rebels (though we are). Not because we're stubborn (obviously). But because here, in Telios, you don't just sit to eat. You sit to see. To speak. To remember where you are.

And no piece of paper, however official, will ever tell a Greek, or a goat, where to point their chair.

CHAPTER FIFTEEN

THE SCOUTS HAVE LANDED

The bins had been emptied. The cats were fighting on the roof again. Katerina was finally de-glittered after wandering off for the day and gatecrashing a kiddie paint party. She had returned after an unfortunate involvement with a glue stick and fairy dust.

And then they arrived. Not soldiers. Not tourists. Worse. Aunties. Two of them. From the distant regions of Mary's extended family tree, which in Greece just means you haven't argued yet. One claimed to be from Volos and smelled of lavender and liniment. The other said she was from Patras, but Maria, the village's resident gossip engine, swore that by the look of her, she hadn't lived in Greece since Papandreou had real hair. They stepped out of the taxi like minor royals at a garden party. Big handbags. Bigger earrings. And sandals that looked like they came with a prescription.

Claude squinted from behind the wine fridge. "Is that… a scouting mission?"

Mary, drying a glass, didn't even look. "Worse. Family."

Theodora squealed like a Eurovision intro and greeted them with double kisses and a speech about local produce, fertility, and the importance of marrying before your eggs went bad and your ovaries withered like an overripe fig.

Alex stood at the kitchen door, arms folded, her expression unyielding. "Brace," she said flatly.

The women took their seats as if presiding over a summit. "We've come to speak about Andonis," said the one with the larger handbag and the sharper teeth.

Mary looked bored. "Of course you have."

"He's very successful," said the other. "He owns a building. In California. Apartments. Possibly even a car park."

"Has he sent a message to Mary, or the family, regarding his intentions?" asked Alex, still unmoving. "Oh no, no," they waved breezily. "He trusts us. We're only here to make sure everything's… aligned."

"Aligned how?" Mary asked, folding her arms.

The answer came via a binder.

"We have a list," one auntie declared. "Do you enjoy yoga? Are you emotionally available on weekends? How do you feel about healthy living?"

Mary stared at her. "I serve fried cheese to hungover Germans. That's as close to emotional availability as you're going to get."

"And Los Angeles?" they asked.

"I like it more when it's over there."

Katerina wandered up, stared at them hard, then turned to Mary.

"She's with me," said Mary.

Then the questions came thick and fast. About Mary's age. About her childbearing potential. About whether she knew how to boil rice without using "devices". It wasn't a conversation any more. It was a cross-examination conducted by women in floral blouses who thought subtlety was a foreign vice.

Alex stepped forward. Calm. Controlled. Dangerous. She had stopped blinking. This, in itself, was not catastrophic. But those who knew her well began to shift slightly in their chairs.

Then she started to laugh.

Not a warm, belly kind of laugh. No, this was the brittle, rhythmic laugh of a woman doing the mental arithmetic of how many forks she'd need to stab everyone evenly and still have enough left to set the tables for dinner.

"You've had your questions," she said, voice level and cold enough to curdle cream. "You've had your answers. Now unless you're ordering food or adopting livestock, I suggest you wrap it up."

The aunties froze. One instinctively reached for her shawl, as if it might shield her from tone of voice.

Mary stayed silent but met Alex's eyes – a tiny nod, a life-line. Theodora jumped in with her best crisis-management voice. "Come now, Alex, they've come all this way–"

Alex turned with the kind of calm that usually means someone is about to get verbally stabbed.

"Hospitality," she said, "means feeding people. Not auctioning off the staff like a prize lamb at Easter."

There was a silence.

Not offended silence. Defeated silence. The kind that happens when someone rearranges your soul without raising their voice.

The aunties murmured apologies and turned their attention back to their pastries. One of them began chewing slower, as if that might help the situation.

Alex rarely spoke of her past. She wore it like heirloom jewellery: beautiful, sharp-edged, and hidden in a drawer. Not because she was ashamed, but because people never really asked the right questions. And when they did, they usually regretted it.

But something in her had shifted. The aunties had pushed too far.

Alex didn't often talk about it. The marriage.

It existed in her history like an old scar, not hidden, exactly, but grown over. Faded by time, but unmistakably there if you knew where to look.

She'd been nineteen. That precarious age when everyone assumes you're both old enough to decide and too young to resist. Her family, with their good intentions and terrible judgment, had come to what they had called "an understanding" with another family. Friends of friends. A quiet word here, a knowing glance there. The boy in question was described as "promising", which in Greece usually means "needs to get out more, with a grandmother pushing for grandchildren".

He needed to grow up. Which, of course, meant marriage.

And so, Alex was offered up like a polite theory: well-mannered, practical, and with enough fire to be interesting but not so much that anyone expected her to burn the building down.

Arrangements were made. Pressure applied. Dresses chosen. Smiles rehearsed.

No one asked if she wanted it.

Alex turned to face the aunties, chin high, a spark catching behind her eyes, the kind of spark that usually ends with someone crying or dancing, and sometimes both.

The aunties stiffened in their chairs, clutching their coffee cups like shields, sensing that something dramatic, and possibly loud, was about to happen.

"I was married once," she said flatly, like reading a shopping list. "He seemed respectable. At first."

Mary stopped moving.

Theodora looked down, not in shame, but in memory, the kind that smells like burnt toast and cheap perfume, that hits behind the eyes before it ever reaches the heart.

"I lasted a year," Alex said. She wasn't bitter, or sad. She just had the quiet exhaustion of someone who survived a tempest that everyone else called a picnic. "Not because I loved him; I didn't. But because I thought… maybe I could learn. Maybe if I said the right things, wore the right dresses, laughed at the right jokes, I could bend myself into something that fitted. Or at least stop resenting the life that had been assigned to me like a civic duty."

She paused.

And for a moment, she looked older. Not in years – Alex never aged like the rest of us – but in experience. The kind that wears down bone. The kind that lives in the spine, curled like a story no one wants to hear.

"When I left him," she continued, "no one asked why. No one wanted to know. They only asked what I had done, what I had failed to appreciate, what I had broken; as if his unhappiness were a priceless vase I'd smashed on purpose. I was the scandal. The shame. The girl who said no too late."

Katerina, in the corner, chewed a tablecloth with less enthusiasm than usual. Even Claude stopped pretending to dust the wine bottles.

"It took years," Alex said, "to trust anyone again. Even longer to trust myself. To believe that marriage wasn't just a polite cage lined with good linens and scheduled compromises.

That saying no was no sin at all, it was survival. That choosing myself was an act of courage, not selfishness, something worth teaching to every daughter who comes after me."

She looked at Mary then; really looked. Eyes soft, voice sharp.

"And that no one, not your family, not your aunties, not some tanned investment with a car that parks itself in California, gets to choose for you."

Mary quietly nodded, slow and solid, like she'd been waiting to hear it.

Alex turned back to the aunties. Their brows furrowed, fingers poised over binders, as if still hoping this was not the end of the discussion. "It ends here," Alex said.

One of the aunties looked up, clutching her cup like evidence.

"We were just collecting data," she began, with the innocence of someone who had absolutely not staged an emotional ambush.

"Mary is not a spreadsheet," Alex snapped. "She is not a project. She is not here to increase your cousin's emotional equity."

The silence after was the good kind, the kind that comes just after truth, and just before change.

And in that silence, Mary smiled.

Because Alex, fierce, fallible Alex, had set the room on fire.

And for the first time in a long time, no one tried to put it out.

Zorba coughed pointedly. Claude whispered something that might have been "bravo" and poured himself a glass of something very red and definitely fermented.

Theodora stepped forward, hands nervously folding a napkin that didn't need folding. Her eyes met Alex's without argument, just understanding. Regret curled into the corners of her smile, but it didn't reach her eyes. "I thought I was helping," she whispered.

Alex nodded. "I know. But help shouldn't come with conditions."

Katerina trotted past and began chewing on one of the auntie's guidebooks.

"Good girl," Mary smiled.

The aunties exchanged a glance. One snapped the binder shut like a final act. "Andonis will arrive soon," she said, as if it were both a threat and a weather forecast.

Theodora squeaked. Mary exhaled through her teeth. Alex swore under her breath in a dialect only spoken by very angry Spartan women. And Katerina headbutted the nearest flowerpot with determination.

As the door closed behind the aunties, normality resumed.

But Mary caught Alex's eye again.

That nod returned, smaller this time, almost invisible,

but this time it meant something else entirely. Trust. Hard-won. Uneasy. But real.

Zorba raised his glass as a farewell to the aunties.

"Cheers to that," Claude said and uncorked another bottle of wine.

Eleni raised a form from behind the counter. "I can file this entire event under 'Resolved by verbal policy enforcement.'"

Katerina peed on the welcome mat.

Alex stepped beside Mary, tucked a strand of hair behind her ear and whispered, "You deserve to be asked. Not arranged."

Mary smiled – small, tired, but real.

Somewhere outside, Spiros coughed, the sound of a man both agreeing and refusing to be caught caring.

The room exhaled. The aunties' voices faded down the street. And for the first time all week, the taverna felt like itself again.

The village returned to its natural state: slightly chaotic, wholly unbothered, and entirely unfit for arranged love.

CHAPTER SIXTEEN

Mary's Counterattack (with Cake)

By the time the aunties had returned to their taxi, one whinging about "a tragic lack of ambition" and the other adjusting her earrings as if bracing for court, the village had already begun to quietly, efficiently, and delightfully revolt.

The match had been proposed. The match had also been, in the collective opinion of nearly everyone at the taverna, politely shoved into the nearest bin and doused with *retsina*.

Mary had said nothing. Which, for Mary, meant everything.

Because Mary silent is like a sky before a thunderstorm: lovely, golden, and absolutely ready to flatten something.

Theodora, bless her eternally hopeful heart and her growing stack of *kourabiedes*, refused to lose faith. "She just needs to *see* him," she insisted, icing a trial cake like it was a contract with destiny. "He owns a building, you know. With a car park!"

"She's not marrying a car park," Claude said, lighting something suspicious and eyeing the ganache. "Although it'd probably be more responsive than a man who sends aunties instead of flowers."

Maria was already drafting her article, "Love in the Time of Overinvestment: The Cross-Atlantic Courtship Nobody Ordered".

Even Dimitri, who generally avoided affairs of the heart unless they arrived salted and grilled, offered his support. He carved "Free Mary" into a crate of sardines and declared it symbolic – and also tax-deductible.

But Mary? Mary had a plan. She hadn't told anyone what it was.

There are many strategies for turning down a marriage proposal in Greece.

You can pretend to be already married. You can claim a spiritual calling. You can announce plans to become a nun, a goat whisperer, or a professional backgammon player. But what you absolutely cannot do is reject a suitor handpicked by your mother *without good reason.*

Especially if your mother is Theodora.

Theodora, who once wrestled a rooster at Easter because it dared wake the baby. Who peels potatoes with the aggression of a retired general. Who believes feelings are real only if served warm, with lemon, and accompanied by unsolicited advice.

Mary knew this. She also knew that simply saying "no" would not be accepted. Not because Theodora was unreasonable – no, no – but because she had already told five women at church and a stranger at the bus stop that "the match was practically sealed".

There was now a fantasy wedding marching towards them like a brass band. The dress had been imagined. The lamb had been mentally seasoned. *Koufeta* almonds had been priced, in bulk. One relative had already offered to DJ with a playlist exclusively made up of Nana Mouskouri and 80s power ballads.

Mary needed a plan.

STEP ONE: DELAY

"I'm so busy this week," she told Theodora, standing in front of the fridge and hoping it would electrocute her rather than prolong this conversation.

"Busy?" Theodora repeated, like the word was foreign. "With what? Stirring things and glaring at tourists?"

"Exactly," Mary said, without irony.

STEP TWO: REDIRECT

"You know who might like him?" Mary said, reaching for the emergency tin of coffee. "Daphne's niece. The tall one. Great hair. Lazy eye. Ambidextrous. Very polite."

Theodora's eyes narrowed.

"She doesn't cook."

"She could learn."

"She once put ketchup on *pastitsio*."

Mary gasped. "I withdraw the suggestion."

STEP THREE: GUILT

"If you really loved me," Mary began.

"I do," Theodora said.

"Then you'd let me choose."

"I *am* choosing for you."

Mary sighed. "That's not how this works."

"Of course it is," Theodora said, then hesitated just long enough to show she knew it wasn't entirely true. "I chose your father, yes. He was the only man who could eat my stuffed peppers without his eyes watering."

Mary folded her arms. "Exactly. *You* chose. That's the point."

"Yes, but I was clever when I was your age," Theodora shot back. "You are… distracted. This is why you need me."

Mary groaned. "You mean I need you to find me a man who won't choke on your peppers?"

Theodora nodded, completely serious. "Love is digestion, *koukla mou*. If he survives my cooking, he will survive you."

At this point, Katerina ambled into the yard, looked between them, and headbutted the empty laundry basket as if casting the deciding vote.

Mary placed a hand on her heart. "See? Even the goat agrees with me."

"She's confused," Theodora said, mostly to herself. "Probably hormonal."

***

Across the terrace, Maria was already sketching the outline of a love triangle story that included betrayal, redemption, and a dramatic bakery incident. Claude, inspired, had begun crafting a play. It opened with a dream sequence set in a vineyard and ended with a wedding conducted by a dolphin.

The village had moved beyond speculation. It had started *rehearsing.*

So Mary tried a different approach. She transformed – overnight – into the most accommodating version of herself that anyone had ever seen. Theodora beamed. Alex narrowed her eyes. Stamos, passing through on his way to deliver dubious electrical repairs, took one look at her cleaning cutlery with serene enthusiasm and complained, "Someone's about to blow something up."

He wasn't wrong.

At the taverna, a worn notebook labelled "Inventory" sat behind the till. It contained no stocktakes, but pages of scribbled notes under the heading, "Make Them Regret This".

Mary had planned this in detail. She had sat under the lemon tree with a notebook, writing it out like a battle plan, and this time she meant to execute every step with precision.

STEP ONE: WIN HEARTS

Mary became the most accommodating version of herself ever seen. She remembered orders before they were spoken. She refilled wine without asking. She laughed at Claude's jokes. Twice.

She even told Father Evangelos that his sermon last Sunday had been "especially relevant".

He hadn't given one. He nodded anyway and blessed the olives.

By the end of the day, the German tourists were so enchanted they threatened to immortalise her in a five-star Tripadvisor review titled: "The Saint of Telios".

STEP TWO: REWRITE THE MYTH

Mary stayed silent, raising an eyebrow at Eleni in the way that meant "go on then".

Within the hour, Eleni had "remembered" that Andonis once tried to trademark the phrase "emotional journey" for his matchmaking app start-up. Maria, sensing a scoop and smelling mischief, ran the story in *The Telios Tribune* under the headline, "The Start-Up Fiancé".

No one verified it, but it spread through the village like wildfire, and by sundown half the tables were debating whether Andonis should be fined for "emotional capitalism".

STEP THREE: WEAPONISE THE GOAT

Katerina appeared at lunch wearing a hand-stitched sash that read: #LetHerSayNo.

No one admitted to making it. Mary claimed ignorance.

Claude declared it a political statement and added a small beret, calling it "performance art".

Katerina stomped pointedly on a pile of bridal flyers, then ate one. The symbolism was not lost on anyone.

STEP FOUR: PROVOKE THE ELDERS

During Friday lunch, Mary turned up the theatrics. She laughed too loudly. She flirted shamelessly with an Australian backpacker named Lachlan who'd come in looking for Wi-Fi and left with a limp.

He proposed, using a breadstick and half a bottle of house wine.

Mary declined with a smile.

"I prefer men who season their own olives," she said sweetly.

Theodora clutched her pearls.

Spiros applauded from the bar.

Step Five: Deploy the Cake

Saturday night. Peak service. Tables full, sun low, wine flowing.

Mary emerged from the kitchen like a goddess of vengeance and ganache.

The cake was three layers tall. Chocolate sponge. Candied walnuts. A swirl of buttercream so perfect Zeus himself would have sworn allegiance.

And across the top, in flawless white icing, one word:

NO.

The taverna went silent.

The breeze gave up and went to watch from the shade.

Then Claude raised a glass.

"Magnificent," he said, voice reverent.

Theodora muttered something that might have been a prayer or a curse – it was hard to tell over the sound of Spiros choking on his wine from laughing too hard.

The taverna erupted. Tourists cheered. Someone took a photo. Katerina tried to lick the frosting.

Only Alex remained still. Watching. Calculating.

Later, as the tables cleared, Alex found Mary in the kitchen, wiping down the counter like she'd just repelled a siege.

Alex handed her a glass of wine.

"You've declared war," she said.

Mary took a sip. "One slice at a time."

"You're not going to marry him."

"No."

"You're going to make sure the village stops asking."

"That's the goal."

Alex nodded. "Need help?"

"Not yet. But keep your flamethrower ready."

Outside, Stamos had taken it upon himself to start a fire, "for ambience", and was toasting sardines with Dimitri using an old car aerial.

Father Evangelos wandered over, took one look at the flaming crate, and sighed.

"Every time I leave you people alone for five minutes, something catches fire. Do you know how many special prayers I've had to invent for this village?"

Then, almost as an afterthought, he made the sign of the cross, "And may the Lord protect whatever was inside."

Inside, Theodora unfurled a catalogue of wedding dresses.

She was the last true believer.

Everyone else had started quietly buying more cake.

The wedding hadn't been called off.

But it was slipping quietly into myth.

Mary had never looked more serene.

She adjusted her lipstick, straightened her apron, and muttered under her breath, "Let them try."

The next chapter of madness was already taking shape.

CHAPTER SEVENTEEN

THE OLD MAN AND THE SEA

There are some mornings when the sea wakes first.

Before the taverna. Before the cats. Before even Eleni's first coffee, which is brewed at a strength that could legally be considered a pesticide.

On those mornings, Zorba walks.

He doesn't walk quickly. Not like the pensioners who power-stride past the pharmacy in Lycra, tracking their heart rates and pretending not to check who's watching.

No – Zorba walks like the sea now. Slow. Steady. A little more careful since the day he slumped forward and made half the village consider CPR training. But there's still that faint air of irritation, as though time itself is an unnecessary nuisance.

He doesn't tell anyone when he does this. He just disappears. Slips out before the bread van honks, before the fishermen return, before Alex has had a chance to command the sun to rise properly.

He walks down to the old beach.

Not the new one, with the umbrellas and the kayak hire and the Instagram people doing squats in front of sunsets. The *real* beach. The one behind the olive grove, past the leaning pine tree that looks like it gave up halfway through growing.

It's just rocks now. Pebbles. Driftwood. The last few bones of a pier that once held up his first grill, a battered rusted frame that sizzled with ambition and the occasional anchovy.

This is where it began.

No menu. Only a cooler box, a grill, and a crate of tomatoes that refused to ripen in sync.

Zorba never advertised; he never needed to. The smell carried across the harbour, and the sea delivered the hungry straight to his tables.

People came. And stayed. And came again.

He had fewer lines on his face back then. Fewer stories too, but more hair.

Now he stands on the rocks, looking out at the water like it owes him something. But the waves are old friends. They bring no news, only the sound of everything staying the same – which, in this world, is a kind of miracle.

Zorba bends, winces slightly, and picks up a smooth, flat stone. He weighs it in his palm, tossing it lightly a couple of times to test its balance, before attempting to skim it.

Badly.

It bounces once and sinks like a broken promise.

He shrugs.

"That's fair," he agreed. "I've been heavy lately too."

He takes a seat on the old jetty stump. It creaks. Everything creaks now. Chairs. Knees. Expectations.

And he remembers.

The early days. When tourists still asked for permission. When menus were suggestions, not contracts. When a table by the sea wasn't a violation, it was a gift.

When he built the taverna with his own hands. Well, mostly his own. And Spiros's back. And a bottle of ouzo that served as both payment and anesthetic. He didn't plan to build a business. He planned to build a place. A place where people could sit. Breathe. Eat. Argue. Laugh. Drink too much wine and forget why they were angry. A place where the fish was fresh and the gossip fresher.

And for a long time, it worked.

But when the rules came, Zorba didn't argue. Not really. He just stopped. He closed the taverna. Folded it up like an old tablecloth. Sat by the sea and waited for the silence to feel like peace.

But it never did.

Because the taverna wasn't a job. It was a song. And when you stop singing, the silence doesn't soothe. It stings.

He runs a hand through his hair, or what's left of it, and sighs.

He doesn't say he misses it. He wouldn't. That's not how he talks. But he hasn't missed a morning at the taverna since the day it closed.

And now it's open again. Different. Messier. Louder. Run by a committee of chaos and caffeine. But alive. And the sea… still close enough to salt the glasses.

Zorba reaches into his pocket and pulls out a small coin. Old. Worn smooth by years of handling.

It was the first tip he had ever received. From a Belgian couple who had asked, with halting Greek and nervous smiles, if he could make something vegetarian.

He had given them bread, olives, and tomatoes. They had wept.

He had kept the coin ever since. Not for its value – it wasn't worth enough to buy an onion – but as proof. Proof that feeding someone well can mean more than speaking their language. Proof that a taverna can be church, therapy, and revolution if you do it right.

He holds it a long moment, thumb brushing over its faded face, the metal heavier now, not because it has changed, but because he has.

Then, with no drama and no witnesses except the sea,

he kisses it once, like a priest blessing bread, and throws it.

It sinks instantly, without even a ripple.

And Zorba smiles.

Because some things don't need to come back.

They just need to be released like smoke from a grill, like a stubborn grief, like a man who has finally remembered why he loves to cook. And whatever comes next, an acknowledgement that his grip on the taverna, like life itself, is not eternal.

CHAPTER EIGHTEEN

THE PAPER TRAIL AND THE PERSISTENT WHISPER

One day, a letter arrived. It was folded three times, stamped twice, signed once, and delivered with the kind of solemnity usually reserved for court summons or bad news from Athens.

"New ordinance," said the courier, a pale young man who looked like he had been seconded from a Volos office against his will and hadn't seen the sun since 2020. "Article 14B. Concerning the lemon grove."

He placed the envelope on the taverna table like it might explode, then fled before anyone could ask questions.

We opened it.

We read it.

And we wished we hadn't.

Nine pages. Printed on paper so thin it was practically translucent. In summary, our lemon grove had been "provisionally designated a Heritage-Adjacent Eco-Cultural Space" and must now be "brought into visual harmony with contemporary visitor expectations".

"They want us to *standardise* the lemons," Alex said flatly.

"Standardise the lemons?" I repeated, sure I'd misheard.

"Yes," she said, tapping the document. "Page three. All branches must conform to a 'sympathetic curve ratio'. Undergrowth must be removed. And spontaneous growth…" – she looked up, deadpan – "is prohibited."

"Spontaneous growth is the only kind of growth we have!" Maria exploded, snatching the paper.

Claude leaned in, scanning the text. "They've even got a section on 'emotional resonance'. What does that mean?"

"It means," Maria said darkly, "someone in Volos thinks they can tell our lemons how to feel."

That was when Eleni arrived.

She took one look at the document, turned the colour of a ripening fig, and snapped, "Give me that."

What followed was a masterclass in righteous bureaucratic fury.

Eleni sat, spread the pages flat like a teacher about to mark the worst exam papers of her career, and read them line by line, hissing comments under her breath like someone personally offended by every comma. "This clause contradicts itself," she said, stabbing the page with one finger. "This section was never properly gazetted. And here – here – they have cited the *wrong subsection entirely*!"

Maria, meanwhile, had already begun her own counterattack. She flipped open her notebook, eyes gleaming.

"'Villagers Outraged at Lemon Grove Sterilisation Plan,'" she murmured. "No. Too soft. 'Telios Faces Cultural Cleansing'. Perfect."

"They can't cleanse a grove!" Eleni snapped.

"They can if I say they can," Maria shot back. "And everyone will believe me."

Thus began the Great Telios Divide: Eleni, armed with regulations, and Maria, armed with gossip.

Eleni marched home and returned with a stack of old permits, coffee-stained and dog-eared, dating back to the 1970s. She spent the afternoon cross-referencing obscure land-use maps and criticising "administrative overreach".

Maria marched through the village, interviewing everyone she could find. "How do you feel about the grove?" she asked.

Kyria Sofia declared that the twisted branches brought good luck to her goats.

Little Yannis said the lemons told him secrets when he was quiet.

Spiros assured us that if anyone touched the grove he would personally glue himself to the biggest tree.

By sunset, Maria had enough material to publish a special edition of *The Telios Tribune* titled, "Voices of the Grove: A People's Testimony".

When Eleni saw it, she nearly fainted.

"You can't put this in an official filing!" she protested. "This is just… feelings!"

"Exactly," Maria said. "The people's feelings. Do you know how many tourists cry under those lemons every year? This is heritage."

"They are lemons, not heritage!"

"They are *heritage lemons*," Maria snapped. "And I have quotes to prove it."

For two days, the campaign raged: Eleni firing off letters, citing obscure case law, threatening counter-complaints for "procedural vagueness"; Maria pinning bulletins in the *kafenio*, stirring public sentiment, feeding gossip to passing bus drivers.

On the third day, Alex intervened.

"You're both right," she said. "And you're both unbearable. Eleni, use Maria's stories in your next filing – call them 'unrecorded cultural narratives'. Maria, cite Eleni's research so your headlines look official. If we're going to fight Volos, we need everyone throwing stones in the same direction."

Reluctantly, they agreed.

The final letter was a masterpiece: part legal brief, part village manifesto. Eleni's precise language was sprinkled with Maria's testimonies, rephrased for maximum gravitas:

The crooked tree by the taverna became "a site of recurring intergenerational gathering".

The wild undergrowth was "botanically significant spontaneous flora".

Even Katerina was listed as "an unofficial custodian of the grove's integrity".

Maria pinned her latest *Tribune* to the *kafenio* wall: "Lemons Under Attack – Village Unites to Save Sacred Grove".

By the following week, the verdict arrived.

"After careful review," the letter began, "the enforcement of Ordinance 14B is deemed impractical at this time due to overwhelming public sentiment and procedural ambiguity."

Translated from bureaucrat-speak: Fine, keep your messy grove. But don't tell anyone we gave up.

Eleni folded the letter, smug but dignified.

Maria read it aloud to the taverna crowd, embellishing heavily, announcing that "The grove is now officially protected – by decree of the people."

That night, we all drank under the lemons, which, in the glow of the fairy lights, looked particularly smug.

Katerina headbutted the notice into the sea.

No one stopped her.

Even Eleni smiled.

And Zorba, who had been silent through the entire campaign, finally raised his glass.

"It was never really about the lemons," he said. "Paperwork or no paperwork. What matters is that everyone knows they're ours. The trees, the grove, the stories that happen under them. That's what we're protecting."

And somehow, that made the lemons taste sweeter.

Spiros lit a cigarette, exhaled slowly toward the grove, and muttered, "Good. Now the lemons have more legal protection than the road."

Claude nodded, topping up everyone's glasses.

"Excellent," he said. "Next week, we get them voting rights."

CHAPTER NINETEEN

The Reluctant Messiah of Municipal Chaos

Spiros had not agreed to run.

That fact was repeated and shouted over three meze platters and a flaming *saganaki*. He had, in his own words, "no interest, no time, and no intention" of becoming mayor. He had other plans. These included sitting on his bench, smoking hand-rolled cigarettes, and dispensing unsolicited life advice in riddles so obscure that even Plato would've asked for a translation.

And yet, somehow, unbeknown to Spiros, he had already been nominated. He was running, officially.

Alex blamed Eleni. Eleni blamed the misfiled "Community Engagement Form". Claude blamed the stars and Mercury in retrograde. Maria blamed the spirits of the ancestors, who were clearly bored and meddling again.

But the truth was simple: the village had decided.

Spiros, like *moussaka* and pointless arguments, was essential. He was Telios. And if Nichos, with his sock spreadsheet and noise-cancellation policies, was the future, then it was up to Spiros to remind everyone of the past. Even if he refused to stand up for it.

At the taverna, the "accidental campaign" quietly shifted gears.

We didn't ask for permission. We just… started helping Spiros win. Quietly. Cunningly. Like all great Greek endeavours.

Mary printed new menus with "Vote Spiros (or Else)" hidden inside the list of starters. Claude updated the drinks board with a slogan that could be read as either a call to civic duty or a threat, depending on how much *tsipouro* you'd had:

Today's Specials:

Wine

Fish

The Last Hope of the Village

(served cold, like revenge)

"He won't change anything," Maria told tourists. "That's what makes him trustworthy."

Even Dimitri got involved, carving "SPIROS 4 FREEDOM" into a large watermelon and displaying it like it was modern art.

Spiros, of course, noticed nothing. Or pretended not to. He simply grunted more often, which in Spiros-speak meant something was definitely happening. He remained firmly rooted to his bench.

And while Spiros refused to participate, Nichos was already preparing leaflets, brochures so painfully beige they may have been printed on actual toast. His slogans included:

"For a Cleaner, Quieter Telios"
"Vote Nichos: Organised by Nature"
"Let's Modernise Telios (Without Emotion)"

It was like watching a well-manicured parking inspector campaign against a bonfire.

But that didn't matter. Because what we were building wasn't a campaign.

It was resistance.

A taverna-led, goat-assisted, olive-oil-fuelled uprising of sheer indignation. A movement against plastic dreams and Wi-Fi cafés. Against the spreadsheeting of our lives.

And Spiros? He was the accidental messiah. The reluctant revolutionary.

Eventually, he would have to be told.

But not today.

Today, he smoked in the sun, complained about olive prices and how figs were sweeter in the 80s, while around him a quiet rebellion baked in the oven, stirred in the soup, and bubbled in the village air like good *tsipouro* and bad intentions.

And Nichos?

He would never know what hit him.

***

It was late.

Not the loud kind of late, when the taverna is still humming and someone's arguing with a chair. But the soft kind. The sea had gone smooth. The fridge had stopped rattling. Even Katerina had curled into some obscure corner of the garden, dreaming of tyranny and half-eaten menus.

Alex sat on the back steps of the taverna with her head in her hands.

Not dramatically. Not even heavily. Just… still.

I watched her from the doorway, a tea towel still slung over my shoulder like I might do something useful with it. I didn't say anything right away. Sometimes, the best way to help Alex was to not interrupt her thinking.

But this wasn't thinking.

This was weighing.

After a while, I sat beside her. She kept her eyes fixed ahead but stayed put; permission enough.

The moon lit her profile. Strong, as always. But her fingers were tapping that nervous rhythm she never admitted was a tell.

"What if we can't hold it?" she asked quietly.

I let the silence sit a while as the breeze drifted in.

"What if it's too much? The taverna. The village. The… everything."

She gestured, vaguely, towards the olive trees, the sea, the chaos of our lives. The unseen paperwork. The volunteer meetings. The fridge repairs and the budget estimates. The goat.

She sighed.

"I fix things. I organise them. But what if–"

She paused.

"What if I'm just keeping everything from falling apart?"

I reached over and took her hand. She didn't squeeze back, not immediately. But she let me hold it, which, from Alex, was a full admission of fear.

"You are," I said.

She turned, startled.

"But here's the thing," I added. "You're really, really good at it."

A long silence.

Then a laugh – soft, tired, but real.

"That's not comforting."

"Didn't mean it to be. Just meant it to be true."

She leaned against me, forehead against my shoulder.

"I didn't want to be in charge," she said.

"I know."

"They're going to vote for Spiros."

"I know."

"And I'll have to clean up behind both of you."

I smiled. "Obviously."

For a long time, we sat there. Tea towel useless. The fridge silent for once. The moon above us, the sea doing its slow, patient breathing.

Finally, she pulled back. Stood. Brushed the dust from her skirt like she was shaking off doubt itself.

"Right," she said. "Back to work."

Because Alex is strong.

But now you know: sometimes, she's scared too.

CHAPTER TWENTY

THE RELUCTANT CANDIDATE

There are certain moments in life that require immense courage: childbirth, war, cancelling plans with a Greek grandmother, and, most scary of all, telling Spiros something he doesn't want to hear.

We'd avoided it for weeks. Whispered. Danced. Dodged. Pretended we hadn't noticed the gathering storm cloud of inevitability hanging over the village square.

But there comes a time in every tale of cowardly conspirators when one poor soul must be pushed forward like a human offering, clutching only a sacrificial plate of pastry and the faint hope that they'll return alive.

That soul was me.

I had known it was coming. The way condemned men sense the hangman's lunch break ending. Everyone else had quietly vanished behind crates, corners, and questionable wine bottles. Even the goat turned her back on me.

"Should we draw straws?" Claude had offered earlier, swirling a glass of red that had no right to call itself wine.

"No straws," said Maria. "Straws favour the fool."

"I nominate Dimitri," I'd said.

"I've already been struck by lightning," Dimitri replied. "I'm on borrowed time as it is."

I turned to Alex, our fearless general.

She blinked once, then stopped blinking altogether.

"No," she said. "I've faced inspectors, angry grandmothers, and a man who tried to pay for lunch with a love poem. I draw the line at Spiros."

And just like that, the silence thickened, and everyone else took one subtle step back. That's how you know you've been chosen.

So now I stood there, alone, like a Spartan child sent into the mountains to prove himself, armed not with a spear, but with a plate of lukewarm baklava and the knowledge that Spiros once made a man cry for suggesting the moussaka was "too eggplanty".

They say Spartan mothers told their sons, "Come back with your shield – or on it" (*è tàn è epì tâs*). I understood that now.

I had no shield, only sticky fingers and the scent of fear.

Spiros was in his usual spot: his bench, his watchtower, angled perfectly to the sea. He hadn't moved in hours, except to light a new cigarette or grumble about how tomatoes had lost their flavour since the EU got involved.

I approached slowly, the baklava trembling slightly in my hand. Each step felt like a final confession.

He didn't look up.

He just sniffed and said, "That better not be store-bought."

I sat beside him, carefully, like a man lowering himself onto a landmine he hopes is only decorative.

"We need to talk," I said.

He exhaled.

"That's never good."

"It's about the village."

"That's worse."

He eyed the baklava. Then me. Then the baklava again.

I cleared my throat. "We want you to run for mayor."

A breeze stirred. A lemon dropped from the tree with a heavy thud, as if even the fruit had chosen this exact moment to register its opinion.

He neither blinked nor spoke, staring out to sea instead as if I'd just asked him to lead a charge on the Acropolis.

"No," he said flatly.

"You haven't heard the argument."

"I don't need to. It's a no."

I pressed on, because I'm an idiot.

"You're the only one people trust."

"They shouldn't."

"But they do."

"Well, they're fools."

"You understand the village," I said, desperately. "Its rhythm. Its stubbornness. Its mysterious bins."

"I understand peace and quiet. You're disturbing both."

I tried logic. Emotion. Civic pride. Even guilt. I mentioned his grandfather. I mentioned democracy.

He sighed.

By now, the others were emerging from their hiding spots like guilty meerkats. Maria ambled up, pretending she was "just passing". Claude arrived with a bottle of something labelled "Emergency Bravery" and passed it around. Dimitri followed with a bowl of soup that smelled like week-old anchovies.

Alex stood by the door, arms crossed. Watching. Waiting. Judging.

Spiros scanned us all slowly, as though he was being forced to choose between root canal or poetry night.

"You're serious," he said.

"We are," I said, voice cracking slightly. Now wasn't the time to tell him the nomination forms had already been signed and delivered.

He shook his head.

"I've spent decades avoiding politics. And now you want

me to stand in it? Waist-deep? With campaign flyers and microphones and strangers asking about parking bays?"

"We'll do all the work," Maria said quickly. "You'd just sit there. Symbolically."

"Like a scarecrow."

"More like a lighthouse," Claude offered. "Strong. Stoic. Useful. Slightly damp."

He lit another cigarette. The flame flared. The silence deepened.

"You're mad."

"Yes," I said. "But it's a collective madness. We're all in it. Together."

He looked at me.

Not through me; *at* me. Properly. It felt like he was deciding whether to throw me into the sea or tell me to walk there myself.

Then he stood.

We all tensed.

He stretched, groaned, adjusted his waistband… and sat back down.

Eleni, who'd materialised like a bureaucratic spirit of fate, quietly stamped a form.

Spiros stayed silent, not agreeing but not leaving either.

And just like that, we knew.

He wouldn't campaign.

He wouldn't smile for posters.

He wouldn't show up to any debates.

But he'd sit.

And in Telios, that was as close as anyone had ever come to saying "Yes."

CHAPTER TWENTY-ONE

It's not often the village priest becomes the most stable person in the story. But in Telios, stability is relative, and Father Evangelos had the look of a man who had once performed an exorcism on a broken boiler and won.

He wasn't your typical priest. He blessed bread with one hand and stirred lentils with the other. His sermons included references to motor oil, ancient Sparta, and once, memorably, *Mamma Mia 2*. But what he lacked in theological rigidity, he made up for in kindness, and the terrifying accuracy with which he could read people.

So when Mary started avoiding the square, ducking behind fig trees, slipping out the back of the taverna, or pretending to rearrange lemon baskets, he noticed.

And when Spiros, increasingly encircled by passive-aggressive campaign posters and a goat with a sash, began grunting more than speaking, he noticed that too. Father Evangelos looked straight through you, not in a cold way, but in a way that made you feel seen all the way down to your soul. The sort of noticing that made people sit up straighter, confess things they hadn't meant to, or abandon a plan halfway through because they knew he'd already seen right through it.

Which is exactly why Mary had to work harder when he was around; he'd catch the glint in her eye before she even picked up the mixing bowl.

One morning, Father Evangelos invited them both for tea.

Not together. He wasn't mad.

Mary came first. She arrived with arms folded and eyebrows raised.

"I'm not marrying anyone," she said, before sitting down.

"Of course not," said Father Evangelos. "That would involve paperwork."

She narrowed her eyes. "I mean it."

"So do I. We've only just had the tax forms translated. A wedding would collapse the system."

Mary blinked. Then, unexpectedly, she laughed.

He poured tea. It smelled faintly of cinnamon and possibly

holy water – or maybe it was just thyme.

"I hear the aunties have been busy," he said.

"They treated me like a prize chicken at an agricultural fair," Mary said. "Except I have more opinions and fewer feathers."

"They mean well," he said.

"They mean control."

He nodded. "And you mean freedom. A fair standoff."

She looked at him, uncertain.

"Do I disappoint them?" she asked, suddenly small.

"No," he said gently. "You confuse them. Which is better."

A pause.

He reached under the table and handed her a *koulouri* wrapped in wax paper.

"You don't owe anyone a performance," he added. "Just be kind. Especially to yourself."

Mary blinked hard and took the *koulouri*. She didn't cry, but she came close.

"Don't worry," he said. "I'll talk to the aunties."

"Will you tell them to stop?"

"No. I'll tell them to pace themselves."

Later that same day, Spiros arrived. Father Evangelos was watering the basil.

"I'm not running for mayor," Spiros grunted.

"Of course not," said the priest. "That would involve standing."

Spiros paused. Then he glared. "I'm serious."

"So am I. You sit. They campaign. Seems to be working."

"It's madness."

"Yes," said Father Evangelos. "But it's our madness."

He gestured to a chair. Spiros remained standing but stayed put, which, by his standards, was practically a hug. "I'm not built for this," he told the priest. "I don't do slogans. Or events. Or…" he gestured vaguely at the sea, "… hope."

"You've been a lighthouse since before the rest of us knew we were at sea," said Father Evangelos.

Spiros grunted, which was not a disagreement.

"There's a rumour," the priest continued, "that you once stopped a bureaucrat with nothing but a raised eyebrow and a glass of house red."

Spiros looked away, muttering something about poor wine and weaker men.

"Leadership isn't speeches," Father Evangelos said. "It's presence. And you've been present longer than anyone."

"I didn't ask for this."

"No one did," the priest replied. "Except the goats. And Claude. And everyone else."

A long pause.

Finally, Spiros sat down. Only slightly. On the edge. As if he was preparing to bolt at any sign of respect.

"Fine," he said. "But I'm not campaigning."

"Of course not."

"I'm not smiling."

"God forbid."

"If they print leaflets, I'll burn them."

"Please do. That paper chafes."

They drank tea in silence. Two men. Two mugs. Three types of rebellion. Then Spiros said, "Mary's strong."

"She is," said Father Evangelos.

"Too strong for marriage."

"Maybe. Or maybe strong enough to wait for the right reason."

Another silence.

Then the priest said, "And maybe you're just stubborn enough to be exactly the kind of mayor we need."

Spiros snorted.

But he didn't disagree.

By sunset, both Mary and Spiros were in slightly better moods.

She returned to the taverna with a fresh koulouri and less tension in her shoulders. He returned to his bench, lit a cigarette, and nodded when a tourist asked if he was "the famous mayoral goat-whisperer".

Later, someone asked Father Evangelos what he'd said to them.

He shrugged. "Sometimes," he said, "people need to be reminded they're allowed to not know yet."

And somehow, that was enough.

But because when the storms come, literal or emotional,

Father Evangelos shows up with coffee. With candles. With calm.

And in a village like ours, that's all you need to be holy.

182

CHAPTER TWENTY-TWO

KATERINA THE CONQUEROR

Dimitri's boat, normally snoring gently at the jetty, was making a noise.

Not a wave noise.

Not a seagull noise.

A chewing noise.

We rounded the corner in time to see Katerina standing proudly on the prow, gnawing the mooring rope like it was the world's toughest strand of spaghetti, and she was determined to finish it before anyone stopped her. With a sound like a sigh, the rope gave way.

The boat drifted free.

And just like that, Katerina was at sea.

She didn't panic.

She didn't bleat for help.

She stood there, square-legged and unblinking, staring at the horizon as if she had been waiting her entire life for this moment.

"She's… leaving," Alex said, shading her eyes.

"She's stolen my boat," Dimitri growled, though there was the faintest note of admiration.

The boat began to drift faster, caught by the current, heading for open water.

By the time it passed the taverna, Katerina had taken on the air of a conqueror. She stood at the prow like a figurehead, the wind tugging at her ears, bleating loudly, either showing off that she now owned maritime property, or crying for rescue.

Either way, we could not let our hairy taverna menace disappear off to Skiathos.

She might find another taverna to terrorise.

And after all, she was family.

"Right," said Alex. "We need a boat."

"There are no boats," said Dimitri. "All the fishermen are out."

"Then we need… something floaty," Mary said.

And that's when Claude spotted salvation.

He paused, shielding his eyes against the sun.

"Look!" he cried, pointing. "Our fleet!"

The toys were everywhere, scattered across the beach like the aftermath of a particularly lazy shipwreck. A few bobbed in the shallows, being ridden by shrieking children, while others lay sunbaked, waiting for their owners to cook themselves into needing to use them. A full flotilla of tourist inflatables.

"Men!" Claude declared, in a tone that suggested we were about to storm the beaches of Normandy. "To the flamingo!"

Within minutes, we had commandeered:

- One enormous pink flamingo.

- Two blow-up dolphins (one missing a fin).

- A unicorn with a perpetually shocked expression.

- An inflatable baby shark that grinned like a psychopath.

- A swan the size of a car tyre.

- A pizza slice with a bite missing.

- And, inexplicably, a flaming gold Pegasus that looked like Zeus's pool toy.

The tourists, delighted rather than offended, gathered in a semicircle with beers in hand to watch the preparations.

Getting everyone *on* the inflatables was an event in itself.

Claude, naturally, took the flamingo, striking a pose so dramatic he looked like a saint in a very strange Renaissance painting.

Alex straddled the unicorn, gripping its neck with a dark expression.

"This had better not end up on Instagram."

Mary ended up on one of the inflatable dolphins, which immediately rolled over and dumped her into the sea. She surfaced, hair plastered to her face, unleashing a string of language normally reserved for tax inspectors, faulty washing machines, and anyone who puts pineapple on *souvlaki*.

Dimitri simply grabbed the baby shark under one arm and began kicking furiously, like Poseidon on his day off.

Eleni claimed the Pegasus, announcing she would "fly over the goat like a hero".

Claude shouted back that this was not mythology, this was an emergency, and Eleni replied, "Everything is mythology if you survive it."

Spiros, who had been sitting on his bench watching with increasing horror, finally stood, complained, "This is madness," picked up the inflatable pizza slice, carried it back to his bench, and sat down. "If I'm going to watch this lunacy," he said, "I may as well be comfortable."

Zorba came out from the kitchen, cigarette in one hand, glass of wine in the other, and took in the entire scene. "You're all insane," he said, then sat back down, which was his way of giving permission.

Theodora refused to get involved but appeared in the doorway with a wooden spoon and shouted tactical advice: "Kick harder, you'll drift left! LEFT! No, your OTHER left!"

A ragged fleet of mythical creatures had hit the waves, paddling furiously with flip-flops, beach mats, and a pink flipper with a picture of Barbie discarded by a little girl on the beach.

From the shore, it must have looked like a children's story book gone wrong:

The Flamingo of Justice.

The Angry Unicorn.

The Shark of Doom.

The Majestic Pegasus, now facing backwards but still committed to glory.

Tourists were cheering.

Someone started taking photos.

Maria began live commentary for *The Telios Tribune*: "Goat Escapes, Village Responds with Naval Engagement".

Out at sea, Katerina watched our approach with mild disdain.

She bleated, a sound that could have either meant "Help me," or "You fools will never take me alive."

The current was carrying her faster now. The flotilla raced after her.

Claude's flamingo was taking on water.

Eleni's Pegasus had spun backwards and was now majestically retreating, slowly, defiantly, as though it had a personal grudge. She lunged, grabbed the pole, and spun it back around to face forwards. It immediately began to swivel backwards again, mocking her. By the third rotation she was muttering darkly about destiny; by the fifth she was threatening to call the mayor; and by the sixth she was riding it like a victorious general who had conquered municipal maintenance.

Mary had one leg in the air, still yelling at her dolphin.

"Faster!" Alex barked. "If she reaches the point, we'll lose her!"

Dimitri finally caught the boat and hauled himself aboard with one heroic heave, still clutching the baby shark.

Man and goat locked eyes.

There was a silence so thick you could hear the tourists holding their breath.

And then, with a weary sigh, Katerina sat down. Defeated. Or possibly bored.

Dimitri started the motor and turned for the shore, our fleet of mythical beasts limping behind.

By the time we reached the harbour, the entire beach had gathered to watch. There was applause and cheering. One German tourist sang the theme from *Pirates of the Caribbean*.

When we reached shore, Katerina hopped off the boat, shook herself off, and strolled back towards the taverna as though nothing had happened.

"She planned that," Alex grumbled, dripping wet.

"She *always* plans it," Dimitri said, tying the boat with a knot so complicated even Houdini wouldn't escape it.

Claude raised his arms, triumphant. "Well," he said, "at least it was dramatic."

Maria scribbled furiously, "Goat Dramatically Rescued by Unicorn Navy: Village Applauds Swift Action, Goat Remains Defiant".

Spiros shifted on his pizza-slice cushion and announced dryly, "Next time, let her go. The goat might open a better taverna."

That night, Katerina was back in her usual spot by the bins, chewing reflectively.

She looked smug. Which was fair. After all, how many goats get their own Viking funeral rehearsal, and a flotilla of mythical creatures sent to bring them home?

The next morning, the harbour was quiet.

Too quiet.

I wandered down with my coffee, half-expecting everything to be normal again.

It wasn't.

Katerina was back on the jetty. Not chewing this time. Not leaping aboard. Just *looking* at the boat. Judging the new knot. Judging the sea. Judging me.

Spiros sat on his bench, still using the inflatable pizza slice as a cushion, cigarette in one hand, coffee in the other, watching her with a patience that suggested he had seen this before.

"She's planning another escape," I said.

"She's planning a fleet," Spiros replied.

Katerina turned her head slowly, locking eyes with both of us, then bleated once, long, low, and ominous, before strolling away.

Spiros exhaled smoke and nodded toward the boat. "Double the knot," he said.

"Why?"

"Because next time," he said, tapping ash into ground, "she'll bring friends."

CHAPTER TWENTY-THREE

A Debate by the Bench

There were no posters, no microphones, no refreshments – unless you counted the open bottle of *tsipouro* Claude had decanted into a recycled water bottle marked "Lemonade (Do Not Touch)".

But somehow, on a Friday evening with no real warning, the first official mayoral debate of Telios's campaign season unfolded.

Spiros, as usual, was on his bench. He hadn't moved all day except to light a cigarette and share his opinion about the state of figs.

Maria, keen to "capture a civic moment", dragged an empty chair out from the back storeroom and placed it opposite him. "A chat," she said.

Spiros grunted.

"Public interest."

"Public nuisance."

Within minutes, the circle grew.

Eleni wandered over, paperwork in hand, saying something about procedural legality.

And then someone, probably Maria, possibly Katerina, said the words, "Let's make it a debate."

Debate is a strong word. What followed was more of a shouting match in instalments, punctuated by coughing, *retsina*, and historical references no one fact-checked.

Spiros, to be clear, had still not agreed to any of this.

"I'm not campaigning," he said.

"You're sitting in the candidate's seat," Maria pointed out.

"I'm sitting where I always sit."

"That's symbolic."

"It's shady."

She turned to the gathering crowd. "As you can see, he's humble."

Spiros stared at her.

Claude stood. "Let us begin. First question: What is your vision for Telios?"

Spiros took a drag of his cigarette.

"Survive the summer without dying."

A cheer went up.

Second question: "How will you address the coastal paving issue?"

Spiros snorted. "Let the sea take it."

More cheers.

Third question, from Dimitri, slightly tipsy: "Where do you stand on mandatory helmets for scooter drivers carrying goats?"

"I stand in the shade," said Spiros. "And I let the goats decide."

At this point, the crowd had grown. Tourists wandered over, assuming it was a show. Someone set up a speaker and played *bouzouki* music softly, as if underscoring the entire scene with national pride.

Zorba, seated at his usual table just outside the kitchen – where he no longer cooked, no longer was in charge, but still held moral authority like a disgruntled sea god – leaned back in his chair and scowled. His scowl said: "You're all fools, but I'm bored, so carry on."

Someone shouted, "Ask him what he's going to do about the taxes."

Spiros replied, "Ignore them."

Zorba raised one eyebrow. Approval – or as close as it gets.

And then, inevitably, Nichos appeared – not in person, but in the form of a press release, printed and immaculately stapled, delivered by a man on a moped who looked frightened of eye contact.

Alex read it aloud in full dramatic tone: "Mayor-elect Nichos pledges to modernise Telios with digital innovation, heritage-sensitive infrastructure, and community-centred regulation."

It painted a glowing picture of a brave new world: digitised forms that never leaked (unlike the roofs), LED signs that told the truth (unlike the fishermen), and public announcements delivered not by shouting over the *bouzouki* player but by village-wide WhatsApp alerts – because nothing says "community spirit" like a notification at 3 a.m. reminding you to renew your septic tank licence.

Silence.

Then Spiros said flatly: "He wants to ban the fishing line again."

Theodora hissed like a kettle.

Claude raised his wine bottle in solidarity.

Maria produced a new headline draft on a napkin: "The People Versus Progress: Spiros Leads the Resistance".

By the time the sun began to dip behind the fig trees, the crowd had doubled. Spiros hadn't moved. He hadn't promised anything. He hadn't smiled.

And somehow, that was exactly what made everyone so sure: he was the man for the job. By doing nothing – magnificently, stubbornly, consistently – he had become everything.

The debate ended not with applause, but with an unspoken agreement that this was happening.

Alex returned to the kitchen, in search of a strong coffee.

Eleni took notes.

Claude proposed a campaign slogan: "Spiros: Too Tired to Corrupt".

Dimitri suggested we make T-shirts.

Katerina chewed on a discarded press release.

The crowd drifted away, murmuring their approval, more convinced than ever that Spiros was the right man for the job.

Spiros lit another cigarette, watched them go, and grumbled, "Perfect. Just what I needed: more responsibility."

But there was a slight twitch at the corner of his mouth.

A flicker of reluctant destiny.

CHAPTER TWENTY-FOUR

THE ARRIVAL THAT HADN'T ARRIVED

He still hadn't come.

Andonis.

Andy.

The Future Husband.

The Californian–Greek son of Theodora's cousin's cousin who emigrated in 1957, made a fortune in whatever it is people make fortunes in over there, and only returned once, to complain about the lack of order and the lack of personal space in villages where everyone knows your shoe size and how many eggs you have for breakfast.

But even though his plane hadn't yet materialised, his presence was already haunting us, like the ghost of a half-finished government tax office building: unwanted, unavoidable, and somehow always looming at the worst possible moment.

It began gradually. A scented letter addressed to Mary here. An email full of emojis there. Even a handwritten postcard that smelled faintly of airport duty-free cologne.

Theodora started humming love songs while stirring the soup.

Maria asked Claude to check the taverna lighting "just in case he turns up shirtless for lunch", and even Katerina was acting skittish, which, in our village, was the surest sign that something unnatural was brewing.

Spiros, watching it all from his bench, exhaled a plume of smoke.

He flicked ash toward the lemon grove. "Good. We were due for a tragedy. Or at least a decent scandal."

Then a parcel arrived. It was a booklet: glossy, and tied with twine that smelled alarmingly of eucalyptus.

Meet Andy:
A Guide to the Man Behind the Muscles

That was the title. And that was only the start.

Inside:

- A foreword from his mother titled "Raising a Gentle Titan".

- A section on his favourite meditation playlists, ranked by moon phase.

- A full account of his time volunteering at a dog yoga retreat, where he'd apparently achieved "emotional union with a Labrador".

- And, naturally, a full-page glossy photo of him paddleboarding in linen trousers, holding a green smoothie like it was a sacred relic.

Mary read it in silence, then used it to balance a wobbly table.

Then came the video.

Claude's tablet, which we use mostly for weather updates and occasionally to Google if something Dimitri caught is legal, lit up without warning.

Andonis appeared on-screen, smiling the way people smile when they're about to sell you a time share.

"Hi, Mary. Or should I say… *Maria mou.*"

Even the Wi-Fi looked embarrassed.

"I just wanted to send love. I can't wait to walk with you on the path of intentional partnership. Relationships are journeys. But so are people. Let's unpack together."

The screen froze on a still image of him blowing a kiss to a cactus.

Claude shut the tablet, said "This is what happens when you ignore NATO," and left to smoke behind the bins.

The taverna, by now, was quietly simmering.

Theodora had picked out her wedding shoes.

Maria was halfway through editing her documentary *Love in the Modern Age*.

But Mary was all smiles. All grace. All terrifying stillness.

She poured wine with robotic elegance, each glass filled like it was part of a choreographed ritual. She cleared plates with the kind of force that suggested every dish was being judged – and found guilty. She gave a five-minute lecture on why Greek coffee should never, under any circumstances, be called "Turkish", leaving the tourist nodding like a repentant schoolchild.

She stayed calm. She held her ground.

But you could feel it. The plates were starting to protest.

"He'll be here soon," Theodora said, clasping her hands. "Maybe next month."

"He's probably waiting for Mercury to go direct," offered Claude.

"Or for his jawline to be symmetrical," added Maria.

"Or his soul to align with a third-century moon god," said Alex. "Honestly, I've lost track."

And then, one final message from the man himself: "I'll be there soon. Just waiting on the universe… and a passport."

Mary poured herself a very large glass of wine, and went back to garnishing salads like nothing had happened.

But something had.

Because the village, which only last week was ready to stage a protest about the price of lemons, was now spiralling into the most dangerous of Greek conditions: pre-arrival hysteria.

The anticipation had fermented.

Worse, Theodora still believed. Believed that if Mary just met him, just once, something would click. Love would bloom. Tradition would be restored. Grandchildren would come.

Mary, meanwhile, skipped the quiet simmer and went straight for a slow, elegant boil.

Waiting. Plotting. Working.

She had no need for a man to sweep in and declare himself. But for her mother's sake, she would let him try. Try to make his move, plant his flag, flex his romantic muscles.

Because when he finally did, she'd be ready, not with sighs and soft-focus glances, but with a plan. With wine, to survive it, or distract him, or just to make sure she had something to raise in victory. With heels, to stand her ground, balanced and un-shakable, ready to look him straight in the eye. And with a goat, ribboned, defiant, a four-legged protest sign that read #FreeMary in careful hand-stitched rebellion.

Because if Andy thought he was stepping into a perfect island romance, he hadn't met the village yet.

And he definitely hadn't met Mary's version of a happy ending.

CHAPTER TWENTY-FIVE

A COLLECTIVE CHALLENGE

He had a notebook.

Not Maria's notebook, which is sanctioned village property and is occasionally waved in the square like scripture.

This was a different notebook.

A large, leather-bound thing, perched on the table at the back of the taverna like it was planning something.

Its owner was a thin man in beige – beige shorts, beige hat, beige socks, even a face that somehow radiated beige energy – who claimed to be a "birdwatcher".

"Interesting fellow," Claude whispered, leaning conspiratorially over the salt. "He says he's here to observe the endangered Calandra lark."

Mary, passing by with a tray, kept walking without missing a step. "If he wants to see a rare bird, tell him to wait until Theodora throws a ladle. They never come back."

But the man stayed.

And every day, he sat there. Binoculars perched on the table, notebook open, sipping water with the slow deliberation of a man who was either profoundly patient or profoundly suspicious.

"Birdwatcher," he said if anyone asked.

"Spy," said Dimitri, narrowing his eyes.

"Auditor," muttered Alex darkly, as though summoning a demon from the underworld.

"Tax inspector," said Spiros from his bench. "I can smell them."

Even the goat refused to trust him. One afternoon she stationed herself by his table, locked eyes with him, and stared until he flinched, which, frankly, only made him seem more suspicious.

The thing is, in our village, birds are not something you watch. They are something you either eat or shout at until they stop stealing your grapes.

Alex and I learned this very early.

One of our first encounters with Dimitri involved birds. He arrived at our house and asked, perfectly seriously, "Do you like birds?"

"Yes," I replied brightly. "I have a bird table in England. I feed them nuts and watch them from the window."

"With a gun?" he asked.

"No," I said. "Just… with binoculars."

Dimitri stared at me for a long time, his moustache bristling with confusion, then gave a slow nod. Clearly he'd decided this was some peculiar English ritual, best not to question.

"Wait here," he said, disappeared to his truck, and returned with a string of ten freshly shot blackbirds. "These," he said, holding them up like a bouquet, "are delicious stuffed with cheese."

And with that, he left, presumably to shoot more.

So you see, in Telios, birds are not to be observed. They are to be roasted. Or at the very least discouraged from living.

Which meant nobody trusted the man with the binoculars. Not because he might be spying on the village, but because he might be wasting perfectly good birds.

By the third day, the notebook was no longer just a notebook. It was evidence.

Maria, who had taken to peering at it on her way past, reported that it contained diagrams – suspiciously detailed ones.

"Tables. Benches. Olive trees," she said, flipping a page in her own notebook for emphasis. "He's mapping us."

"Mapping us for what?" I asked.

"Commercial development," said Theodora, grimly.

She offered no explanation for how she knew. This was how conspiracies start in villages: quietly, over coffee, and usually by someone who has been wrong about everything since 1994.

But once the seed is planted, it grows.

By lunchtime, the entire cooperative had declared war.

Claude volunteered for surveillance duty. He wandered past the man every ten minutes, "accidentally" dropping philosophical remarks like, "Ambience is such a fragile thing, don't you think?"

Mary sharpened her sarcasm until it could cut glass. When the man asked for a straw, Mary handed him one, raised an eyebrow, and said, "We serve water. Not cocktails with umbrellas. But sure, live dangerously."

He blinked, clearly not used to being challenged over hydration.

Claude, who had been eavesdropping with the intensity of a cat by a mouse hole, suddenly appeared with a spoon. "In case you want to stir your observations," he said gravely.

Maria followed up by placing a napkin next to him. "For your tears," she said, already scribbling "Telios Faces Straw-Related Spy Crisis" in her notebook.

Even Dimitri joined in, slapping a fish on the table. "This one has seen everything," he said. "You can interview it."

By now, half the taverna was watching. The man cleared his throat and said, "I'm only here for the birds."

"Us too," said Spiros from his bench. "Roasted. With oregano."

Katerina wandered over, stared him down until he shifted

uncomfortably, then stole the notebook clean off the table and trotted away with it.

"That settles it," Mary said, dusting her hands. "If the goat doesn't trust you, neither do we."

Theodora, hearing about the situation, came out of the kitchen holding a spoon like a weapon.

"What is this?" she demanded, eyeing the notebook.

The man, to his credit, explained that he was "simply noting the flight patterns of the lesser kestrel".

Theodora nodded.

"Eat," she said. It was lamb stew.

He hesitated.

"Eat," she repeated, louder, until he ordered something.

Theodora stood there until he took a bite, as though the stew itself were part of the interrogation.

By day four, the whole taverna had joined in.

Dimitri blocked the man's view with fishing nets.

Eleni started humming loudly every time he opened the notebook.

Claude adjusted the lighting so his sketches came out crooked.

Maria began drafting a new headline: "Suspicious Stranger Thwarted by Culinary Resistance".

Even Spiros got involved, by refusing to move from his bench so the man had to sit at an awkward angle to see anything at all.

And then, when we had all agreed he was a spy, a developer, a surveyor, and possibly a foreign agent, the man packed up his notebook, stood, and said, "Thank you for your hospitality. Your taverna has one of the healthiest barn swallow populations I've seen in years."

He left money under the plate, tipped his hat, and walked off towards the bus stop.

There was silence.

The next morning, the cooperative held an informal meeting under the olive tree.

Claude suggested we hang a sign that read "Taverna: Swallow Sanctuary".

Mary vetoed it.

Alex declared that any future "birdwatchers" must submit a request for seating at least 24 hours in advance.

Theodora, having already started prepping the day's stew, simply said, "If they eat, they stay. If they don't, they go."

And just like that, the matter was settled.

The tables were back where they belonged.

The goat had stopped glaring.

And for the rest of the summer, the swallows nested undisturbed under the tin roof, singing above the lunchtime clatter, like a tiny feathered choir blessing the chaos below.

CHAPTER TWENTY-SIX

MARY MAKES A MOVE

The thing about Mary was this: she didn't shout.

She didn't fling plates.

She didn't threaten to move to Athens or marry the first tourist who owned a functioning passport.

She didn't cry in the kitchen unless the onions truly deserved it.

No – Mary simply… adjusted.

So when it became painfully, laughably, cosmically clear that Andonis was coming in person, Mary put on her best lipstick – the one that could charm a German accountant *or* silence a disruptive child with a single glance – and went shopping.

Not for a dress. Not for perfume. Certainly not for a wedding folder. No, Mary went shopping for leverage.

Her first stop? The elders.

In Telios, everything important is passed through three filters: gossip, garlic, and the opinions of pensioners.

If Mary was going to weather this storm, and come out dry, she needed the elders fed, flattered, and firmly on her side.

So she began the Baklava Offensive.

Small parcels, lovingly wrapped in foil. No note, no fanfare. Just dropped on doorsteps and plastic tables, accompanied by a nod that said: "You know who's looking after you."

Auntie Fotini declared Mary "a national treasure" and phoned her daughter in Athens just to say, "She's too good for that smoothie boy."

Word was spreading.

Next, she turned to the tourists.

Now, Mary had always been kind to tourists, that delicate mix of curiosity and confusion that wandered into the taverna every summer like polite, sunburnt cattle.

But this time, she launched a campaign. She complimented hats. She gave Greek lessons.

She quietly rescued a newlywed from buying a €9 keychain made in China, steering her instead toward Theodora's homemade spoon sweets and a bottle of dubious but heartfelt olive oil.

Within 48 hours, the TripAdvisor page had a new headline:

"The Mary Effect: Come for the sunsets, stay for the revolution."

Two Australian couples promised to hold a sit-in if she was forced into a union without informed consent. Claude printed them leaflets.

Eleni made badges saying "just say no". Dimitri took the badges as a personal slur on his original use of "herbal oregano".

Her third stop: Katerina.

Now, Katerina had been many things: mascot, menace, minor influencer – but thanks to a mysterious overnight sewing effort, she now wore a sash that read: "INDEPENDENT WOM-AN".

Mary fed her pomegranate seeds like bribes and whispered, "You're the only one I trust."

Katerina responded by headbutting a tourist who asked if the goat was part of the dowry.

The village began to notice.

Theodora, bless her well-intentioned chaos, tried to stay positive.

She invited Mary for coffee and laid out bridal magazines like weapons on the table.

Mary arrived with her own folder. Inside: an employment contract for a summer beach bar in Santorini. Just in case.

Theodora blinked.

Mary smiled.

No words were exchanged. But the message came through loud and clear, wrapped in lace and paperwork.

Meanwhile, Alex, who had been watching everything like a crow perched above a war map, finally intercepted Mary behind the wine fridge.

"You're plotting," Alex said flatly.

"I'm surviving," Mary replied, adjusting the wine bottles into alphabetical order.

"Same thing," said Alex, handing her a pastry.

Mary was ready. Whenever "Andy" finally appeared, she would be ready.

She knew power. And above all, she knew how to win. Not with shouting. Not with sabotage.

But with quiet, precision-crafted grace. With a smile, and if necessary, with a goat in a sash.

Because when the village wrote its next chapter, Mary intended to hold the pen.

And she was already writing in capitals.

CHAPTER TWENTY-SEVEN

THE MANIFESTO THAT WROTE ITSELF

It was supposed to be a quiet evening.

A little gentle plotting under the lemon trees, a few plates of meze, and a discreet nudge to keep Spiros's accidental candidacy shambling forward.

Claude had promised *simplicity*, "just a few friends," he said.

An informal gathering.

A light civic exchange.

"Philosophical murmuring beneath the lemon trees," he added, which in Telios is usually code for: brace yourself, someone's going to end up dancing on a chair.

And sure enough, by the time the sun hit the horizon, Claude's grand vision of calm, dignified politics had been flattened, trampled, and drowned in *retsina* by the village's much louder, much drunker idea of political engagement.

It began, as most questionable things do, with Claude. He had arrived early, trailing the scent of aftershave and misplaced ambition, dressed like a diplomat on sabbatical, and sipping retsina from a teacup. He claimed the teacup was ironic. The linen suit was not.

Maria showed up next, clutching a shiny homemade press badge and a notebook already half-filled with imaginary quotes. Dimitri followed with a plank of wood repurposed as a campaign sign that read, "Spiros: Because Change is Exhausting". It had glitter on it.

Then came Theodora, bearing a tray of *koulourakia* iced with the phrase "Vote Wisely", and Eleni, who arrived with a clipboard and the quiet certainty of someone already filing the paperwork you haven't agreed to yet. The final straw, however, was the podium: constructed from fish crates and decorated with a disco light from Kostas's wedding. It flickered like a political fever dream.

Spiros, entirely unaware of the plan, sat in his usual spot with a cigarette in one hand and a growing sense of foreboding in the other. As far as he was concerned, it was just Thursday. The figs were disappointing. The moon was up to something.

And there were far too many people arriving for anything whole-some.

It wasn't until the microphone appeared – technically it was a karaoke machine from the kafenio, last used during a regretta-ble rendition of "My Heart Will Go On" at Theodora's name day – that Spiros spoke.

"What is this?"

"A gathering," Claude beamed, arms open as if welcoming a revolution.

"It's a mistake," Spiros said flatly, eyeing the crowd, which now included several curious tourists, a confused dog, and Kat-erina, wearing what looked suspiciously like a campaign rosette.

Claude began the evening with an announcement – grand, theatrical, and slightly misjudged.

"Ladies and gentlemen, we gather tonight to celebrate not just a man, but a movement. A figure of reluctant leadership. A prophet of potholes and patience…"

Spiros narrowed his eyes.

"I don't want to be a candidate."

Eleni ticked a box on her clipboard and said, "But you are now."

That was the moment. The exact moment when the vil-lage, powered by *retsina*, boredom, and a deep, unspoken need for someone to blame for the bins, decided that Spiros, grumpy bench-sitter and professional pessimist, was their future.

Zorba, watching from his usual corner with a glass in hand

and judgment on his face, gave a single nod. "Could be worse," he said. And in Telios, that was an endorsement.

And so, it began.

Someone lit a lantern. Someone else uncorked more wine. Claude, inexplicably, began quoting Rousseau. Eleni distributed leaflets freshly printed barely five minutes earlier. Katerina bleated with approval and headbutted an old olive oil tin.

The night spiralled into campaign fever.

Alex arrived in time to witness the chaos and whispered something that sounded like "Dear gods, they've actually done it", before joining the crowd with the weary grace of a woman who's seen worse, but only slightly.

Spiros was asked to speak.

He stood up with the energy of a man returning a faulty appliance. His expression was part confusion, part indigestion.

"What do you want from me?" he asked, scanning the faces around him.

"You already sit down a lot," offered Dimitri, unhelpfully.

"You've been angry for fifty years," Maria added. "It's practically a political career."

Someone shouted, "Manifesto!"

Spiros looked skyward, possibly in prayer.

"I don't want to be the one who arranges pothole repairs."

Applause.

"I want the tax office to stop sending letters written by lunatics."

Cheers.

"And I want to be left alone."

Silence.

Then the chant began. Slowly. Softly. Then louder. "*Spi-ros! Spi-ros! Spi-ros!*" Even the goat joined in, in her own way – by chewing a corner of his bench.

He sat back down, lit another cigarette, and muttered, "Idiots."

He still hadn't said yes. But the village noted that he hadn't *explicitly* said no, either. And in Telios, not saying no is as good as winning anyway.

By midnight, campaign posters were already being designed. Claude had big plans for olive-inspired colour schemes. Maria was workshopping headlines. Alex was already drafting contingency plans involving plausible deniability.

And Spiros? He finished his wine, looked at the moon again, still suspicious, and said to no one in particular: "If anyone wakes me up before ten, I'm quitting."

But everyone knew the truth.

The candidate had risen.

And nothing in Telios would ever be quiet again.

CHAPTER TWENTY-EIGHT

The Cheese-Shed Incident

You should never trust Stamos, our resident builder, philosopher, and prophet of pessimism. Not with your tools, not with your secrets, and certainly not with your lunch (especially if he's decided to "improve" it on the BBQ).

Hand Stamos a hammer and he'll swear he's "just fixing a hinge", but somehow end up dismantling half your balcony, declaring it an "essential improvement" to "improve airflow" or create a "second deck level". He'd likely leave you with a bill for his unsolicited efforts. Give him your fishing net to mend, and he'll return it strung with bottle caps and perhaps even sea urchins, swearing it now "catches only the good fish". He certainly has no intention of following any modern mending codes anyway. Once, someone asked him to watch their goat for an hour, and he brought it back with a haircut and a tattoo (well, technically paint, but it caused a scandal anyway). In all likelihood, he had probably also installed a swing for it.

Stamos has that special glint in his eye, the kind that says he's about to solve a problem no one asked him to solve, or construct an entirely new structure out of thin air and spite. The last time he "helped" at Zorba's, we ended up with a slightly crooked open-air seating plan, complete with columns like the Parthenon (which is impressive when you realise we already had one), and potentially a new third entrance "for good luck". He once caused the bathroom to flood after "improving the plumbing" with an old snorkel and mismatched garden hoses.

He is charming, persuasive, and entirely unreliable – a dangerous combination in a man who owns both a toolbox (often filled with suspiciously rusted tools) and a collection of home-made fireworks. He enjoys setting fires for "ambience", and once turned a lamb roast into a "pagan bonfire visible from the mainland". He is truly a "tinkerer of doom" who genuinely believes any appliance can become a pizza oven.

And yet, somehow, we all keep trusting him. Because when Stamos is involved, things are never boring, as chaos is another form of craftsmanship in his eyes.

George, our village shepherd and semi-professional feta

philosopher, had been *meaning* to fix his cheese shed for months. Or possibly years. Time, like his brine, was a flexible concept.

It was the same stone shed that used to be his uncle's garage, or perhaps his cousin's – the exact lineage was charmingly disputed by three different branches of the family and one lawyer who gave up sometime in the 1990s. The shed leaned slightly to the left, or to the right, depending on the wind, the moon phase, and George's mood. Ask him about its structural integrity and you'd get a single, quiet "We'll see," which in George's language meant, "Don't rush me, I'm ageing cheese *and* excuses."

The door was a masterpiece of rustic defiance: it only closed on Sundays, and then only if you swore heartily in dialect while delivering a swift kick to the bottom hinge with a properly soled boot. Tourists thought this was charming. Theodora thought it was grounds for divorce.

Inside, the air smelled of feta, smoke, and something that might technically be described as "lactose", but which had long since ascended to a higher, more philosophical state of matter. The scent was not unpleasant, just… committed. It was the smell of old wood, goat gossip, and the kind of fermentation that fought against EU food-safety standards.

The roof was a four-season experience: it leaked faithfully every winter, roasted its contents to the edge of legality every summer, and always looked as if it might collapse entirely if you so much as mentioned building inspectors within earshot. The fridge inside wheezed like a donkey with a chest cold, and its electricity supply was rumoured to involve at least one highly illegal wire and a deal with a cousin in the power company.

This peculiar little building, steaming gently in the morning heat, existed to irritate not merely sheep and cheesemakers, but – most importantly – Theodora. Each time the feta delivery was late, her sighs grew more pointed, her eyebrows sharper, until George would reluctantly shuffle in its direction, as if heading into battle. He'd sit on his rickety stool, goat hoofprints stamped on the seat, nodding sagely at the sky while Theodora's fury built to what we called "the vinegar cycle": a stage at which even Zorba himself quietly left the taverna, muttering something about urgent fishing nets that needed untangling.

So, on a bright morning, Stamos appeared. "Today," he declared, "we rebuild."

George, who normally communicated in three words or less, merely nodded. He was a man of few opinions, but a leaning cheese shed was one of them.

Within minutes, they had assembled a work crew. Which is to say: Stamos, George, and an enthusiastic sheep who believed herself to be project manager.

The plan, if you could call it that, was simple: reinforce the roof, straighten the door, maybe add a shelf for the feta. But then Stamos found a stack of tiles "left over" from the church restoration project (a statement that would later be contested by the priest), and George found a bag of cement, and before anyone could stop them, they were halfway through building a second floor.

"This will be the finest cheese shed in all of Evia," Stamos said proudly, balancing on the roof with a hammer and no visible regard for gravity.

"This will be a church," George replied, mixing cement in a wheelbarrow. "For cheese."

By lunchtime, the cheese shed had grown buttresses. By early afternoon, a passing tourist asked if they could book it for a wedding.

And on this particular day, Theodora was already irritated.

She had an order of *saganaki* to prepare for Table Five, and there was no cheese.

"Where is George?" she demanded, brandishing a ladle like a weapon.

"In the field," said Dimitri.

"In the *kafenio*," said Maria.

"Building the Acropolis," said Claude, who had seen the cheese shed that morning and now refused to call it anything else.

Theodora stomped out of the kitchen and across the square, apron flying like a battle flag, in time to see George and Stamos putting the finishing touches on what looked suspiciously like a religious monument to dairy.

"What is this?" she demanded.

"My shed," George said.

"A masterpiece," Stamos corrected.

"It is three metres taller than it was yesterday!"

"Growth is natural," Stamos said solemnly.

Theodora was still glaring when the municipal inspector arrived, summoned by the sound of power tools and Stamos shouting, "More tiles!" from the roof.

The inspector stared at the structure, pencil trembling over his notepad. "You can't just… build a second storey."

"Not a second storey," Stamos corrected. "A mezzanine."

George kept mixing cement.

"Do you have a permit?"

"Do you have a soul?" Stamos shot back.

It went downhill from there.

By sundown, George was sitting in the back of a police car, calm as you like, as though this were simply the natural conclusion of a productive day.

Stamos was seemingly nowhere to be found. "I was never here," he insisted from behind the *kafenio's* fig tree, even though everyone could still see him.

Now, here's where we must pause to explain the Greek planning system, a phrase that really ought to come with a warning label and perhaps a shot of *tsipouro*.

In most countries, if you build something you shouldn't, you get a polite letter from the council. Maybe a fine. Perhaps a sternly worded reminder that rules exist for a reason.

In Greece? You get the police.

Build a wall too close to a river? Arrest.

Add an extra room to your house? Handcuffs.

Construct a BBQ big enough to roast a goat? You'll be explaining yourself down at the station while your *souvlaki* goes cold.

And yet, people still build. And, astonishingly, they often get away with it.

It depends who your cousin is. Or which official owes you a favour. Or whether someone is willing to produce the mysterious *blue stamp*, which appears like a blessing from the bureaucratic gods and somehow makes everything legal retroactively.

Nobody truly understands how this system works, possibly not even the people running it, but Stamos has always lived by one principle: "It's better to ask for forgiveness than permission."

So far, it's worked for him. Mostly.

Well… except for that time he decided to "improve" our small, friendly dwarf wall by replacing it with something roughly the height of Hadrian's. By the time we returned from Athens, we owned what looked like a fortified compound, complete with battlements, two new gates, and a suspiciously defensive aura.

The wall had blocked out the light for half the village. The *kafenio* was in shadow. Even the goat had been disoriented, and stood outside staring at it like a hiker who'd discovered a mountain that hadn't been there yesterday.

Maria had been the first to react, naturally. She produced a special edition of *The Telios Tribune* with the headline: "Local Couple Build New Monastery – Village Seeks Pilgrim Donations"

Claude had declared it "postmodern land art" and suggested selling tickets for guided tours.

Spiros had shaken his head for three full minutes, muttered "the Berlin Wall of Telios", and ordered another cigarette.

Father Evangelos had blessed it, of course, but only after muttering something about the Battle of Thermopylae and whether we were preparing for another.

Theodora had claimed it ruined the airflow for drying her peppers and threatened to knock a hole in it with a ladle.

We had been duly arrested, despite having been 200 kilometres away when the whole thing went up.

The police report simply stated:

Structure: illegal.

Owners: guilty by proximity.

And so we found ourselves explaining, under oath, that we had no knowledge of the wall's construction, its architectural plans, or why it appeared to have its own defensive moat.

But that, as they say, is another story.

***

Back at Zorba's, Theodora slammed her ladle onto the counter.

"No feta," she hissed. "No feta: no *saganaki*. No *saganaki*: no customers."

"This is the first time anyone's been arrested for cheese," Alex said, pouring herself wine.

Claude was sketching the shed on a napkin. "You have to admit, it has gravitas," he murmured.

Spiros sipped his ouzo. "*Olokliri katastrofi*," (complete disaster) he pronounced, which is what he says about nearly everything, but it somehow carries the weight of prophecy.

The next morning, George returned from the police station, dusty but unbothered, with a tray of feta under his arm, as if nothing had happened.

"They said it was illegal construction," he said.

"It was a cheese shed!" Theodora snapped.

"They said it was a public danger."

"To what? Lactose intolerance?"

That night, Stamos bought George a drink at the taverna.

"It was worth it," he said.

The new cheese shed – or as Stamos now called it, The Dairy Pantheon – stood gleaming in the moonlight. It had survived the inspection mostly intact, though the council ordered them to remove the dome.

So now it has a pergola.

And every time it rains, the cheese tastes faintly of victory, like it knows it survived a council inspection and wants to brag.

CHAPTER TWENTY-NINE

THE ALMOST CANDIDATE
AND THE ALMOST BRIDE

The taverna was quiet.

For once.

No broken glass. No impromptu jazz. No drone hovering above the *tzatziki*. Just the hush that comes after a long day in Telios, when the sea exhales, the last tourists vanish into their mosquito-netted rooms, and even the wine bottle knows better than to ask for more attention.

The tables had been cleared, the chairs stacked – mostly evenly – and the last of the stray cats had been fed and dramatically dismissed. Claude had departed hours earlier, leaving behind his wine glass, a crumpled linen scarf, and a half-finished sketch of Katerina in a laurel wreath titled, "Democracy, 2025". The goat had eaten the bottom corner. Everyone agreed it improved the composition.

Mary was behind the bar, stacking glasses and avoiding her own reflection in the window. Spiros was exactly where Spiros always was: just beneath a knotted olive tree at the far corner of the taverna's front, from where it overlooks the sea. His bench is positioned perfectly in the shade, angled like a philosopher's perch, offering a full panoramic view of the sea, the boats, and the surrounding area, like a monument no one dared repaint.

He nursed his *tsipouro* slowly, like it was medicine or memory. The overhead lights buzzed gently. A cricket near the wine fridge launched into what sounded like its opening monologue.

Mary wiped her hands on a dish towel, poured herself a glass, and walked over. She didn't ask if she could join him. She just did.

The kind of silence that followed wasn't awkward. It was earned. Telios silence. The kind that lives between people who have seen each other in storm season – literal and emotional – and still pass the olives.

They sat like that for a while. Two people, one bench, and all the chaos of the village orbiting somewhere just out of frame.

Then, without turning, Spiros said, "So. You're not getting married."

Mary took a sip of wine.

"Not this decade," she replied.

He nodded. "Good."

There was a pause. Not for effect, but to let the next truth arrive when it was ready.

"You?" she asked.

"What about me?"

"You're running for mayor."

Spiros made a sound that was part cough, part scoff, and part ancient curse. "I'm sitting. They're the ones running around shouting."

"You have a poster."

"I didn't ask for it."

"You have a slogan."

"I didn't approve it."

"You have a goat in a sash."

"That… I did approve."

She smiled. They drank.

Mary leaned back against the bench. Her wine glass caught the light, refracting it onto her shirt like an unintentional badge of honour.

"It's strange, isn't it?" she said.

"What?"

"This village. These people. The way they pick you up like furniture and carry you into a future you never agreed to."

Spiros chuckled. "I've been carried. Literally. Once.

During the wine shortage of '97."

Mary laughed, imagining the image. "Was that the one where you climbed onto the olive press and declared a state of emergency? My father told me that story."

"They still never opened the second barrel," he said, shaking his head with mock disappointment.

There was a softness in the quiet that followed. The quiet of people who had made their peace with being misunderstood.

"I said no," Mary said eventually. "That's all I did. No to the wrong person. And suddenly I'm Joan of Arc with a corkscrew."

Spiros studied her for a beat.

"You said no and they turned it into a movement."

"You sat down and they made you a candidate."

He raised his glass.

"To inertia."

They clinked.

The taverna creaked in the heat's final breath. Somewhere in the back, a pan settled loudly. Both of them flinched on instinct.

Mary stared out across the empty tables. The place looked different without noise. Like it had taken off its makeup for the night.

"I don't want to argue with them," she said. "I just want them to stop deciding my life for me."

Spiros nodded. "You want control."

"No," she said, after a moment. "I want peace."

"Same thing."

There was wisdom in the way he said it. Not wise in the "sage on a hill" kind of way. More in the "survived enough nonsense to stop caring what anyone thinks" kind of way.

The lights above flickered, but held. A warm glow. Like the building was trying, even now, to be hospitable.

"What will you do now?" he asked.

Mary shrugged. "I'll keep saying no. Until they hear it."

"You think they will?"

"Eventually. Or they'll get tired and bother someone else."

They drank again.

This time, Mary's glass was nearly empty. She stared into it like it might offer a prophecy. It didn't. Just the reflection of someone trying very hard not to become a symbol.

Then Spiros, voice low and a little amused, asked, "What if we both win?"

She looked at him.

"Win what?"

"You don't marry. I don't mayor. And somehow, the village survives us both."

Mary smiled the kind of smile that creeps up when someone surprises you with truth instead of pressure. "That would be something," she said.

They raised their glasses again.

"To not winning."

"To surviving."

"To never giving them what they expect."

Clink.

The cricket tried a new rhythm. The sea murmured in approval.

And from inside the kitchen, the goat sneezed.

The taverna settled back into itself. A little older. A little wiser. A little more stubborn.

Just like them.

CHAPTER THIRTY

BETWEEN THE TSIPOURO AND THE STORM

The mood in Telios had turned… festive.

Not quite celebratory.

Not quite anxious.

Something in between.

Like the feeling just before a thunderstorm when the air goes too still and everyone knows something's coming but refuses to name it.

There were two things stirring the wind:

1. Spiros, the newly-anointed candidate for mayor, who had still refused to make any official comment other than "don't talk to me".
2. Andonis, the almost-fiancé, who still hadn't arrived but had begun to haunt the village like a sponsored spirit.

Claude called it "a convergence of political and romantic myth".

Zorba called it "nonsense".

Theodora, on the other hand, had fully entered pre-arrival nesting mode.

She baked. Constantly. *Koulourakia* shaped like hearts. Baklava in the shape of a map of Greece. A giant spanakopita shaped like the initials A & M. She insisted on lighting incense "for good energy", which set off the kitchen fire alarm. Twice.

She mopped the taverna floor even though Mary had just done it.

"We want it to shine!"

"It's stone."

"Then let it gleam!"

Even the cats were nervous.

Eleni had printed a full schedule for "The Arrival Week", complete with possible weather disruptions, backup table arrangements, and a 20 per cent buffer time in case of goat interference.

Claude began sketching a welcome mural. It featured a fig tree, the Acropolis, and Andonis's face. No one asked him to do this. He simply said he was "moved".

Maria, of course, had gone full tabloid. The latest edition of *The Telios Tribune* ran the headline, "Love and Politics: Which Will Win Telios's Heart?"

It included a timeline of "key romantic moments" in Mary's life, none of which were accurate, and an anonymous source quote which Mary recognised as Dimitri after his second *tsipouro*.

There were whispers. Plans. A subtle shift in how people looked at Mary, with hope, with scrutiny, with quiet, insufferable matchmaking eyes.

Even the tourists knew something was up.

A Dutch couple asked if they needed to book for the wedding.

A German woman donated a bottle of champagne "for the betrothal toast".

Two Australians offered to livestream the ceremony and brought a drone.

Mary smiled. She brought out the octopus. She cleared the plates. She delivered the retsina. But inside? She was building something.

"I've seen that look before," Alex told me, watching her move.

"Which one?" I asked.

"The 'I'm going to politely destroy everyone' one."

"Ah. Yes. That is a good look on her."

Mary's counteroffensive was quiet. Measured. Beautifully passive-aggressive.

She replaced one of the menus with a handwritten note that read, in perfect cursive, "Marriage? Try the sardines first."

She instructed Katerina to sit, quite pointedly, in the middle of the reserved table that had been set up "just in case" for Andonis and his entourage.

Katerina complied. And glared. She sat like a sentinel of scepticism. A furry, horned warning against romantic optimism. Every now and then, she'd sniff the cutlery with mild disdain, as if deciding whether to throw it or just judge it silently.

Spiros, for his part, refused to be involved.

"Romance is a distraction," he muttered from behind his cigarette.

Then he drank an entire glass of Claude's experimental fig liqueur, winced, and fell asleep under the grapevines, complaining about the price of onions in 1983.

Then came the email. From Andonis himself.

He had been delayed. Something about his passport not arriving, but it was more likely he'd tried to cash in some cryptocurrency to pay for the trip and discovered – too late – that the company's founder had absconded with everyone's investment and relocated to a country with no extradition treaty and very good mangoes.

The campaign rolled on, untouched, not ended, not even dented, merely postponed. A bureaucratic hiccup, while the Greek passport office recalibrated its printer and the crypto police investigated some unusually creative offshore accounting.

But still – something was building.

You could feel it in the atmosphere.

In the way the napkins were folded a little more sharply. In the way Claude started humming the wedding march under his breath while chopping mint. In the way the sunset lingered, like it knew something the rest of us didn't, the village agreed on one thing:

Andonis would come.

Not today. Not tomorrow. Maybe not until the tourist season was over and the figs had been picked and eaten and turned into jam.

But he would come eventually.

Because that's what happens here: gossip ripens into certainty, and certainty turns into a date on someone's calendar, even if nobody knows whose.

CHAPTER THIRTY-ONE

The Trouble with Perfection, and Something New

Perfection, like a well-behaved cat, exists only when unobserved.

At least, that's what we've learned in Telios.

On postcards and filtered Instagram feeds, we are the epitome of Mediterranean perfection: crooked olive trees, sun-soaked ruins, and a goat chewing reflectively in the background. But the reality, the delicious, sunburned, occasionally soggy reality, is far messier.

And far better.

It's in the slightly chipped plates, the menu that changes depending on what Dimitri hasn't caught today, or has, but he doesn't want to admit to snaring another endangered sea creature. The fact that Zorba's Taverna now doubles as a campaign headquarters, a matchmaking salon, and an unofficial goat sanctuary.

But with Andonis delayed, the village relaxed a little.

It was a collective sigh of relief, disguised as a week of not having to take Andonis seriously on Mary's behalf.

Even Theodora stopped sighing over her *dolmades* for a few days.

It was as if the whole village had been holding its breath, and now, finally, it could go back to the important business of complaining about the price of tomatoes and speculating about whether the new postman dyes his moustache.

Even Claude took a break from matchmaking and instead devoted himself to his painting, an eternal work-in-progress he claimed was titled "Sea and Silence" but was, in reality, just the same patch of wall at dusk, viewed through four empty glasses of wine.

"I'm capturing the moment between shadows," he said.

"Try capturing the bill," Alex suggested.

Even Mary seemed lighter. Not joyful, exactly. But less braced. As though some emotional weather had passed and she could finally take off her raincoat.

We were all still worried about Zorba, though none of us

were foolish enough to say it out loud. Mentioning his health would have been like insulting the sea: pointless and likely to earn you a storm.

Alex, ever-watchful, kept finding her eyes drawn to Zorba's corner. Every time he reached for his coffee instead of the glass of water Theodora had started placing at his elbow, her brow would crease slightly, a silent sigh that only those of us who knew her well could read.

Zorba never drank the water. But he never moved it either. It sat there between them like a treaty neither of them wanted to discuss: Theodora's quiet plea, Zorba's equally quiet refusal.

In the kitchen, Theodora stirred her lentils with her usual fierce precision, but every so often her spoon would slow just enough for her eyes to flick to Zorba. It was a mother's glance, sharp as basil and twice as green, carrying that small, new edge of worry that had been there ever since he showed he was not indestructible.

Spiros noticed too, of course. He always did. But his version of concern was to take a long drag on his cigarette and say, "If he starts drinking the water, we'll all know it's over."

Zorba said nothing, just kept drinking his coffee, which was as close as he'd ever get to saying, *I'm fine.*

It was during one of these golden hours, that unrepeatable time when the sun makes even cracked tiles look romantic, that I noticed him.

A new boy.

He wasn't a tourist – he didn't have a sunhat, a guidebook, or any urgent demands for ice.

He was seated alone, just beyond the olive tree, where the tables tilt ever so slightly towards the sea as if in prayer. He wore joggers and a loose cream shirt and the kind of necklace you only buy from someone who also sells healing crystals and homemade soap.

Claude had delivered him wine and peanuts, entirely un-prompted, which was his version of a welcome mat.

The boy sat quietly, not looking at his phone, not fidgeting, simply watching the horizon like it had said something impor-tant and he was trying to remember what it was.

I approached. Because I am nosy.

"First time in Telios?" I asked.

He nodded, slowly. "Got in today. On the late boat."

"Holiday?"

He hesitated, then smiled. "Escape."

Now, *that* was an answer.

And he told me, in that careful, almost apologetic way some people have when they're used to being misunderstood: a Greek–American father with an obsession for Mykonos and mint sham-poo. An English mother with a fondness for correct cutlery and unresolved emotional inheritance. A youth spent between places, between expectations, and between disappointing them both.

Finance hadn't stuck. Nor had the penthouse or the idea of legacy.

So he'd run. To Greece. To something less polished.

He worked kitchens. Learned the language. Fixed boats. Slept on rooftops and deck chairs and once, he claimed, inside a pizza oven (cold, he clarified).

"I like it here," he said again, staring at the water like it owed him peace and was beginning to pay him back.

He didn't notice Mary right away.

But I did.

She swept past, tray in hand, hair loose, expression unreadable.

She saw him. He saw her. There was a flicker, not of recognition, but of possibility. That old magic. The one that makes you check your reflection in a spoon.

She nodded. He nodded. She disappeared inside.

Seconds later, she returned. Dropped a knife. Swore under her breath.

He chuckled. Not in mockery. Just… timing.

She walked on, gaze fixed ahead, as if the horizon held all the answers. He remained rooted, a quiet pause in her retreat, letting the space between them speak.

It was the quietest beginning imaginable. Not even a spark. Just a temperature shift.

Claude appeared beside me like an over-involved weathervane.

"Who's linen boy?" he asked.

"Paulo."

"Hmm," said Claude. "Looks like trouble."

"Or company," I said.

We looked towards Paulo. Then towards Mary. Then Claude poured another glass.

The taverna hummed softly. The sun dipped lower.

A moment suspended.

Later that night, I watched Claude write a new special on the chalkboard:

TODAY'S CHEF SUGGESTION:

Grilled Sardines

Red Wine

A Possibility, Lightly Salted

He added a smiley face.

And for once, I didn't correct him.

Because in Telios, perfection never arrives the way you plan. It arrives on a late boat, wearing linen, sitting quietly until it's time.

And Mary?

She's not ready yet. But the table is. And that's enough.

For now.

CHAPTER THIRTY-TWO

THE RESET

The suspicious humming noise was our first clue that the fridge was about to die. Our ancient, wobbling, wheezing, aggressively humming fridge, the one we affectionately called "The Compressor of Dreams", finally gave up. Not with a bang, or a puff of smoke. Only silence. A long, menacing silence that made everyone in the kitchen freeze, spoons mid-stir, as if a ghost had entered.

"It's fine," Alex assured us, already on her knees, performing CPR with a hammer and a prayer. "It's just sulking."

But no. The fridge had passed on. Off to the great cooler in the sky. The feta wept. The octopus looked smug. We stood there, in the cold(ish) void, knowing exactly what it meant:

The gods were angry.

And they weren't done yet.

Ten minutes later, Dimitri stumbled in, smelling of salt and diesel.

"No fish," he said, tossing his hat on the counter. "Force eight in the straits. Boats didn't go out."

Alex looked up from the fridge, grease on her forehead and vengeance in her eyes. "What do you mean, *no fish*?"

He shrugged. "We have anchovy paste."

Then the gas ran out.

Not metaphorically. Literally.

The stove sputtered like a dying goat, coughed one last flame, and died. Theodora slammed a pan down on the counter with a clang that made the cutlery jump like startled cats. "I haven't even sautéed!" she howled. "This isn't a kitchen. It's a tragic poem."

Claude, emerging from the storage room with a garland made of spoons (don't ask), declared, "The charcoal is delayed. The delivery truck broke down outside Karystos."

"Of course it did," said Alex, wiping her hands on a napkin now labelled "Emergency Resignation Letter".

We had no gas. No charcoal. No fridge. No fish.

We still had yoghurt. But no one felt like negotiating with dairy.

And then, as we were debating whether to close for the day or set the taverna on fire and start anew, Eleni came sprinting across the square, hair flying, clipboard flapping like a distressed seagull.

"It's here!" she gasped, breathless.

"What is?" we asked, collectively bracing for impact.

"The bus."

A silence fell that no one dared break – not even Katerina, who appeared briefly in the doorway, sniffed the air for signs of danger, and wisely retreated to the lemon grove.

Moments later, the bus arrived. A large one. The sort of bus that makes you question your life choices and whether your insurance covers "acts of God".

Out poured twenty-seven tourists, all wearing matching hats and expressions of moderate culinary entitlement.

"We're here for the lunch tasting!" one of them announced brightly.

There was a pause so deep you could hear Spiros's cigarette ash fall onto the pavement.

"We don't do lunch tastings," Alex said flatly.

"You do today," the tourist said. "We pre-booked."

No one had heard of them.

"Who did you speak to?" Alex asked, narrowing her eyes.

"Someone named… Claude?"

We all turned slowly. Claude, crouched over a crate of decorative sea pebbles, looked up and froze.

"Ah," he said. "That bus. I thought that was next Wednesday."

By the time anyone could argue, the tourists had flooded in, filling every table, asking for menus, ice, and gluten-free, sugar-free, anchovy-free options.

Someone wanted almond milk.

Someone else asked if our goat was certified emotional support livestock.

Maria tried to open a bottle of wine. The cork snapped. Dimitri tried to light the grill with driftwood, which immediately exploded in a minor – yet deeply symbolic – fireball.

Claude offered to read a poem about hospitality. No one wanted poetry.

And then came the final insult: "Is your olive oil extra virgin or just… regular promiscuous?"

Theodora put her head in her hands.

"No more!" she roared. "No more requests. No more substitutions. No more tofu!"

Alex stormed out of the kitchen, muttering darkly. "I did not move to the village to explain hummus," she growled.

By 2:37 p.m., still no food had appeared from the kitchen, only rising smoke and despair. Alex finally grabbed a pot and banged it with a ladle so loudly that even the cats scattered.

"Everyone out!" she commanded.

The tourists laughed nervously.

"This is not a joke," Alex said, raising the ladle again. "The taverna is closed."

"But we're hungry!" someone protested.

"Then be hungry somewhere else!"

Mary began shooing them gently toward the door. Dimitri fanned the smoke towards them for dramatic effect. Katerina positioned herself squarely in the doorway and glared until the last tourist backed out.

We stacked the chairs, turned the sign, and sat in silence, listening to the bus drive away.

We made coffee. Strong, black, illegal-strength coffee. We drank it in silence. Eleni mumbled something about retroactive filing amnesty. Dimitri announced he was quitting the sea and becoming a monk. Claude read us all a haiku. We ignored him.

And then, after the dishes had been ignored, the tablecloths scorched, and the tourists deposited safely at the bus stop, we all looked at each other.

"We need a day off," said Alex.

"Tomorrow?" I asked.

"Tomorrow," she nodded. "No taverna. No food. No fish. No feelings."

And with that, we declared a full reset.

The taverna would reopen when, and only when, the fridge

hummed, the fish returned, and we'd all agreed that anchovy paste was not a main course.

Until then?

We closed the taverna. We took our coffees to the sea. Theodora laid down flat in the lemon grove and refused to move. Claude painted the quiet. Alex wrote a list that simply read: "NO." Dimitri went fishing. Without bait. Just peace.

And tomorrow we would have a day off. A glorious, silent, non-negotiable day.

And for twenty-four golden hours, no one asked if our olives were certified organic, or whether the bread could be steamed.

I went for a walk. Sometimes, Greece has a way of making you think. Not casually, but deeply, unexpectedly. It's as if the spirit of the ancient philosophers still lingers in the air, slipping into your thoughts between sips of coffee and the sound of cicadas. You don't just visit Greece; you catch something timeless.

We're not meant to be happy all the time. Life doesn't work like that. Not in Greece, not anywhere. It ebbs and flows, like the sea we sit beside and pretend to understand.

There's this strange pressure these days to always be cheerful, to always be achieving something, to create a life full of sunshine and smiles. But the truth is, we need the quiet moments too. The ones where nothing is happening. The ones where a bit of sadness settles in like a familiar friend, and we finally sit still long enough to listen.

Sometimes, it's good to let a melancholy song play and

just… be. Let the music dig up old memories, let your mind wander to the things you didn't say, the chances you didn't take, the people you miss, and the version of yourself you once imagined you'd become.

It's not wallowing in self-pity. It's balance.

I live in what I often call the most beautiful place in the world, a village hugged by pine trees, kissed by the sea, lit each evening by sunsets so rich they feel almost undeserved. But beauty doesn't shield you from feeling. If anything, it invites it.

There are days when something calls me, not loud, but persistent. I walk to the far end of the beach, where the sand gives way to rock and the cliffs rise up like a quiet amphitheatre for your thoughts. I sit on the warm stone, stare out at the horizon, and let the stillness take over.

I don't try to solve anything. I don't make grand plans. I let myself remember, all of it. The good, the messy, the missed moments. I let the breeze untangle what's been knotted inside, and I breathe.

And in that space, with the salt in the air, the rhythm of the waves, and the weight of a thousand silent thoughts, I find something that feels like completeness. Not joy. Not sadness. Just truth.

Because the truth is, we are all made of both. We are laughter and tears, success and failure.

To reflect isn't to regret. It's to remind ourselves how precious it all is. How fast it moves. How beautiful and fragile and completely unscripted this thing called life really is.

So, if you ever feel the weight of a quiet day, let it come. Sit with it. Walk to your version of the rocks at the end of the beach. Listen.

And you might just realise… that still, aching moment?

That's when you're most alive.

***

And that's exactly where I was. Perched on the rock like a less glamorous siren, lost in thoughts about existence, impermanence, and life, when Dimitri's boat came coughing into view.

The motor sputtered and sent up three separate plumes of smoke, one of which smelled suspiciously like old sardines.

"Peterrrrrr!" he shouted, waving one arm and holding something indistinctly slimy in the other. "I have brought something you must see!"

That's never good.

He was grinning. Which meant either something had gone incredibly right, or something had gone so wrong he was now using faith as a flotation device.

He docked – if you can call ramming into the rocks "docking" – and jumped out with what appeared to be a net full of movement.

"It tried to bite me," he said proudly.

"Dimitri," I said, standing up and brushing existential peace off my trousers, "what is that?"

"I don't know," he beamed. "But I think it's edible."

"No, it isn't."

"Then it's decorative."

"It's twitching."

"All the better!"

And just like that, I was no longer a philosopher by the sea. I was a man standing next to an overexcited fisherman trying to convince a possibly endangered sea creature to hold still while he posed with it for a selfie.

Greece gives you the silence to think.

And just as quickly, it gives you Dimitri.

Balance.

I returned to the taverna with a smile.

The taverna was still closed. Everyone was still there, sitting on the steps, passing around leftover wine and stale bread. The music was gone. Even Katerina had taken the night off. It was just us.

We talked. We laughed. We watched the sea, and for the first time in days, nobody tried to film it.

Even the fridge, given up for dead, which had almost been given its last rights, seemed to sense the shift. It shuddered once, cleared its throat like an old man about to tell a story, and began to hum again.

By sundown, it felt as though something had been put back in its proper place. Not rebuilt. Not rebranded... remembered.

The next morning we reopened, quietly, without ceremony. No theme nights. No special menus. Just a blackboard, a few mismatched chairs, and the sound of the sea doing exactly what it had always done.

CHAPTER THIRTY-THREE

MARY'S DISAPPEARING ACT

Mary started taking days off.

At first, we didn't think much of it. She'd earned them. She hadn't taken a proper break since… well, no one could remember. Possibly the time she had mild sunstroke and had to be physically dragged to lie under a fig tree. Even then, she returned after an hour to yell at Claude for "arranging olives in a way that suggested emotional instability".

So yes – days off. Long overdue.

But Mary didn't *announce* them. She simply wasn't there.

The first time, we assumed she was late.

The second time, we thought she might have gone to the market.

By the third time, even Theodora looked concerned, which is saying something, because Theodora doesn't get concerned. She gets furious, then fixes things with soup.

"I don't know where she is," she said, standing in the courtyard with her hands on her hips, scanning the horizon like Mary might emerge from the sea like Aphrodite with a day planner.

"She said she needed… time."

"Time for what?" Claude asked, genuinely baffled.

"She didn't say," Theodora replied. "Which is how I know it's serious." Mary's absences weren't dramatic – no slammed doors, no grand exits. She came and went like the breeze, slipping through the taverna, rearranging the air, and vanishing again before anyone could hand her an apron.

And when she returned, there was no sign of tiredness or stress. She looked lighter. Not in a bad way, just… noticeable. Her face, already beautiful in that fierce, unapproachable sort of way, had softened. Her laugh came quicker. Her hair seemed to fall differently. She didn't roll her eyes as often, which meant Alex had to carry the sarcasm quota alone (a responsibility she shouldered with dignity and considerable flair).

The rest of the village, meanwhile, went into full speculation mode.

"I think she's painting," Eleni said, in the hushed tone usually reserved for scandal.

"I think she's in love," Dimitri offered, and was immediately sprayed with the hose Theodora had been using to wash down the terrace.

Claude said nothing, which was more suspicious than anything.

Maria began compiling a list of "Possible Mary Activities" for the next issue of *The Telios Tribune*. It included pottery, smuggling, and a silent vow of revenge against a man who once short-changed her at the bakery.

But Alex and I knew better.

On our nightly loop past the old boatyard, we sometimes caught a glimpse. Not of anything dramatic, but of a quiet presence.

Paulo, the new boy, was often there, mending nets with the same meticulous care he brought to everything. And sometimes, just as the light was fading, we'd see Mary nearby, sitting on an overturned bucket, watching him work – just *being*. Or walking with him along the most deserted stretch of beach, collecting seashells like children.

There was no grand gesture, no public display. Simply the soft murmur of two people finding a little pocket of peace away from the taverna's constant hum.

Mary would return from these absences glowing.

Her eyes sparkled in that dangerous way that makes poets start bad habits and married men forget themselves.

She was still Mary, sharp as a knife, quick as a cat, but somehow better. Recharged. Renewed.

Theodora, in a rare moment of maternal intuition unburdened by matchmaking, said to Alex one evening, "She's finding her own light, that one."

And Alex, who saw more than she ever let on, just nodded.

The tables felt a little emptier without her, and the hopeful young men still wore their best shirts for nothing.

But for the rest of us, it was enough to see Mary, finally, simply happy.

Because when someone you care about finally starts looking like themselves again, the real version, the one buried under months of long shifts and half-cleaned kitchens, you don't ask questions.

You just make sure there's a quiet chair waiting in the shade.

And maybe, if you're lucky, she'll come back one day with a story. Or someone.

Until then, we set an extra place, not for a man, not for Andonis, but for whatever came next for Mary.

And if she didn't take it, Katerina the goat usually did.

Which felt like the universe keeping it warm until Mary was ready.

CHAPTER THIRTY-FOUR

POSTERS, POLITICS, AND
A PROBLEM CALLED NICHOS

It was supposed to be quiet.

Just a modest event. Not a festival, not a parade, and certainly not what it became: a full-blown open-air political spectacle featuring a goat in a sash, an unsanctioned candidate, and a minor incident involving propaganda flyers, a flying chair, and someone's bruised shin.

The plan, such as it was, had been Claude's. "Elegant and symbolic," he said. "Nothing theatrical. No fireworks." A simple unveiling of a campaign poster, a soft ripple of polite clapping, and everyone back to their ouzo and conspiracy theories before sunset.

"We're unveiling a visual narrative," he told us, as though the village square was the Louvre.

He promised restraint. Muted tones. A tasteful quote from Plato. "No nudity," he added, unprompted.

Alex waved it through with her classic blend of menace and charm. "Fine," she said. "Just don't make it embarrassing." Which, as we all knew, guaranteed something unforgettable.

Eleni signed off the paperwork with her usual flourish, without reading it, which, by local standards, made it legally sacred.

Maria promised "light press coverage", which translated to: front-page feature, dramatic adjectives, and a photographer from Volos named Ilias, who owned both a drone and a loud opinion about artistic licence.

The setting was poetic, in a tragic way: the wall near the bins, beneath the faded remains of "DOWN WITH FETA TAX-ES" from the Great Cheese Uprising of 2011. Claude arrived early, dressed entirely in black, claiming he needed "creative neutrality" to finish painting the poster. He used oils, watercolours, and something he called "intent". He refused to elaborate.

Theodora brought snacks. Naturally. Cheese-filled. Olive-stuffed. Politically ambiguous.

Dimitri appeared with a pot of leftover paint, a brush in his toes, and no explanation. We didn't ask. He was humming.

Spiros had not been told the truth.

Normally, he was as permanent a fixture as the bench itself – weathered, unshiftable, and always in position, facing the sea like a living monument to patience and tobacco.

But on this day, someone had coaxed him away with the promise of "planning the bench improvement ceremony". The meeting, naturally, was being held in the square, because in this village, no decision about a bench is ever made anywhere near the actual bench.

Rumours swirled of fresh varnish, a new plaque, perhaps even an awning to keep the August sun off his head. Spiros, suspicious but curious, had allowed himself to be lured inland, muttering that if anyone so much as touched *his* bench, they'd better be ready to sleep on it themselves.

He was halfway through his cigarette, imagining what font they might use for the plaque, when he noticed the crowd gathering in the square, right where the campaign poster was about to be unveiled.

There were locals. Tourists. Children with balloons. A German man holding a map and looking lost, like he'd walked into an opera mid-performance.

"Why are there streamers?" Spiros asked, eyeing the square.

"Atmosphere," said Claude.

"Why is Maria holding a microphone?"

"Acoustics."

"Why is the goat wearing a sash?"

Alex didn't even flinch. "Katerina is politically active."

Claude took the stage, which in this case was a crate and a slight incline, and gestured dramatically. "Today," he declared, "we unveil the future."

He pulled the sheet with all the gravitas of a man revealing a prophecy.

And there it was.

The poster.

Spiros, hand-painted, bathed in dramatic light, wearing an expression that landed somewhere between reluctant hero and a man who'd just found out his name was on a petition he didn't remember signing. One eyebrow loomed. His left eye stared directly into your soul. The right seemed to have wandered off towards Albania.

Above him, the slogan read, "Spiros: The Least Bad Option". And underneath, in delicate calligraphy, "No Promises. No Problems."

There was silence.

Then Eleni clapped.

Then the goat.

Then, somehow, the village erupted in cheers. Applause rang out. Someone shouted "opa!" Someone else dropped a *koulouri*. It was glorious. Confusing. Loud.

Zorba, watching from his usual seat beneath the olive tree. He stared in what was possibly approval; possibly wind.

Spiros squinted at the poster. "What the hell is this?"

"Your candidacy," said Claude proudly. "You're a symbol now."

"Of what?"

"Ambiguous hope," Maria replied, scribbling.

It could've ended there. Should have. But fate has a flair for drama.

From the edge of the crowd came a voice, "I'm running too."

Silence fell like a dropped plate.

Enter: Nichos.

Pressed shirt. Shiny shoes. The kind of confident grin usually worn by a man about to announce plans for a luxury resort and a golf course. He walked like someone who had practised this entrance in the mirror. Repeatedly. He took the microphone, without asking, which in Telios is considered both rude and legally questionable.

"This village," he announced, "needs structure. Vision. Energy. I have a plan for digital infrastructure. For sustainable tourism. For better bins."

He handed out flyers like they were gold leaf.

"Meet Lena," he added, gesturing to a woman in beige with the eyes of someone who regrets accepting freelance work from cousins. "She's my campaign manager and web designer." She waved. No one waved back.

"I believe we should ban scooters from the square," Nichos declared.

Spiros exhaled smoke. "What square?"

"I believe in cleanliness. In regulation. In order."

And that's when Katerina made her move.

She trotted forward, quiet as fate, and headbutted Nichos square in the shin.

He yelped. The crowd froze. A bird flew off a power line in dramatic solidarity.

Spiros looked up. Still unmoved.

"I believe," he said, "you've already lost."

Applause exploded. Someone threw a fig. Kostas got it on drone footage from three angles. The German man finally found the *kafenio*.

Claude turned to Alex. "We're going to need a second poster."

Alex nodded. "Make the goat the running mate."

Spiros lit another cigarette. He didn't smile. He didn't wave. He didn't say thank you. But then, he never did. And that, of course, was what made him perfect.

For the village, this wasn't a campaign launch so much as a seasonal ritual, like the fig harvest, or someone inevitably crashing their scooter into the olive press.

As the sun dipped behind the bins and Katerina's mayoral sash fluttered like a flag of reluctant revolution, it was clear to everyone: the campaign, or at least this week's version of it, was officially in full swing.

By nightfall, we had three broken folding chairs, one goat who looked dangerously close to taking office, and Spiros, who hadn't moved an inch.

If the popular vote were counted in cigarette ash and muttered disapproval, Spiros had just been elected in a landslide.

CHAPTER THIRTY-FIVE

THE CREATURE FEATURE SPECIAL

Dimitri had caught another strange sea creature. The third this week.

It was late afternoon at Zorba's, and, against all known odds, everything was… suspiciously normal.

The sea was doing its sparkly thing. The chairs were upright. Eleni was fighting the receipt printer again. Mary was slicing lemons with her usual blend of grace and mild aggression. Katerina was licking the napkin dispenser like it had wronged her in a past life.

Then the back door slammed open.

Three spoons jumped out of a drawer. A tourist let out a startled yelp. And in came Dimitri.

Dripping wet, barefoot, shirtless, and radiating the energy of someone who had either survived a shipwreck or started one.

"MAKE WAY!" he shouted, flinging a sodden net onto the prep table. "Dinner has arrived!"

The thing inside twitched.

Everyone stared.

Mary slowly stepped back, knife raised. "It moved."

"It's fresh!" Dimitri beamed. "Caught it myself. Beyond the jetty. Might be a new type of squid. Or an eel. Or… something else."

"It has… knees," said Claude, peering around a crate of onions. "Are squid supposed to have knees?"

"No," said Alex flatly, entering from the pantry. "Also, you're dripping on the pastry tray."

"It tried to eat a pepper," said Theodora, calmly reaching for a frying pan.

"Which means it has taste," Dimitri said. "Perfect for olive oil and garlic."

"It winked at me," Mary added.

Eleni walked in, saw the puddle, the twitching, and the trail of wet footprints, and immediately began filling out Form 12-B: Unexpected Seafood Event.

Theodora drew a breath. "Dimitri. No. Put it back. Or bury it. Or donate it to science."

But Dimitri was already rolling up his sleeves.

He took it outside and returned with a tray of fillets and tentacles.

"Pan's hot," he said. "Let's be brave."

And before anyone could organise a resistance, he flipped the tray, released the thing – whatever it was – and declared, "opa!"

It hit the pan with a splatter and a hiss. The smell was instant and unforgettable: salt, fish, fear, and a top note of old rope.

Claude began composing a haiku.

Alex unplugged the toaster, just in case.

The creature sizzled. A few tourists applauded.

"We are not serving this," Theodora said, already reaching for the bin.

But the tourists, emboldened by wine and a misguided sense of authenticity, insisted.

So Dimitri plated it, added lemon, and declared it "the catch of the day".

One tourist took a bite. Chewed. Grimaced. Nodded. "It tastes… alarming," he said. "But honest."

Mary muttered, "So does petrol," and wiped down the counter with more force than necessary.

We figured that was that. Another day, another mystery fish, another apology to health and safety – should they ever ask.

But they didn't need to.

Because the next morning, Eleni burst in with her clipboard, three pens, and the face of someone braced for a fight.

"The inspector is coming," she said.

Everyone stopped.

Even the goat.

"He'll want paperwork," said Eleni.

"We don't have paperwork," I said.

"Exactly."

And she was right: if he wanted receipts, we were finished. We'd have to produce a receipt for the fish, and we weren't even sure it *was* a fish. It might have been something that had wandered down from the forest, taken a wrong turn, and fallen into the harbour out of sheer despair.

And receipts for meat? Forget it. Theodora's butcher was a cousin who accepted payment in cash, gossip, and occasional favours involving tractor repairs. The last time anyone saw a receipt from him was sometime around 1987, and it was handwritten on the back of a lottery ticket.

Maria, who had been listening intently, suddenly perked up.

"I can write them," she said, already pulling out her glittery notebook. "One mystical forest fish, slightly glowing. Two heroic lamb chops, obtained under mysterious but entirely legal circumstances. Three chickens of excellent moral character."

"Maria–" Alex began.

"Do you want receipts or not?" Maria said, already adding flourishes. "I can even draw the goat."

Katerina, who had appeared in the doorway, stared at her approvingly.

Cue panic.

Alex went full commander: cleaning, barking orders, stashing the glow-in-the-dark *tsipouro* Dimitri brewed as a 'conversation starter'.

Theodora stirred her pot of beans with the serene defiance of someone who'd outlived regulations, electricity, and at least one revolution.

Mary tried to hide the fishy pan. Claude pasted a sign on the door: "Closed for Metaphysical Recalibration".

At 10:01 a.m., the inspector arrived.

He wore a grey suit. His shoes didn't creak, but his eyes did. He walked in and said one word: "Seafood."

Not "hello", not "good afternoon", not even "who's in charge here?" Just *seafood*, like a man delivering a verdict.

Word had already reached him, through the harbour master's cousin's brother-in-law's neighbour, who'd overheard the entire debate in the *kafenio*. By the time the inspector arrived, the story had been through four rounds of retelling and now came with footnotes.

Some said it was a mutated octopus, the result of years of swimming too close to the ferry exhaust. Others insisted it wasn't an octopus at all but a monkfish that had seen things no monk should ever see. Spiros claimed it was "part fish, part municipal council", which everyone agreed explained its expression.

We all turned to Dimitri.

"Technically," he said, "it was a sea… thing."

"Where is it?"

"In the bin."

Alex tried to smile. "We serve only recognised fish. Local. Responsible. Alive until moments before consumption."

"I'll need to see your freezer," he said.

"We don't have one," I said.

"Then your stock list."

"Dimitri swims," said Claude.

The inspector blinked. "This is not protocol."

"It's Telios," Alex said.

There was a silence. Long. Tense. Measured in heartbeats and lemon rinds.

And then Theodora stepped forward.

"Have some beans," she said, holding out a spoon like a peace offering. "You look hungry."

He hesitated.

He tasted.

He closed his eyes.

He exhaled.

And in that tiny moment, you could feel bureaucracy buckle. He left twenty minutes later with three jars of spoon sweets, a thank-you note from Katerina written in goat hoof, and one fewer "formal warning" ticket in his book than when he arrived. So, no, we didn't get shut down.

Mostly because what remained of Dimitri's "catch", after the tourists enthusiastically devoured most of it, was so unidentifiable it could only have been classified with the help of a DNA lab and a priest.

There was no proof it had ever existed.

No fine came. No one ever named whatever it was Dimitri dragged out of the sea. But a new house rule appeared in chalk above the stove: "Nothing goes in the pan unless it has fins, gills, or at least a recognisable Latin name."

Claude painted it on driftwood and nailed it above the door.

And in small print underneath, Alex added: "If it glows, it goes."

I stood in the corner, sipping someone else's wine, notebook in hand, watching a glowing seafood cryptid get served next to fries. And all I could think was:

This place.

This ridiculous, beautiful, insane little taverna.

This is home.

Where the wine is homemade, the goat is judgmental, and the menu occasionally hisses.

Just another normal day at Zorba's.

CHAPTER THIRTY-SIX

STARS, SCANDALS, AND
A MAN NAMED PHILIPPE

He was wearing a scarf. That should have been the first clue.

It was thirty-four degrees in the shade, and this man was still committed to his look: head-to-toe linen, a waft of something expensive enough to have its own Instagram account, and a scarf – the kind that didn't keep you warm so much as announce your profession.

He had chosen the best table, the one under the olive tree where the sunset turned everything cinematic and the breeze tasted faintly of oregano. He sat alone, back straight, cross-legged, expression unreadable.

And he ate.

Slowly. Deliberately. Like he was taking communion.

One bite. Pause. Scribble.

Another bite. Sip. Scribble.

He even photographed the bread, and then the shadow cast by his wine glass, which caught the late light in a way that made our accidental smudges look deliberate.

Maria confirmed it within the hour, armed with a half-loaded web page, a grainy headshot, and the infamous "Do Not Engage" list taped to the fridge.

It was him.

Philippe.

Senior reviewer, Pan-European desk, *Global Gastro Guide*. The kind of man who could make or break a restaurant with a single phrase: *"lacking soul"*, or *"a triumph of chaos over cuisine"*, or, worst of all, *"charming in its resistance to seasoning"*.

And now, he had come to us.

We froze. We whispered. We rearranged napkins with trembling hands.

Alex nearly fainted when she noticed he was left-handed, a clear sign of refined cruelty.

Dimitri suggested undercooking something on purpose.

Mary threatened to throw salt in her own eye to be excused from service.

But it was too late.

Philippe had already tasted the lentils.

And, God help us, he had smiled.

A Greek smile is the warm, toothy, belly-deep kind that invites you to share in the joke. This was a French smile: the tiniest twitch at the corner of his mouth, a subtle acknowledgment that what he had eaten was… good.

Then he stood, bowed, and left a card. It said:

"Wonderful. Unspoiled. Worth returning to. –P."

And beneath it:

Three Stars.

Neatly printed.

Irrevocable.

We stared at it. Half-elated, half-terrified.

Then we erupted.

That night, we celebrated like fools.

We poured wine. We shouted "opa!" Claude began sketching a new logo involving laurels and dramatic serif fonts. Maria drafted a press release titled "From Beans to Brilliance." Even Theodora smiled, which made us all slightly nervous.

For four hours, we believed we had won.

Then the review went online.

Zorba's Taverna:
A Wild, Honest Triumph on the Edge of the Aegean

The title alone was a problem.

But the quotes were worse:

- "Service that crackles with soul." (Mary, shouting at Claude.)

- "Simplicity that sings." (Theodora's lentils.)

- "The goat alone deserves an award." (Katerina. Uncredited.)

There were photos.

Of the food.

Of the olive tree.

Of the hand-painted menu board with the eternal typo ("aubergime") that was now likely to be preserved forever in online guides.

And then came the final blow: "Book ahead. Worth the detour. Possibly the best-kept secret in Greece."

Alex threw her clipboard. Claude dropped a spoon in mourning. Dimitri suggested a celebratory drink and was immediately silenced.

Because we all knew.

The bloggers would come.

The influencers.

The linen-wearing lifestyle pilgrims who speak of "sacred simplicity" while demanding almond-based feta alternatives.

We had crossed a line.

Zorba didn't say much – he never did – but from his usual seat under the tree he muttered a phrase that froze us all: "We'll lose the soul."

And he was right. This place had been built out of stubbornness, old recipes, salt, smoke, and the kind of laughter that only comes after a storm. And now it risked becoming curated.

Maria folded the article and placed it under the nearest glass. "Right," she said. "Meeting. Now."

And so we gathered.

Claude. Maria. Eleni. Dimitri. Even Father Evangelos, who brought nuts and a notebook.

The courtyard looked serene. The air shimmered like heat. But the tension? You could cut it with a bread knife.

"We can't stop people from writing things," Eleni said.

"No," Alex replied. "But we can stop giving them something to write about."

Claude leaned forward. "You mean… fight back?"

"Yes," Alex said grimly. "But not with charm. With chaos."

So there and then, we decided to make Zorba's as unappealing as possible.

Day One: The Linen People

"Do you have a QR menu?" asked a man in perfectly coordinated linen, to his partner, who had perfectly coordinated teeth.

Mary handed then a napkin that just said "No".

Claude handed them a stone from the courtyard. "This is our ordering system," he told them. "Throw it. Whatever it hits, you eat."

Katerina wandered over. Mary gestured at her. "She'll decide for you. She has a nose for *moussaka*."

"Is that… it?"

The man put his elbow on the table and it dropped a few inches to one side. "Is the table supposed to wobble?"

Claude looked at them, solemn as a priest. "It represents impermanence," he said.

Katerina climbed onto the next table, stared at him, and chewed the corner of the napkin until the word *No* became just a dangling o.

"See?" Claude said. "She approves."

Day Two: The Wellness Group

"Are the sardines sustainable?" asked a woman in expensive hemp trousers.

"They were alive this morning," said Mary. "They're furious."

"What kind of oil do you use?"

"The angry kind."

"Do you offer gluten-free moussaka?"

Theodora didn't even look up. "Do I look like a clown to you?"

One of them cried. They left mid-hummus.

Day Three: The Food Blogger

"I'm here to document authentic culinary experiences," announced a man with a camera so big it required its own chair.

Alex handed him a single fork.

"No spoon?" he asked.

"You'll earn it," she said.

He requested a seat with "optimal light".

Alex led him to a table directly behind the bins.

He asked about "the chef's vision".

Theodora replied, "Hot food. Warm heart. Leave me alone."

"And the terroir?"

Spiros wandered past. "You want dirt? I'll get you dirt."

The blogger left looking like he had been spiritually mugged.

***

By the end of the week, nobody had posted a single reel.

Claude looked wistful. "I miss the shouting," he said.

"Then shout," Alex told him.

"It's working."

We were fighting back. Not with billboards or slogans or marketing campaigns, but with deliberate chaos, skewed tables, mismatched plates, illegible menus, and one extremely judgmental goat.

The stars would stay.

But so would we.

CHAPTER THIRTY-SEVEN

The Man Who Wouldn't Campaign

With two weeks left until the election, the village was in a frenzy.

There were banners. Flyers. Speeches. A debate scheduled near the lemon grove with backup chairs.

Nichos had even arranged a campaign podcast, which consisted of him talking into a microphone and waiting for applause from Lena.

Meanwhile, Spiros was under a tree.

He wasn't hiding. That would've required effort. He was simply… sitting. In his usual spot, with his cigarette, watching the sea and ignoring history.

"We need to organise something," Maria said, pacing the taverna like a general without an army.

"He won't come," I said.

"Then we'll take the campaign to him."

"He won't speak."

"Then we'll quote him."

"He doesn't say anything."

"We'll interpret the silence."

The village tried everything:

- A friendly meet-and-greet at the kafenio: Spiros arrived late, said "don't be idiots", and left.

- A proposed photoshoot: he wore his usual shirt and refused to face the camera.

- A "Walk and Talk" with voters: he walked. He did not talk.

Even Father Evangelos tried to help.

Now that Spiros had "agreed" to run, in the sense that he hadn't physically walked away, Father Evangelos took it upon himself to deliver a gentle lecture about service, duty, and representing the people.

Spiros listened, then asked if the priest had any cigarettes.

We tried everything after that. Guilt. Bribery. Claude even turned up with a donkey, a flag, and a half-written campaign anthem that rhymed *ouzo* with *manifesto*.

Spiros lit another cigarette, watched the donkey eat half the flag, and said, "This is why democracy fails."

Nichos, meanwhile, was doubling down.

He'd upgraded to campaign polos. He was offering policies. Plans. PowerPoints. He even produced a colour-coded voter engagement chart so offensive that Zorba stood up mid-sardine and left the *kafenio* without a word.

And yet… every time we checked in with the village, Spiros was still ahead.

"You know what it is," Theodora said, one afternoon. "He doesn't want it."

"Exactly," said Mary. "And that makes him trustworthy."

Nichos held a rally with finger food and a slide show. Half the crowd left when he used the phrase "municipal brand identity".

Spiros attended. He sat in the back. He heckled, with a single cough. It brought the house down.

By now, even Spiros was beginning to suspect something had gone terribly wrong.

"I'm doing nothing."

"Exactly," I said.

He narrowed his eyes.

"You all think I'm clever."

"No, no," I said. "We think you're… inevitable."
He groaned, loudly, for emphasis.
As of that day, the campaign consisted of:

- One broken sign.

- A goat in a ribbon.

- An old man with a bench.

And somehow, a real chance at victory.

CHAPTER THIRTY-EIGHT

Zorba Returns (God Help Us)

A fresh article.

A new headline.

And this time, it wasn't Philippe.

It was worse.

It was Telios.com, the blog beloved by the kind of visitors who arrive in matching linen, speak of "the energy of the land", and ask if our goat is available for photoshoots.

The title blared, "Zorba's Taverna: Telios's Hidden Culinary Gem", which was rich, considering we had spent the better part of last week trying to make ourselves look *distinctly unappealing.* We'd hidden menus, discouraged hashtags, and politely (well, mostly politely) told three separate influencers to go eat at the next village. And yet, somehow, someone had still eaten here, enjoyed themselves, and written something glowing enough to ruin our peace and quiet.

By lunchtime, it had been shared a hundred times. By evening, a thousand.

And by the next morning, a line of pilgrims had formed, snaking from the jetty to the taverna door, each clutching the article and quoting lines about "the primal honesty of the grill" and "the transcendental poetry of beans".

Maria read it aloud. Nobody moved.

Claude made the sign of the cross.

Eleni asked if we could bribe the man to delete it.

Father Evangelos offered to excommunicate him.

Finally, Alex stood up. Her voice was calm. Too calm. "There's only one way left."

The courtyard fell silent.

Somewhere, a goat stopped mid-chew.

"We bring back Zorba," Alex said.

The words dropped into the courtyard like a stone into a well.

Zorba had been retired. Or semi-retired. Or was in voluntary exile, depending on which version of the story you believed.

But every day he still came and sat beneath his tin roof, a cigarette in one hand, coffee in the other, watching, silently judging, as though the entire taverna were on probation.

He was the original force of nature behind the kitchen: the man who had built the place with his own hands, seasoned it with his own sweat, and run it on a philosophy of smoke, instinct, and the occasional bellow loud enough to startle the next village into better behaviour.

When Alex explained what we wanted, he didn't move. He just looked at us – slow, suspicious, the way a saint might look at sinners begging for a second miracle.

Zorba grunted, and laid down his rules.

The Rules of Zorba

- No menus. The kitchen decides. You eat what arrives.

- No substitutions. "If you ask for almond milk, I will serve you the almond tree."

- No photographs. "The last man who tried is still apologising."

- If you complain, you get more food. Twice as much. Hotter, saltier, louder.

And finally:

- "The goat stays."

(Katerina bleated her approval like a queen reinstating her court.)

That first night, the pilgrims came early, clutching guidebooks, cameras, and expectations.

"Do you have a vegan option?" one asked hopefully.

"Yes," Zorba said. "Wine."

Another tried to order grilled chicken.

Zorba shook his head. "Chicken orders you."

Then the food arrived.

Fish came still glaring, as if personally offended by the cooking process.

Beans were so smoky they stained the walls and possibly the air.

Meatballs landed on tables with a force that made glasses rattle.

At first, the pilgrims looked horrified.

Then they tasted the food, and everything changed.

The taverna erupted into something primal: plates scraped clean, wine poured recklessly, strangers laughing like cousins at a wedding.

Even Claude forgot himself and danced with a chair.

By midnight, the place looked like it had survived a small but meaningful earthquake – overturned chairs, broken glasses, a tablecloth still smouldering – and yet the tourists cheered.

Zorba didn't just cook, he conducted.

Every slam of the pan was a commandment. Every slice of the knife, a sermon.

He barked orders at Theodora, who barked back louder, and together they created food that felt less like a meal and more like a dare.

Claude whispered, "It's not cooking, it's theatre."

Dimitri shook his head. "It's not theatre. It's justice."

People cried over their lentils. Even Spiros gave a single nod, which in village terms was a standing ovation.

The next day, the internet had done its work.

A fresh headline appeared: "Forget Michelin: Telios Has Zorba".

We sat in silence, shell-shocked. Claude put his head down on the table. Mary groaned into her coffee.

Zorba poured himself a glass of wine, sat under the olive tree, and lit another cigarette.

"You cannot stop them," he said finally. "But you can outlast them."

He raised his glass towards the taverna, smoky, loud, still vibrating from the night before, and nodded, as though approving of the chaos.

Theodora rolled her eyes, but her mouth twitched like she was trying not to smile.

Mary muttered, "God help us."

And Katerina, smug as ever, climbed onto a chair and stole Zorba's bread.

That evening, Zorba stayed long after the others had drifted away, smoke curling around him in thin grey ribbons, like punctuation marks in a story only he could read.

I sat with him for a while, not speaking, letting the night do the talking. The taverna was winding down around us – the last plates drying in the rack, the chairs stacked in quiet, lopsided towers, Katerina crunching something in the shadows that I was fairly sure wasn't food, but which I decided was not my problem.

The air was thick with the smell of charcoal and vinegar, and something in me ached – the kind of ache you get when you realise you are standing in the middle of something rare, and fragile, and alive.

It struck me then: this is what people came for. Not the service, which was inconsistent at best and occasionally hostile. Not even the food, good as it was – some nights it was better than others. No, they came for this.

The hum. The clatter. The sense that here, at least, nothing was pretending to be something else.

In a world of polished surfaces and curated experiences, this place was unapologetically itself. A little crooked, a little smoky, a little too loud, but real. And maybe that was why the world had found us. People were thirsty, not just for wine, but for something honest. And the cruel trick was that our very effort to stay honest, to stay a little rough, a little wild, might one day be the thing that broke us.

We couldn't stop the world coming in. But we could try, at least, to hold the line.

When Zorba finally stood and stubbed out his cigarette, it wasn't just a gesture. It was a full stop. A promise.

He was reminding us what it was for.

Not to impress.

Not to trend.

But to feed – simply, fiercely, honestly.

And that, we could never let go.

CHAPTER THIRTY-NINE

The Goat Who Needed a Hug

Katerina was not herself. Not a single headbutt had been administered all day. No flip-flops had been chewed, no menus sampled, not even a casual nibble at a passing napkin. Instead, she drifted through the taverna like a tragic heroine from a village soap opera, doing the goat equivalent of sighing, and staring into the middle distance, as though contemplating the futility of existence, or at least the sudden lack of chaos.

"She's depressed," Maria whispered, handing her a piece of melon with solemn ceremony. "You can see it in her shoulders."

We all had theories.

Perhaps she sensed the rising tension, the politics, the paperwork, the romantic weather systems moving in from America which threatened to rain on Mary. Perhaps she felt threatened by Spiros's change of mood. His suspicion that there were more things going on that he hadn't been told about. He carried a new energy of reluctance she couldn't quite place.

Or maybe, and this became the leading theory, she was broody.

Her adopted kittens had moved on. They'd stopped snuggling. They no longer followed her through the lemon grove or used her as a warm pillow. They were independent now. Teenagers. The kind who ignore you all day and then show up at lunchtime pretending to care, only to steal your food and vanish again.

"She wants company," Theodora declared, eyeing Katerina. She had matchmaking on the mind. "Not cats. Her kind. A proper boy goat."

"A broody goat?" Claude said. "We need a suitor?"

"Preferably one with strong haunches and emotional intelligence," added Maria, who had recently taken up goat astrology. "Taurus, ideally. Earth signs pair well with stubbornness."

Alex crossed her arms. "No."

That was it. One syllable, flat and immovable, like a boulder dropped in front of a bad idea.

"No?"

"The last thing we need around here is another goat," she said. "We are not a farm. We are not a sanctuary. We are definitely not a petting zoo."

"But she's lonely," Theodora insisted.

"She's judging us more than usual," said Dimitri.

"She's sulking in the lemon grove," added Mary. "She ignored an entire bucket of chips."

Alex remained unmoved. "Katerina is not sad. She's thoughtful. It's different. And if we bring in another goat, what's next? A donkey with commitment issues? A sheep commune? No. Absolutely not."

But it was too late.

Because, as Theodora pointed out with the serene menace of someone who has won many arguments with pie, "Democracy was invented in Greece."

And in Telios, that democracy now included a surprisingly well-organised goat-lobbying group, consisting of three pensioners, two bored teenagers, and a tourist who thought the entire discussion was a form of entertainment.

So Alex was overruled.

The vote was held behind the taverna, using a show of hands, a horn of approval from Katerina herself, and a ballot box previously used to collect bread orders.

The result?

Unanimous.

Well, except Alex, who wrote "No more goats" on a napkin and stapled it to the lemon tree.

But the village had spoken.

And soon, Telios's most eligible bachelor goat was en route, whether Alex liked it or not.

He arrived in the back of a pickup at dusk, blinking through the dust like a mythical creature reluctantly returning to the mortal realm. His name was Vassilis. He had soulful eyes, uneven horns, and the demeanour of someone who'd once been left behind on a ferry.

He looked at Katerina.

Katerina looked at him.

Something passed between them. Recognition? Interest? Mutual goat confusion?

She took a few steps forwards.

He bleated, a soft, hopeful bleat.

She huffed, turned away, then, as if rethinking things, turned and gave him a single, dignified headbutt.

We assumed this was love.

And for a few days, it was. They shared wall space behind the bins. He tried to follow her around the taverna. She tolerated it. He attempted to impress her by climbing things, headbutting things, and once, unsuccessfully, eating an ashtray.

She ignored most of it.

By day four, the cracks appeared.

He bleated too much. He chewed too loudly. He stood too close to her spot under the fig tree.

By day five, she had moved three metres to the left and begun glaring at him like he'd served her overcooked aubergine.

He attempted to woo her with a sprig of basil. She responded by climbing onto a roof and refusing to come down.

"He's trying," said Dimitri.

"She's finished," said Alex.

And just like that, it ended.

Not with drama. Not with tragedy.

But simply with boredom.

He was sweet. He was sincere. But she was Katerina. And Katerina, as it turns out, prefers being an only goat.

By the end of the week, Vassilis had been diplomatically rehomed to a nearby olive grove with a view and less judgement. He seemed grateful. Or at least relieved.

Katerina returned to her patrol. She judged. She glared. She resumed her rightful position on the wall behind the bins and resumed glaring at tomatoes for being too smug.

The balance was restored.

Not every goat wants a love story. Some want their chair, their view, and the right to decide who's allowed to eat near the lemon tree. She was never meant to share her reign. She is the Goat of Telios.

And she walks alone.

But now she walked with purpose. She leapt onto her favourite chair, after headbutting a stool as she passed just to prove she still could, and chewed the corner of the tablecloth with renewed enthusiasm.

And then she climbed onto a table in the centre of the terrace, stood there like a victorious general surveying her troops, and let out a long, triumphant bleat.

The message was clear: the goat was back in charge.

CHAPTER FORTY

ACCIDENTAL ICONS

It was meant to be temporary.

A one-week return. A nostalgia stunt. A culinary purge.

Zorba had come back to the kitchen like a storm in denim, barking, frying, refusing to acknowledge special requests, and ensuring that no plate left the pass with anything remotely resembling finesse.

We'd expected complaints.

We got applause.

At first, we thought people were too scared to complain.

But then they started coming back.

The same customers who'd been mortally offended by the lack of menus were now standing in line for a plate of lentils and whatever Zorba decided "meat" meant that day.

The reviews kept flooding in. A man from Athens wrote a review titled: "Finally, Someone Told Me No."

A woman from London posted a photo of a half-burnt sardine with the caption: "Real Food. Real Menace. 5 Stars."

Someone launched a hashtag: #ZorbaDoesNotCare.

To Zorba's horror, it trended. Katerina was tagged in most of them.

And we realised, with slow, dawning dread, that we had become cool.

We were just being aggressively, uncooperatively ourselves, rather than "curated" or "rustic-chic". And people loved it.

Tourists began *requesting* to be shouted at. Someone asked Alex if she could "be meaner".

Zorba had come, cooked, and terrified an entire generation of bloggers.

He'd shouted, he'd grilled, he'd turned culinary trends into ash, literally, and then, like a summer storm, he was gone. Not dramatically, not with a speech. Just… gone. Back to his corner table, leaving behind a taverna that smelled of smoke, salt, and divine retribution.

The menus had vanished overnight, as if they'd never existed. The specials board now bore a single word, chalked in letters so bold you could feel them in your chest: "FOOD".

And that was all there was to say about it.

The influencers retreated to their rental villas, ring lights clutched to their chests, wondering if they'd witnessed genius or madness. (Or possibly both.) Their reviews spoke of "authentic terror" and "smoky transcendence", which, in our book, counted as five stars.

Zorba made no declaration of victory. He offered no grand announcement that his work was done. He simply sat back under the tin roof, lit a cigarette, and gave us that look – the one that says: You know where to find me when you lose your minds again.

But something had shifted.

What was supposed to be one glorious week of shouting and grilled truth had, in classic Telios fashion, turned into an indefinite extension. The heat of the grill had done something to Zorba, burned away the last of the silence, sparked something deep in his chest.

He still grumbled, still judged, but there was a lightness in him now. His movements had purpose again. His insults landed with more accuracy. The smoke rose in perfect, disciplined columns, as though the taverna itself had been holding its breath and was finally allowed to exhale.

It was as if, by dragging him back to the grill, we had coaxed him back to life.

And in a village where miracles are rarely tidy and never quiet, that counted as a recovery.

But instead of fading into obscurity, we became… something else.

Maria was the first to notice.

"Look at this," she said one morning, slapping her notebook on the table. "They're calling us the 'punk-rock of Aegean hospitality.'"

Claude's eyes went wide. "Oh no. We're edgy now."

And he was right.

The more chaotic, uncurated, and downright unhelpful we were, the more they loved us.

A blogger posted a photo of Zorba shouting at a tourist with the caption "The Real Greece: Served Hot." It got fifty thousand likes.

Someone filmed Claude's "chair installation" and called it "performance art".

Mary served without smiling once and still got called "an icon of Greek hospitality".

Even Spiros, who contributed nothing except sullen silence from his bench, was photographed and labelled "the philosopher king of Telios".

TripAdvisor reviews went from cautious praise to near-religious devotion:

- "I came for dinner. I left changed."
- "The goat spoke to me – spiritually."

- "Five stars. Would get yelled at again."

Maria christened it The Zorba Doctrine: the less we tried, the more they came.

Zorba, of course, refused to acknowledge any of this. He simply grunted, as Theodora found her rhythm again, hurling pans around like a woman possessed.

We hadn't just survived the onslaught.

We had accidentally created a movement.

People came not despite the chaos, but for it. They wanted to earn their food, to be chastised, to be ignored and shouted at in equal measure.

And we, against all reason, gave it to them.

The next morning, we heard the unmistakable sound of a bus pulling in to the square.

Not the usual rickety blue one from Istiaia; this one was gleaming white, with tinted windows and a slogan on the side that read, "Seek Chaos. Find Yourself."

The doors hissed open and out stepped thirty identical people: matching tracksuits, matching notebooks, matching expressions of reverent hunger.

Maria nearly dropped her coffee.

Claude whispered, "We're a cult now."

Theodora crossed herself twice for emphasis.

Alex set down her glass of wine with the kind of precision that made everyone else go quiet. She stood, scanned the bus full of eager faces looking for chaos, and said, "Right. More chairs. And double the wine. If they're going to find themselves, they might as well do it drunk."

And with that, the goat trotted up to the bus steps, planted her hooves like a gatekeeper, and bleated, a single resonant sound that echoed down the square like the starting bell of some great and terrible festival.

CHAPTER FORTY-ONE

THEODORA'S LAST HOPE

We knew he was coming.

Mary prayed he wouldn't.

Theodora prayed harder that he would.

The rest of us didn't care either way, we just knew it was going to be entertaining.

And of course he didn't arrive on a weekend, when there might have been a ferry crowd to disguise him or a Sunday service to absorb the gossip. No. He arrived on a Tuesday. Mid-week absurdity.

The kind of arrival that cuts through a siesta, startles a chicken off its perch, and makes someone shout, "Did anyone switch the fridge back on?"

First came the sound: not the reassuring rattle of a moped or the battered cough of a fishing van, but a sleek, self-satisfied hum that sounded like it had been imported along with its own playlist.

And then it appeared: a white Tesla, gliding into the square like a swan that had wandered into the wrong pond, silent and certain of its own magnificence.

It stopped in front of the kafenio, right where the old men sit and measure time by the length of their cigarettes. They stared at the car like it had landed from another planet.

Then Andonis stepped out.

White linen trousers, salmon-pink shirt, sunglasses large enough to provide shade for the entire village. In one hand, a leather weekender bag. In the other, a drone. He wore no socks. Naturally.

He turned a slow circle, inhaled as though he were personally blessing the air, and said, "Ah… authenticity."

Behind him, his luggage followed like loyal disciples. Five matching suitcases, monogrammed, colour-coded, and wholly unnecessary for a two-week visit to a village with one road, two functioning clocks, and no concept of brunch.

From her kitchen window, Theodora watched.

Mary was clearing table four when the world tilted. She stepped outside, dishcloth in hand, blinked into the sun – and froze.

There he was.

Andonis.

Fresh from the ferry, glistening with confidence, dressed like a man who believed linen shirts counted as character.

He beamed, a smile as bright as the Tesla parked behind him. "*Maria mou!*"

Greek code took over. Hospitality is muscle memory, baked in, like oregano into beans.

She gave a smile. Small. Perfectly polite. The kind you'd offer a stranger at a bus stop, one you hoped was going somewhere else.

"Welcome," she said, because anything else would have had Theodora lighting candles for her soul.

He took a half-step forward, all choreography and shine.

"Or is it Mary now? I respect your journey."

Her smile held. Her eyes, however, narrowed like shutters in a windstorm.

"It's still no," she said gently – not cruel, not dramatic, just clear – and turned back inside.

Theodora's wooden spoon clattered in the kitchen. Claude let out a sympathetic hiss.

Alex arrived, surveyed the scene, and muttered, "Well. That's going to need wine."

Outside, Andonis adjusted his sunglasses, muttered something about "resetting the energy", and wheeled his luggage towards the guesthouse, leaving a faint trail of cologne and unresolved tension in his wake.

Lunch was a blur. Theodora served plates like a woman possessed, banging pots with the force of a small earthquake. Mary stayed busy at the counter, lips pressed thin.

When the last table was cleared and the tourists had drifted away in search of sunsets and Wi-Fi, Theodora wiped her hands on her apron, nodded to Alex, and said, "Sit."

Mary hesitated.

"Sit," Theodora repeated.

Alex poured wine and sat between them like a referee.

There was a long silence, broken only by the cicadas outside and a lone cat knocking over something fragile.

"You know why we are talking," Theodora said finally.

Mary crossed her arms. "Because you want me to marry him."

"No." Theodora's voice softened. "Because I want you to be happy. And because he came all this way. That must mean something."

Mary opened her mouth, but Alex raised a hand. "Let her finish."

Theodora sighed, staring at her hands. "I had doubts too. From the first letter. From the aunties' visit. Even today, when I saw him step out of that car like he was arriving at a film premiere. I thought, 'No. This is wrong.'"

Mary blinked, caught off guard.

"But," Theodora continued, "I also saw his face when he tasted the baklava. For a moment, he looked like a boy. Like someone who had found something he didn't know he had lost."

Mary stayed quiet.

"Perhaps we give him a chance," Theodora said gently. "You get to know him. See who he really is. I will accept any decision you make, but let us not throw him into the sea before we have even heard what he has to say. At least let him try to prove himself to you. To all of us."

"Even Katerina?" Alex asked, half-smiling.

Theodora nodded gravely. "Especially Katerina."

Mary groaned. "Fine. But if he uses the word 'mindfulness' again, I'm putting him on the ferry myself."

"Fair," Alex said, topping up her glass.

And so it was agreed, not as a surrender, but as a stay of execution.

That evening, Andy lingered after dinner, quieter than before.

"You know," he said softly, "I haven't eaten like this since my Yiayia died."

Mary paused mid-polish. Theodora stopped wiping the counter.

"In Jersey," he went on, "everything's fast. Even when it's

hot, it's cold. But this, the smells, the shouting, the way food just… appears… I miss it. I miss her."

His voice was smaller now. Not performative. Not hash-tagged. Honest.

Mary stared at him for a moment, then put down her cloth and walked over with a plate of honey cakes.

"You eat these with your hands," she said.

He smiled – real, unguarded – and reached for one. Honey dripped down his fingers.

For a moment, there was peace.

Theodora watched, and though her face stayed stern, something in her shoulders softened.

There was hope.

Slim. Slightly ridiculous.

But hope nonetheless.

****

Andy's first day began with a sunrise yoga session.

Nobody asked for it.

At 6:03 a.m., the village square was silent except for the ci-cadas, until an electronic chime shattered the peace. Andy stood barefoot on a woven mat, framed by the first gold of morning, playing "soothing whale noises" from his phone.

"Come join me!" he called to anyone within earshot.

No one did.

A single cat wandered over, sat on his mat, and washed

itself pointedly. Katerina the goat watched from the terrace, chewing contemplatively.

Mary, bleary-eyed, walked past on her way to fetch bread.

"Good morning, *Maria mou*," Andy said, beaming.

Mary raised an eyebrow. "You're blocking the bakery."

"Just breathing in the sunrise."

"Breathe somewhere else," she said, and kept walking.

To everyone's surprise, the first day went well. Andy offered to help with lunch prep and turned out to be good with a knife, the culinary kind. He chopped tomatoes with surgical precision, humming softly.

Theodora hovered nearby, arms folded, as though ready to snatch the knife from him if he so much as looked at the garlic wrong.

Mary kept her distance, wiping down tables that were already clean.

At service, Andy carried plates to tables with the exaggerated reverence of a man presenting offerings to a minor god. The German tourists loved him. Claude applauded. Even Zorba grudgingly nodded when Andy refilled the olive oil without spilling.

That night, he sat under the fig tree with everyone, asking questions about the village and, more impressively, listening to the answers.

"This is the happiest I've been in years," Andy said softly.

Theodora's lips were pressed tight, in the look she wore

when she wanted to smile but didn't trust the moment enough to risk it. There was a flicker of something: the dangerous, impossible hope that maybe this match wasn't doomed after all.

Day two was more… Andy.

He launched his drone over the beach, which caused three fishermen to throw stones at it and one *yiayia* to cross herself. Andy suggested renaming the daily specials "seasonal offerings of intentional nourishment". Theodora said something about renaming Andy.

By lunch, Mary's patience was wearing thin.

"He talks like an inspirational fridge magnet," she whispered to Alex.

"Give him a chance," Alex said. "He did peel fifty potatoes."

Mary narrowed her eyes. "He peeled them with a smile. That's suspicious."

Day three: disaster.

Andy decided to "optimise" the taverna flow by reorganising the tables according to "energetic principles". This involved moving table three closer to the olive tree and table six halfway into the road.

"This is not Feng Shui," said Theodora, storming out of the kitchen.

"It's energy alignment!" Andy said cheerfully.

"It's blocking the delivery van!" she snapped.

Mary intervened, resetting the tables with the quiet efficiency of a woman who had endured many men with theories.

By the end of the first week, the charm had started to thin.

Andy was not unpleasant, but he was relentless. He followed Mary around like a well-moisturised shadow, offering unsolicited advice on sleep cycles, sea swimming, and why carbs were "emotional crutches".

Mary did not throw anything at him. She simply began disappearing again. One extra morning off. A longer trip to the market. Walks on the beach that somehow took all afternoon.

She wasn't being rude. She was being evasive, which in Greece is a much higher art.

Theodora noticed, of course. She had eyes sharper than a basil-stalk switch.

That night, when the last table had been cleared and Andy had gone to bed, Theodora gathered Mary and Alex.

"We need to talk," she said.

Mary crossed her arms. "About him?"

"Yes." Theodora's tone softened. "I wanted this match. I wanted it very much. But I see you, *koukla mou*. I see you hiding."

Mary said nothing.

Alex poured wine and sat like a mediator at a peace summit.

"Perhaps we should give him a real chance," Theodora said. "Not only to hover around you. To prove himself. If he is wrong for you, fine. But let us be sure."

Mary's jaw tightened. "And if he is right?"

"Then I will dance at your wedding and fatten your children with *loukoumades*," Theodora said, smiling sadly.

There was a silence.

Finally, Mary sighed. "Fine. One more chance."

"Good," Alex said, raising her glass. "Because I already have a plan."

Mary's days were carefully arranged to force "natural" encounters with Andy, and to make sure half the village witnessed them.

She was sent to buy flour (Andy carried the sacks).

To collect fresh eggs (Andy got chased by a rooster).

To deliver *koulourakia* to the priest (Andy accidentally rang the church bell and summoned half the village).

Each day ended with a small dinner under the olive tree, Theodora watching quietly from the kitchen window.

And slowly, almost imperceptibly, Andy stopped talking quite so much. Stopped posing for invisible cameras. Stopped calling himself a "wellness strategist".

For a moment, the taverna was quiet.

But the village saw the writing on the wall before Mary did.

Andy had been "just visiting" for a week, which in village time is approximately three harvests, one minor religious festival, and two meltdowns over the price of fish.

He wasn't exactly unwelcome. But villagers had developed the remarkable ability to look in the opposite direction whenever he approached, a collective facial-avoidance system, triggered by his sandals.

He wandered the square in white linen, calling feta "low-intervention dairy" and explaining to Zorba why his "aura reads dark".

Zorba didn't respond. But he did casually move his chair one inch closer to the kitchen knives.

So the decision was made, with a nod over coffee, a shrug near the mopeds, and one slow, deliberate blink from Zorba.

Andy had to go.

Enter Alex: the general, the strategist, the woman who once organised an entire olive harvest using three broken baskets and a teenager named Vangelis with no sense of direction.

"We'll ease him out," she said, over a bottle of wine and a plate of confusingly spicy tzatziki.

"No confrontation?" asked Maria.

"God, no," said Alex. "We're Greek. We'll bury him in politeness."

Suddenly, there was an about-turn in tactics. Mary's "days off" became mysteriously filled with very solo social responsibilities: visits to sick aunts (real or invented), errands for the church, volunteer pastry testing for the village festival.

Andy offered to join once. She handed him a box of olives and told him to count them. In the sun.

Any time Andy tried to talk to Mary, someone else intercepted. Claude would swoop in with a poem. Dimitri would challenge him to a backgammon match (and cheat). Eleni would need urgent help translating the recycling schedule into "emotional language".

At one point, someone asked Andy to teach a "yoga-for-goats" class. He said yes. Katerina glared at him, turned her back, and deliberately chewed the washing line until two pairs of underpants hit the ground.

Message received.

By week's end, the entire village was in on it. The butcher offered him "meat for the broken-hearted". The baker labelled a loaf "Closure". Children started calling him "Uncle Maybe". And Andy, bless him, remained cheerfully oblivious.

"This village," he said one evening, sipping mountain tea through a stainless-steel straw, "is so healing. I feel seen."

Alex nodded, smiling thinly.

"Oh yes," she said. "We see you."

They all did.

And soon, just as politely, just as softly, they would see him off.

But not yet.

First: the election.

Then: the departure.

And somewhere, in the distance, the goat farted, which, let's face it, was the only endorsement that truly mattered.

CHAPTER FORTY-TWO

WELCOME TO THE RESISTANCE (TABLE FOR TWO?)

We didn't mean to start a movement.

Honestly, we barely meant to open on time.

All we wanted was to serve fish, grumble about the weather, curse the power cuts, and argue about whether the oregano was fresher last year. Our job was to keep the chaos safely corralled behind the kitchen door, not to accidentally launch a cultural rebellion.

But somewhere between the cracked plates, the overcooked lentils, and the way Zorba could command a room by adjusting one eyebrow, something happened.

People were still talking about us.

Not the usual gossip; we were used to that. This was stranger. Louder. Digital. Suddenly, photos of our uneven tables were trending under hashtags like #AuthenticityGoals. A visiting blogger called us "a love letter to the past", which was flattering until someone else described us as "post-ironic dining with subversive undertones", which made Theodora threaten to throw her ladle at them.

We didn't understand it. We had done everything possible to put people off: no QR codes. No English menus (unless you counted Alex's handwriting, which even the locals struggled to decipher). No Instagram-ready lighting, unless you considered a single dusty lightbulb swinging over table six "mood".

But the more we resisted, the more they came.

Bloggers. Influencers. Self-described "culinary pilgrims". One woman showed up claiming she had flown from Berlin to "experience radical imperfection". She cried when Katerina stole her shoe.

The *Global Gastro Guide* sent another critic. Then a photographer. Then, inexplicably, a podcast team.

Somewhere along the way, we had become… a concept.

Zorba's was no longer a restaurant, or a taverna. It was a manifesto. People began writing about us like we were some sort of edible protest movement, with headlines like, "Zorba's Taverna: The Last Bastion of Resistance Dining" and "No Menu, No Mercy: Why Greece Is Leading the Anti-Foodie Revolution".

We hadn't set out to be revolutionary. We just didn't want to serve anyone tofu.

Claude, of course, loved it. "We are no longer simply a taverna," he announced one evening, draping himself dramatically over a chair. "We are the beating heart of the gastro-resistance."

Zorba grunted, which we took as approval.

Theodora crossed herself and went back to stirring the beans. "God help us," she said. "Now we'll never get rid of them."

And she was right.

By sundown, there were two food critics, three bloggers, and a pair of earnest documentary-makers camped out under the lemon tree, waiting for something profound to happen.

And all we had was fish.

One day an email arrived from Bologna. "We are filming a documentary about anti-establishment gastronomy. May we visit your taverna to capture the philosophy of refusal?"

Alex printed it out, read it twice, then, in one fluid motion, walked outside, set it on fire in the ashtray, and returned without comment.

For half an hour, she didn't speak, which was how we knew we were in trouble.

Then came the Dutch man. Quiet. Polite. Dressed like a weathered librarian. He ordered lentils and grilled bread, took no photos, made no eye contact, and spent the entire meal writing in a cracked leather notebook.

At the end, he stood, nodded at Zorba, and said to Mary, "What you're doing is showing that everything is pointless. It's beautiful."

She said thank you. Then she threw away his tip.

It was already too late.

The article appeared three days later. Not in a travel blog, not in a food column, but in a *philosophy journal*. With footnotes. "Zorba's Taverna and the Ethics of Anti-Hospitality".

They quoted Zorba. ("No substitutions.")

They quoted Spiros. ("What square?")

They even quoted me, though all I'd said was, "Can I clear that?"

And once again, we weren't just a taverna. We were a destination. Just not the kind with overpriced sunbeds or laminated menus in six languages – we'd done that dance already, survived the bloggers, endured Philippe, and terrified a generation of influencers into never asking for "deconstructed *moussaka*" again.

This felt different.

This wasn't fame.

This was… philosophical.

People weren't just coming to eat. They were coming to *ponder*. To sit under the lemon tree and discuss life, death, and whether the goat was a metaphor. An *agora*, they called it, in one of the reviews.

Not a place to eat, but a place to think.

A place to swirl your wine and wrestle with life's big question, like the futility of modern romance or why Theodora refuses to measure salt. A place where chairs faced the sea not just for the view, but for "existential alignment".

Which, irritatingly, we agreed with. Not because we're philosophers (though Claude started wearing his most flamboyant scarf and quoting Plato for a week), but because it sounded exactly like the sort of pretentious nonsense we'd probably write about ourselves if left unsupervised.

Claude offered to design a mural titled "Epiphany Over Aubergine".

I sat very still and wondered how a taverna we'd reopened purely to give the village somewhere to argue and eat in peace had become a site of culinary enlightenment.

A statement. A symbol. A hashtag.

Guests were now arriving not just for lunch, but for *answers*.

"What would Zorba do?" one asked, when faced with a choice between grilled halloumi and moussaka.

"Would Mary be interested in opening a retreat?" asked another, mistaking her stern silence for spiritual wisdom.

Even Father Evangelos was approached, mid-*souvlaki*, and asked if he offered table blessings. He blinked, pointed at the salt, and said, "Use this liberally."

At some point, someone left behind a notebook titled "Thoughts I Had While Eating Lamb".

Another visitor mailed us a handwoven tapestry embroidered with the phrase "Eat. Think. Repeat."

And the worst part? We didn't do anything to cause it. We hadn't changed the food. We hadn't staged a single photo. Alex had banned slogans, and the menu still lived on a chalkboard so unstable it fell over if you breathed near it.

But somewhere between the grilled octopus and the goat wearing protest sashes, we'd become a message.

About slowness.

About soul.

About… olives, probably.

They came like pilgrims, not the sandal-and-incense kind, but the kind armed with linen shirts, and notebooks full of questions nobody asked them to answer.

They didn't want food. They wanted meaning.

One man from Copenhagen asked to "immerse himself in the tension between comfort and defiance".

Alex handed him a broken chair and said, "Sit carefully."

A Parisian woman cried into the lentils and declared it "a metaphor for post-war survival". Mary rolled her eyes and refilled her wine.

A Berlin visitor asked if we offered workshops.

"Workshops?" Alex blinked. "We barely offer chairs." He booked anyway.

Someone filmed reels. Someone wrote a paper. A man from Barcelona described the grilled octopus as "like tasting identity fragmentation in a post-authenticity era". Mary served him the head and walked away.

Someone asked if Katerina was "symbolic".

"She's symbolic of goat," I said. "Chews, headbutts, may or may not bless your dinner. That sort of thing."

Then the madness spread. Someone gave Katerina a Twitter account. Posts appeared like:

"Chew the rope. Bite the fence. Reject the bowl."

Within a week she had more followers than the mayor.

Claude, naturally, leaned into the whole thing. He designed a poster with the slogan, "WELCOME TO ZORBA'S – Where Nothing Is Curated and Everything Is True."

Alex confiscated it. Then she framed it and hung it in the loo, next to the leak.

Soon, no one asked what was on the menu, they asked what wasn't.

They didn't want *tzatziki*; they wanted the absence of *tzatziki*.

They didn't want service; they wanted stare-downs.

They didn't want Instagram; they wanted to feel judged.

And we… did what we always did.

We served what we had, when it was ready, without garnish.

Sometimes still moving.

No apologies.

No hashtags.

No theories.

But the theories came anyway.

It became clear we weren't just feeding tourists any more. We were feeding a crisis of modernity, one plate at a time.

And somehow, this messy, smoky, mismatched taverna – with its yelling, its wrong orders, its fearsome goat, and a specials board that simply read "FOOD" – had become a sort of sanctuary. A final refuge for people who didn't want things explained.

They came because they'd been offered too many options elsewhere. Because they were tired of curated experiences. Because they were hungry for something real. They came for silence. They came for salt. They came for Spiros saying "No" like a benediction. They came to be rejected – and they loved it.

And Zorba?

He didn't react. He sat, smoked, watched them arrive with their canvas bags and complicated shoes. Watched them lower themselves onto slightly wobbly chairs and pretend not to be terrified of Theodora's soup. He didn't speak. He didn't move. He just stared. As if to say: You're not supposed to understand this. You're supposed to eat it. And then leave.

So we didn't build a brand. We didn't make merch. We didn't lean in – we leaned back. Zorba's had become – accidentally, gloriously – a resistance. Against pretension. Against polish. Against the idea that things need improvement.

And that, somehow, was enough.

And now?

Now, every time someone pulled out a notebook instead of ordering dessert, we knew: this wasn't just a taverna any more. It was an idea. And there's nothing more dangerous than that.

So if you're reading this and thinking of visiting – please do.

Just don't expect instructions.

And for the love of all things holy, don't ask for almond milk.

CHAPTER FORTY-THREE

THE NIGHT THE TAVERNA FORGOT TO SIT DOWN

It started, as these things always do in Telios, with someone shouting a wild idea. This time it was: "Let's do a dance night!"

Just the declaration, shouted into the ether like an invocation. And as with most things here, no one questioned it. No one mentioned the fact that the last one ended with a twisted ankle, a ruined clarinet, and Dimitri unconscious with his feet in the sea and his head on a melon. Because in Telios, a shout is as good as a contract. A suggestion becomes a movement. A movement becomes a night no one will forget, even if they wake up wondering why there's a goat in their lap and oregano in their shoe.

Claude, naturally, took creative control. He declared the theme to be "Mediterranean Moonlight", which meant more lanterns, less logic, and a terrifying number of chiffon scarves. "The aesthetic must *breathe*," he said, while draping a fishing net over a fig tree.

Maria launched into research mode, interviewing everyone who'd ever twisted an ankle or broken a promise on a dance floor. Within hours, she'd published a one-off edition of her gossip sheet titled: "Bouzouki and Broken Promises: A Retrospective", featuring three false engagements and one confirmed elopement (to Albania, of all places).

Dimitri offered to "sort the drinks", which should have set off more alarm bells than it did. This is, after all, the man who once brewed wine in a washing machine and swore it "tasted even better with fabric conditioner".

The band arrived around four, in a battered van full of dented instruments. One man named Stelios introduced himself as a "percussionist of fate". They unpacked three bouzoukis, a tambourine, a saucepan duct-taped to a mop handle, and a PA system held together by hope, twine, and the local church's extension cord.

Alex, of course, took over. She always does.

"Chairs to the side! We need a dance floor!" she barked, waving her clipboard like a sceptre. "Mary, crowd control. Eleni, check the power won't explode again. Dimitri, stop lighting things. Spiros–"

"I'll sit here," said Spiros firmly, not moving an inch.

"Perfect," said Alex, without missing a beat.

By sunset, the taverna was glowing. Not romantically, but in the way things glow right before they catch fire. The tables had been rearranged into something vaguely amphitheatrical, the floor swept by volunteers and one particularly determined chicken, and the octopus line cleared to prevent strangulation incidents.

Bottles of Dimitri's *tsipouro* sat ominously on every surface. Some had labels. Some had warnings. None had instructions.

The tourists looked delighted. The locals looked wary. And the air, thick with pine smoke, garlic, and barely contained potential, was electric.

And then… it began.

In Greece, dancing isn't performance. It's history in motion. It's protest and joy and flirtation and communion, all wrapped into one wild swirl of arms and feet and declarations.

Most visitors to Greece believe that *Zorba the Greek* is the traditional national dance. It isn't. Not in most villages. Not on most islands.

The famous "Zorba dance" is actually called *Sirtaki*, and although it's arguably the best-known Greek dance internationally, it only dates back to the 1960s. Composer Mikis Theodorakis created it specifically for the film *Zorba the Greek*, blending slow and fast steps from three older dances: the *Hasapiko*, the

Hasaposerviko, and the *Syrtos*. The result is a dance that starts slow, ends fast, and feels like it's carrying you somewhere you didn't quite expect.

It's danced in a line or a circle, arms draped across your neighbours' shoulders – a mix of camaraderie, choreography, and just enough chaos to make you feel alive.

Every region of Greece has its own folk dances, and no one knows them all. In most villages, the most commonly danced is the *Syrtos* itself – a family of gentle, gliding line dances that form a slow-moving semicircle. Each area has its own version, its own steps, its own tempo.

The best-known of these is the *Kalamatianos* – faster, brighter, more spirited, and often called Greece's national dance. It's what you're most likely to see at weddings and festivals, where the lines grow longer, the feet tap faster, and someone eventually shouts *opa!* whether it's needed or not.

They even teach traditional dancing in Greek schools. That's where Alex caught the bug as a small girl. Somewhere between arithmetic and the alphabet, she fell in love with rhythm. Over the years, she honed her skill so finely that she could leap up and join any dance at any moment, as if her feet had simply been waiting for permission.

Greek dancing often combines tears and smiles, moving through a full range of emotions. *Sirtaki*, for instance, is all smiles, starting slow and building up into a wild crescendo until the whole group collapses in laughter and exhaustion.

Other dances, though, are pure emotion, often expressing sorrow.

Tonight, the first dance was Alex's alone. She chose the *Zeibekiko*.

Greece has always lived with invasion.

First came the Persians, sweeping across the Aegean with ships and fire. Then the Ottomans, who stayed for centuries, folding the country into their empire. And in living memory, the Germans and Italians during the Second World War, when villages were burned and people were starved into silence.

And then there was the loss that still haunts the people, the catastrophe of 1922, when millions of Greeks were forced from their homes in Anatolia. They came across the sea with what little they could carry: icons, recipes, stories, music. They brought with them grief and memory that has never quite left.

The *Zeibekiko* was born from that grief. There are no steps, no count, no pattern to follow. Only movement, improvised from the heart, as if the earth itself is pulling the dancer's feet. It isn't a performance. It's a confession. A prayer made public. A plea for understanding.

Its roots lie in Asia Minor, among the displaced, the defeated, the ones who carried whole villages in their pockets. It is danced alone, not for applause, but for truth.

And for Alex, whose own family had known deportation, hunger, and despair, it was sacred.

When she dances the *Zeibekiko*, she does not dance for an audience. She dances for those who lost everything and still stood up again. She dances for the memory of homes that no longer exist, for the mothers who cooked with empty cupboards, for the fathers who rebuilt walls with bare hands.

She dances because Greece remembers, in music, in words, and most of all, in movement.

Alex stepped into the centre as the musicians struck the first sombre chords. She kept her face still, her gaze low. She moved slowly at first, a soft sway of sorrow. Then a twist, a crouch, a sudden upward lunge. One moment she was seated, lost, broken. The next, she was rising, hands pressed together in prayer, eyes lifted to the sky like she was begging for answers.

When the final note fell, there was a stunned silence. The kind that sits on your chest and refuses to leave.

I looked around the terrace. Eyes wide. Faces streaked with tears. One clap. Then another. And then, the whole taverna stood and applauded. Not the kind of applause that comes from entertainment. The kind that comes from being reminded, just for a moment, of everything we carry, and everything we survive.

Alex returned to the table and sat beside me. She stayed silent, but her tears spoke for her.

***

Then, as if on cue, the *bouzouki* brightened. The rhythm quickened. The second act began. Eleni, the village's quiet architect of order, had one glorious exception to her meticulous routines: the precise, communal chaos of Greek dancing. She was first on her feet, dragging the shy and the slow from their chairs. A circle began to form, hands linking, feet tapping. The *Kalamatianos* had arrived, upbeat and unbothered, leading us gently from grief into joy, as only Greek music can.

I was still seated when Alex looked at me, raised one eyebrow, and pulled me up.

The dance floor was waiting. And in Greece, you don't say no to life when the music starts.

Then, after a short interlude the mood lifted a notch more.

The first strum of the *bouzouki* rang out across the taverna like a gauntlet being thrown to the gods: Zorba the Greek.

The opening bars alone have a gravitational pull. It's not a song. It's a summoning. Alex moved first, as she always does. The spark before the storm. She swept through the tables like a woman possessed, grabbing hands, sleeves, elbows, and at one point, a startled Canadian. "Up! No one escapes sober or seated!"

And just like that, the circle formed. Tourists, villagers, one baker, and a postman who only came to return a borrowed spatula.

The *bouzouki's* cry rose, slow, sly, deliberate. The rhythm crept in. A toe tapped. Someone clapped too early. Anticipation crackled like kindling.

Then: ignition.

The beat snapped. The strings wailed. And the village

launched itself into chaos with the enthusiasm of a toddler on a sugar rush.

Feet stomped. Plates clattered. Elbows flew.

Claude attempted a jazz-adjacent interpretation involving shoulder rolls and interpretive arm spirals. Vassiliki twirled with a wooden spoon still in hand, serving philosophy alongside pastry. Theodora clapped in time, eyes sparkling with the kind of mischief only a woman who's buried three baklava-related feuds can muster.

Even Spiros, our permanent bench fixture, patron saint of Not Getting Up, tapped a toe.

I stood at the edge, glass in hand, dodging elbows, writing mental notes and wondering, again, how we'd ended up turning a broken taverna into something halfway between a celebration and a minor natural disaster.

Mary entered next. Graceful. Dangerous. Spinning like a ballerina. One earring flew off. A man from Sheffield caught it and proposed on the spot. She thanked him with a kiss on the cheek and a generous glass of luminous *tsipouro*.

At some point, Eleni entered the dance floor, in heels, holding a folder of permits and two glasses of wine. She passed one to Alex, tucked the other under her chin, and danced without dropping a single page.

Tourists filmed. Old men wept. Children ran in circles with ribboned spoons. The music swelled. And then, in the way only fate can time, Spiros rose.

It was biblical. A resurrection. A seismic shift in the balance of the known world.

He lit a cigarette. Looked at the circle like a general surveying a battlefield. Then stepped in.

And good God.

The man moved like liquid marble. Grace in denim. Every step was memory. Every turn was proof that no matter how old you are, you never forget the steps that make you feel alive. He danced like the war had ended. Like the taverna had been saved. Like he'd remembered what it meant to be twenty and full of fire.

And when the song ended, loud, defiant, eternal, the village erupted.

"Cheers."

Glasses were raised. Plates were shattered.

Claude threw his arms wide and announced the moment "divinely chaotic".

Maria, ever the philosopher, said it was "a spontaneous act of intergenerational healing", which was generous considering someone had just tripped over the olive oil tin.

Eleni, meanwhile, was two moves ahead of everyone, and of officialdom.

She calmly texted the insurance agent to pre-empt a claim for the evening's inevitable damages… then immediately blocked their number, thereby achieving what she later called "a flawless act of bureaucratic self-defence".

The band struck up for the next song. Theodora served

souvlaki mid-spin. Mary deflected two more proposals and one very hopeful phone number. Dimitri refilled *tsipouro* bottles with an air of innocent menace. And yes, the goat joined in. Katerina was led to the centre by a child named Stavroula, who insisted she was "essential to the dance".

No one questioned it. The band just played louder.

Zorba watched from under the fig tree. He didn't dance. He never danced. But the corner of his mouth lifted – a smile, or the memory of one. When asked if he was enjoying himself, he grumbled, "Too much thyme," and took another sip of wine.

By midnight, the power went out.

By 12:03, it was back on, thanks to Eleni threatening the fuse box with a spatula and the full authority of a woman who once filled out seventeen forms in a single day.

More plates broke. Claude threw his scarf into the air. Dimitri sang a sea shanty he insisted was "historically accurate". Theodora danced with a meatball skewer like it was a baton of divine justice.

At 1 a.m., someone proposed to the wrong person. At 1:01, they realised. At 1:03, everyone applauded anyway.

At 2, the *bouzouki* cracked a string. At 2:01, someone replaced it with twine. The music didn't stop.

I sat with my notebook open, my heart full, and a suspiciously full glass in my hand, watching a village lose its mind in perfect harmony.

This wasn't a party.

It was proof.

Proof that in a world full of quiet disasters and endless forms, there is still a place for laughter, *tsipouro*, and dancing until the sky forgets it's night.

This was our taverna.

Our madness.

Our joy.

Every step was an argument with the darkness, every turn a promise to keep going. The floor shook, the glasses rattled, the tables surrendered their plates and became drums. Even the shy ones were dragged in, caught in the orbit of music that cared less about rhythm and more about whether you had a heartbeat.

We danced because the sea was watching.

We danced because grief was listening.

We danced because joy demanded it.

We danced because it mattered.

We danced because it always matters.

And when the song ended, breathless and shining, we danced again.

CHAPTER FORTY-FIVE

ELECTION DAY, OR THE DAY
THE VILLAGE HELD ITS BREATH

It was election day, and no one was speaking to each other, which, in our village, meant everything was going perfectly.

The *kafenio* was full, but the conversation was suspiciously polite. The taverna was closed, but the kitchen was bustling with unsolicited advice and nervous wiping of already-clean counters. Spiros was on his bench, arms crossed, chewing a toothpick, staring at the sea like it might reveal the results early.

Andonis turned up in a crisp linen shirt and… a bow tie.

Which should have been our first warning that something else apart from the election was brewing.

"He's brought pastries," Maria whispered, as if announcing a plague. She peered over a tray of *bourekia* with the same suspicion usually reserved for unexpected phone calls from Athens.

"Good ones," added Dimitri, chewing thoughtfully. "Too good. Something's wrong."

Andonis had been here for two weeks.

Two weeks of smiling, helping, and wearing that hat, the one that made him look like the brand ambassador for a boutique olive oil company called *Soul & Soil.*

He had carried crates, swept terraces, and somehow mastered the art of stacking wine glasses on one arm like a seasoned waiter, a skill that impressed everyone except Mary, who simply said, "He's showing off."

He had even learned to shoo chickens out of the kitchen without swearing, which earned him a rare nod from Zorba and a suspicious glance from Theodora, who didn't quite trust a man who could move poultry politely.

Mary hadn't said a word about him in days. Which, as Eleni observed, "is how women prepare to flee or kill."

And yet, today was his move.

The Grand Gesture.

The kind of sweeping declaration that works in films, with soft lighting and violins, but rarely survives contact with a Greek village, where the soundtrack is more likely to be a goat bleating and a distant Vespa stalling on the hill.

I found myself feeling unexpectedly sorry for him. It wasn't that he'd been awful. Quite the opposite. He was kind, earnest, and genuinely helpful, if slightly relentless. But no one in the village, except perhaps Andonis himself, believed he belonged here.

He didn't love Mary, not really. Not in the way that meant staying, fighting, becoming part of the story.

And Mary, well, Mary had been patient. She had tried. For the sake of her mother, for the sake of peace. She'd given him time, conversations, even a handful of near-civil smiles. And in doing so, she'd proved to herself that her first instinct had been right.

She couldn't see herself spending another day with him, let alone a lifetime.

Theodora, who could read her daughter's silences better than any words, had begun to see it too.

There was no malice in it. No villain here. It was just mismatch so fundamental that even if Andonis had offered her exactly what she claimed to want – a quiet life, a kitchen of her own, and a man who understood the correct ratio of cinnamon to clove – it still wouldn't have worked. He may as well have been inviting her to New Jersey with colour-coordinated towels, a Costco membership, and a Peloton bike in the corner. Because he didn't really know Mary.

He liked the idea of her, the concept of marriage, the promise of being chosen. But he hadn't thought it through past the picture-book version. Past the wedding photos and the congratulatory Facebook posts.

What he was about to do wasn't selfish. It was, in his mind, brave. A leap of faith. The only way he knew to turn the tide before it slipped away for good.

And that, perhaps, was the saddest part.

Claude claimed he'd heard a guitar. Whatever Andy was planning, it was coming.

And for a moment, just a moment, we all wished it could work, for Theodora, for Mary, even for Andonis, who was about to pour out his heart in a village that had already, politely, decided its answer.

He had a speech, but he wasn't sure how he would deliver it. He paced. Not the purposeful kind of pacing. Not the kind you do before making a business pitch or setting a world record in a triathlon. This was the kind of pacing reserved for men on the verge of doing something very foolish in a very public place.

He paused outside the taverna and peered through the door like a man checking for tigers. Outside, Spiros was in his usual spot. Zorba had claimed the shade. Dimitri was doing something inexplicable with a fishing line and a teacup. The usual.

Andonis sat down awkwardly, fiddling with the eco-leather strap of his watch.

"Can I have some *tsipouro*?" he asked me. "Local. Organic if possible."

I stared at him. A full, extended, silent stare. The kind you reserve for goats in the kitchen or when Dimitri tries to explain organic fishing again.

Because Andonis, Mr Gluten-Free, Mr Alkaline Smoothie, Mr Activated Almond, had just asked for *tsipouro*.

This was the same man who had claimed he could "smell it from the next village" and had described the taste as "like swallowing a lit sparkler". He had even suggested, in full earnestness, that it should come with a warning and a priest.

And now?

He wanted it. Local and organic, no less.

"Are you sure?" I asked, already reaching for the bottle.

He nodded. "I think… I need it."

That was new.

Because no sane man wants *tsipouro*. *Tsipouro* happens to you. It's not so much a drink as a rite of passage and a mild act of self-destruction. It is what you consume when the fridge breaks, the fish don't arrive, the goat eats the tablecloth, and someone suggests you host a wedding for 80 people with no warning and half a bag of chickpeas.

It is, in short, liquid resignation.

Dimitri calls it "emotional disinfectant".

Claude refers to it as "truth serum for cowards".

Zorba just drinks it and lets his eyebrows do the rest.

And now Andonis – linen-clad, drone-operating, yoga-in-the-morning Andonis – had entered the arena.

I poured him a measure. A proper one. No lemon. No ice.

No mercy.

He lifted the glass. He paused. Then he sniffed it, sighed, and drank.

His eyes widened. His throat staged a protest. Somewhere deep in his soul, his natural gut bacteria packed their bags and left. But to his credit, he didn't cry – much.

He slammed the glass down and said, "It's like… being punched."

Dimitri grinned. "It's working."

Alex, passing by with a tray of tomatoes, glanced at the scene. "If he asks for a second one, don't give it to him. It means he's about to propose."

And he did. Because that's what *tsipouro* is. It's not only a drink. It's a decision-making lubricant with no regard for consequences. And today, apparently, it was also an engagement cocktail.

"You okay?" asked Dimitri, who had somehow managed to loop the fishing line around his own ankle.

Andonis took a breath. "I'm going to propose to Mary."

There was a pause – the kind of pause you get before someone drops a fish.

"Today?" said Spiros.

"Yes."

"In public?"

"Yes."

"At the election?"

"Yes."

Zorba looked up. "Do you have a will?"

Andonis ignored him. He stood, dramatically, with the energy of someone trying very hard to appear confident while his insides turned inside out.

The square was that particular kind of full where the air feels thicker and the small talk starts to ferment.

It was election day, which in Telios meant democracy via pastry queue. Eleni was at her folding table with the ballots, a stamp, and a look of holy authority. Claude had turned up with a bouquet of basil and a small poem in his breast pocket "in case of historic outcome". Katerina had already eaten one pencil.

Andonis hovered at the edge with a small bouquet of wild flowers. Waiting.

He watched Mary emerge from the bakery, balancing a tray of *bougatsa* and a weary kind of grace. She hadn't seen him yet. He took a deep breath.

Now or never.

He stood, in full view of the bakery, the *kafenio*, the old men playing cards, and the queue of villagers waiting to elect their new mayor, most of whom had turned up primarily to watch the chaos unfold. He cleared his throat. He stepped forward.

"Mary," he said. "I've come all this way because I believe in something. In us."

Mary stopped halfway across the square, her expression unreadable.

Andonis pressed on. "I know we haven't had much time. But I've seen the way you run this place. The heart. The passion. The… the goat."

Katerina bleated, as if on cue.

"You are the bravest, most beautiful, most stubborn woman I have ever met. And if you will let me, I would like to stay. Not just for the summer. Not just for a season. But for a life."

He dropped to one knee.

The square collectively inhaled.

Even Katerina stopped chewing a ballot paper.

"Mary," Andonis said, holding out the flowers like a peace treaty, "will you marry me?"

For a moment, there was silence.

Then Mary stepped forward.

She took the flowers gently, as if they might bruise. She looked at him, really looked at him, then at the village, which was now holding its collective breath.

"Andonis," she said softly. "You are kind. You are good. And you are wrong."

She placed the flowers back in his hand.

"I don't want this. Not from you. Not from anyone. Not now."

She wasn't cruel. She wasn't angry. She was just certain.

Theodora was standing in the square; her face didn't move, but her shoulders dropped the smallest fraction. Relief.

Andonis swallowed. He stood up.

"Thank you," he said quietly. "For telling me straight."

He turned, nodded at Zorba, who gave the smallest of nods back, the kind men give when they've seen something inevitable play out.

Andonis walked across the square, past the tables, past the goat, past every pair of eyes that had gathered to watch his heart break in real time.

At the edge of the square, he paused, looked back once, and managed a small smile.

And then he was gone.

The square was quiet for a long moment.

Mary stood very still, then exhaled.

Alex slipped an arm around her shoulders.

"It's done," she said.

Mary nodded, and for the first time in weeks, she smiled.

Somewhere nearby, the goat belched, loudly enough to make three tourists jump.

It was, we all agreed, the most appropriate benediction possible.

The entire cast of Zorba's was there, apart from Spiros, who was, of course, still welded to his bench at the taverna.

George, Mary's father and master of cheese, stood near the back, his arms folded like a man expecting to be disappointed but hoping for a miracle.

Stamos the builder perched on an upturned bucket, mumbling calculations under his breath, as if ready to rebuild the entire square should the result go the wrong way.

Dimitri prowled like a lion before feeding time, trident balanced casually over one shoulder, clearly preparing to dedicate the outcome to Poseidon.

Claude had stationed himself dramatically under the bougainvillea, one hand over his heart, as though he were about to conduct the national anthem.

Maria was scribbling into her notebook with the intensity of a court stenographer preparing to deliver a verdict. She straightened her glasses, cleared her throat, and looked around the square with the solemn air of someone about to announce the election results, or possibly declare war.

Theodora went back to the taverna, put on a pot of water, and began kneading dough for tomorrow's bread. Because life, like bread, had to rise again.

Mary stood at the edge of the crowd, her chin high but her fingers twisting the dishcloth she hadn't realised she was still holding.

Alex was beside me, arms crossed, eyes narrowed, the general waiting for the battle cry.

And me? I was writing it all down, as always, trying to capture this moment before it slipped away.

And Katerina, well, Katerina had climbed onto the steps of the kafenio for a better view and was chewing somebody's hat.

***

Nichos was already there, standing as though he was rehearsing for his own statue unveiling. The square was packed. Every chair had been dragged out, every yiayia was perched on the edge as though expecting to witness the Second Coming, or at least a very good scandal. Even the cats had stopped yowling and were crouched under the tables, eyes gleaming like tiny, furry reporters. The air was thick and expectant, charged with that peculiar village tension that feels exactly like the moment before a summer storm, the kind where you can taste the electricity and start mentally securing your washing before it blows into the neighbour's olive grove.

And at the very centre of it all stood Maria.

The drama with Mary and Andonis had barely cooled – you could still feel the heat of it rising off the stones – but the village had moved on, as villages do, to the next great event: the election results.

The votes had been counted in the *kafenio* under the watchful eyes of three pensioners, one priest, and a goat who refused to leave until given an almond biscuit. The results had then been placed in a sealed envelope, a dramatic touch suggested by Claude, and ceremoniously delivered to Maria, who accepted it as though it contained the secrets of Olympus.

Now she stood in the square, clipboard in one hand, envelope in the other, shoulders back, chin lifted like an oracle about to deliver the word of the gods.

She looked around at us slowly, milking the silence for all it was worth, until the tension stretched tight enough to hum. Dimitri spat once into the dust for luck. Somewhere, a spoon clattered to the ground. Even the cats held their breath.

Maria tapped the envelope once against her clipboard, savouring the moment. She cleared her throat, glanced down at the clipboard, and then back up at the sea of faces.

"The next mayor of Telios," she said, her voice perfectly pitched, "is…"

She paused.

The entire village leaned forwards in unison.

Even Katerina stopped chewing.

"…Spiros!"

The square exploded, Telios-style. One fisherman dropped his bucket of fish in excitement, another popped a cork that pinged off the church bell, and Claude began humming a triumphant bouzouki riff into the pepper grinder like a man possessed.

Maria flung her arms in the air, Theodora banged a ladle on the counter of the *kafenio*, and Dimitri shouted, "Poseidon is satisfied!" before running a small victory lap around the fountain.

It was chaos. Beautiful, glorious chaos.

Just across the road, within sight of the square, Spiros was still at the taverna on his usual bench. He heard the commotion, squinted towards us through the heat haze, and asked, deadpan, "Was there an election today?"

"Yes!" we shouted back, still cheering.

"Ah." He lit another cigarette. "Did I win?"

"Yes!"

He tilted his head once, the slow, measured tilt of a man who had just been told the price of tomatoes was holding steady, and went back to staring at the sea.

Katerina, sensing history being made, rushed over to the taverna, climbed onto the bench beside him, turned three circles, and sat down solemnly, like a furry vice-mayor taking her oath of office.

Someone set off a firework. No one knew where it came from. Possibly Claude's emergency happiness box.

And then came the actual figures:

- **Spiros:** 288

- **Nichos:** 12

- **Katerina:** 1

- Two ballots that simply said "No." We gave those to Spiros.

Our new mayor, by a landslide.

A silence followed.

Not the stunned, jaw-dropping kind. This was the gentler, quieter silence of a village that had collectively dodged a bureaucratic bullet and knew it.

Nichos requested a recount.

Eleni looked at him over her glasses. "Do you want it alphabetically or by blood type?"

He sat down again.

And then, right there in the middle of the square, Mary laughed.

Not the small, polite laugh she'd been rationing these last few weeks. A real laugh – loud, head-tipped-back, shoulders-shaking.

Alex caught her eye and raised a glass.

Mary nodded, still smiling, and for a moment it felt like the whole village had been holding its breath for her, waiting, just as they had for the election results, for this release, this decision, this yes to herself.

Theodora didn't say a word, but she reached out and touched Mary's hair as she passed, soft as a blessing.

Back at the taverna terrace, where the sun had shifted but Spiros had not, Zorba had returned and was dozing in the shade like a retired god. Spiros was still on his bench, carving nothing into the air with a toothpick.

Maria came running up the path, sandals flapping like distant applause, waving a wine-stained paper.

"You won!" she cried. "You won!"

"I didn't want it," he said.

"And yet, here we are," Maria grinned, thrusting the paper at him like a sacred scroll.

Zorba sipped his coffee. "At least now they'll stop asking me."

Spiros sighed. "You told them I'd say no."

"We did," said Maria. "But you didn't shout."

Spiros stood up slowly – as if he was about to inspect a roof, or bury a mistake.

He followed Maria back down the lane, Zorba trailing behind with the air of a reluctant chaperone to fate.

By the time they reached the square, the crowd had parted like the Red Sea for a very tired Moses.

Mary, beaming with the weary pride of someone whose village had come to its senses, kissed Spiros on the cheek.

Claude, ever the showman, tossed a handful of oregano confetti into the air. Unfortunately, he misjudged the wind and seasoned Spiros instead.

Spiros did not flinch. He simply muttered, "Now I'm the main course."

Then someone brought out the microphone, borrowed from the karaoke machine and smelling faintly of *retsina* and stale coffee, and offered it to Spiros like a crown.

He took it reluctantly. He looked out at the crowd – his neighbours, his tormentors, the *tsipouro*-soaked conspirators. He coughed. He cleared his throat again. Then he said, "I don't want the job."

And then he sat down.

There was another pause. Then a shrug. Then someone poured more wine.

The election was over.

Alex clapped. "Perfect," she said. "As we've been telling you, Spiros, a mayor who doesn't want power is the most Greek result possible."

Spiros exhaled smoke, unimpressed. "So I'm a cliché now," he muttered, and lit another cigarette.

Everyone cheered anyway.

Somewhere nearby, Katerina the goat let out a single, majestic burp.

Claude declared it an omen.

We raised our glasses.

To Spiros.

To Mary.

To the taverna.

To all of it.

OPA.

CHAPTER FORTY-FOUR

THE FINAL WEEK OF NOT CAMPAIGNING

It was the last week before the election, and the whole village was humming like a badly tuned refrigerator. Even the goats seemed nervous. Maria called it "The Week of Nerves". She wasn't wrong.

The taverna buzzed with speculation. Who would win? Would Spiros actually take the job if he did? Would Nichos pave the lemon grove, install a parking meter outside the taverna, and introduce a "Council of Strategic Vision" to discuss bin collection schedules over coffee?

Nobody slept properly.

Alex started keeping a list of "things Nichos will ruin" on the back of her shopping receipts:

1. The road to the beach ("He'll widen it.")
2. The view of the sea ("He'll put up a noticeboard.")
3. The soul of Telios ("He'll laminate it.")

Even Theodora was showing cracks. "If that man wins," she said grimly, "I will be forced to leave the island."

"You'd really go?" Alex asked, alarmed.

"No," Theodora replied. "But I will say it loudly in the square so everyone knows how close I came."

Nichos, meanwhile, had entered what could only be described as a full, slow-motion implosion.

His campaign headquarters (his aunt's spare room) was a riot of charts, maps, and spreadsheet schedules. He stormed through the square one morning shouting about "infrastructure optimisation", waving a rolled-up blueprint like a sword. When he caught sight of Spiros, as usual, sitting on his bench, Nichos stopped dead, went red, and began yelling. "This is not fair!" he bellowed, loud enough for the chickens to scatter. "You don't campaign, you don't debate, you don't even smile at people!"

Spiros exhaled smoke.

"That's why they like me," he said.

Nichos spun in a circle, clutching his head as if he had been bested by a riddle.

"This is weaponised laziness!" he cried.

Maria scribbled it down immediately.

"That's going in the next *Telios Tribune* headline," she said.

By Friday, the pressure was unbearable.

"Please," Alex said to Spiros, cornering him by his bench. "Please just… say something. Anything."

"No."

"You don't even have to promise anything. Just reassure them."

"They'll find out after."

"Find out what?"

"That I wasn't lying."

Even Dimitri tried to intervene.

"If you lose," he said darkly, "Nichos will install parking meters by the lemon trees, issue fishing permits with barcodes, and make us wear matching polo shirts that say 'Telios: *A Curated Rural Experience*." Spiros didn't reply.

He just sat, watching the square as if the answer might wander across it at any moment.

That night, before closing, I saw him still sitting there, cigarette glowing in the dark, coffee long gone cold.

He wasn't grinning. He wasn't even scowling. He was just… thinking.

For a moment, I thought he might finally say something.

Instead, he ground out his cigarette, stood up, and said, "I still don't want the job."

Then he left.

The village held its breath on the eve of the vote.

Even the waves seemed quieter, as though waiting.

Maria stayed up half the night, scribbling predictions, re-writes, and conspiracy theories.

Claude baked bread "for the symbolism".

Theodora sharpened her knives.

And Spiros?

He went home early. Because of course he did.

A few moments before midnight, there was a crash outside the taverna.

We rushed to the square to find Katerina standing proudly beside one of Nichos's campaign posters, now lying face-down in a puddle.

She stared at us, chewed thoughtfully on one of the poster's corners, then gave a single, triumphant bleat, the kind of sound that carries on the night air and feels suspiciously like a verdict.

No one spoke.

No one dared.

Finally, Maria said what we were all thinking, "Well. The goat has spoken."

And that was how we went into election day, sleepless, tense, and just slightly afraid of what might happen if we ignored a goat's prophecy.

CHAPTER FORTY-SIX

The Man Who Mistook Rejection
for a Retreat

The day after the election – and the proposal heard awkwardly around the village – dawned suspiciously quiet.

Not metaphorically. Literally. The goat had lost her voice.

"She's grieving," Dimitri said, solemnly feeding her leftover *koulouri*. "She was counting on that council seat."

Zorba didn't look up from his coffee. "She made more sense than most politicians."

Andonis, however, was not grieving.

He was packing. Elegantly. As if folding linen shirts into a monogrammed suitcase was part of his yoga practice.

He moved slowly around the taverna, placing his possessions – power adaptor, drone controller, and powdered protein – in the case with ritualistic care. Occasionally he paused to scribble something into a notebook titled "Unfolding: A Soul's Journey Through Unexpected Terrain".

Down in the square, no one said much. The villagers had shifted into that discreet, highly-skilled Greek silence that means "we've had enough now, but we're too polite to shout about it".

Mary had vanished for the day, again.

Claude, noticing Andonis was on his third farewell espresso, leaned over and pointed, "He's still here?"

"He's leaving," said Alex. "Today."

Claude nodded. "That's what he said yesterday."

Alex placed the tray of glasses on the counter, sighed, and went to his table.

Andy was staring out at the sea, shoeless, sipping from a glass that had once held water but now contained something that looked suspiciously like almond milk with turmeric.

"You're not journaling again, are you?" she asked.

Andy looked up and managed a sheepish smile. "Just reflecting."

Alex sat beside him.

There was a pause. Just waves. Cats. The faint clink of plates being stacked in the distance.

"You know," Andy said, "I thought it would be easier. Mary, I mean. The idea of her."

Alex turned to look at him, curious.

"I had this whole version in my head," he said. "A strong, beautiful, traditional-but-modern woman. I thought if I showed up and said the right things, the rest would fall into place. Like… I don't know. An Amazon delivery."

Alex gave a short laugh. "Marriage isn't a parcel," she said. "And Mary isn't a subscription service."

Andy winced. "Yeah. I got that."

Another silence. Softer, this time.

"I think I liked the idea of belonging," he said. "Of finding something… real."

"You can't just arrive and be handed real," Alex said gently. "You have to stay long enough to earn it. To annoy people. To help bury someone. To fix a fence badly. That's how you get woven in."

Andy nodded slowly.

"I wasn't ready for that," he admitted. "I thought effort was the pitch. Not the work after."

Alex stood. "Well, now you know."

He looked up at her.

"Thanks," he said. "For… not mocking me."

She shrugged. "It's early."

He laughed – a small, genuine laugh that didn't sound rehearsed.

Alex took one last look at him, then said, "Don't be a stranger, Andy. Just… don't be a tourist either."

And with that, she walked away.

Later that afternoon, Andonis wheeled his matching luggage to the square. The Tesla, always clean, waited like a loyal robot dog.

He turned, took a breath, and said to no one in particular, "Thank you."

Katerina bleated hoarsely in return. It might have been forgiveness. It might have been indigestion.

He climbed into the car, started the engine, and glided away without drama, without fanfare.

The square exhaled.

Mary reappeared half an hour later, radiant and relaxed.

Theodora offered her a spoonful of lentils and said, simply, "He's gone."

Mary smiled. "Good."

And the village, once again, adjusted its rhythm.

One story richer.

And one boy, almost grown up.

***

Three weeks after Andonis left, a postcard arrived.

Yes, an *actual*, physical postcard.

On the front was a photograph of a Santorini infinity pool at sunset.

The pool was empty except for a single glass of something aggressively green, a pair of designer sunglasses abandoned on the tiles, and a very small dog wearing a sunhat and staring directly into the camera like it was waiting for applause.

On the back, in handwriting so neat it might have been font-tested, it read:

Dear Telios,

I've been thinking.

Thank you for humbling me. Gently. And occasionally with cutlery.

I didn't find love there. But I may have found something better: a sense of scale.

Mary, thank you for your honesty. I'll stop trying to fix things that aren't broken.

Claude, tell the goat I still think she has leadership potential.

Alex, I'm trying to sit still. It's hard.

Also: I've joined a ceramics class. My bowl is terrible. I'm weirdly proud of it.

Living my truth. Hydrated. Grateful. Sending light to the whole village, especially Mary.

Namaste.

Andy

We stuck it to the fridge – the old one, above the freezer, that never closes properly.

Later that week, Claude composed a poem about it. Theodora said something about "finally curing one foreigner", and Katerina tried to eat the postcard.

And somewhere far away, on a different island, a man once known only for linen and lunchbox philosophy was trying, perhaps for the first time, to make something with his hands.

CHAPTER FORTY-SEVEN

THE DAY THE TAVERNA COOKED ITSELF

Theodora had been summoned to Edipsos for a christening. Not just any christening.

This was the grandchild of Theodora's third cousin's *koumbaros*, which, for anyone not fluent in Greek village relationships, is somewhere between a best man, a co-conspirator, and a blood relative acquired through wine. In village terms, this was one step down from a coronation and one step up from an exorcism.

It required three full days of preparation, six pies, four blouses, and one brand-new pair of shoes (because apparently,

God notices these things). It also required a stiff drink for courage, which Theodora took before leaving, in case the holy water didn't quite take.

Zorba, meanwhile, had disappeared to Kymi. Allegedly "to visit an old friend with a goat farm". But he packed two bottles of wine and took his favourite chair with him, which suggested something closer to a spiritual pilgrimage, an elopement, or possibly an intervention.

So not only had we lost our kitchen queen, but the only possible replacement as chef had left in pursuit of goat-related enlightenment.

And the tourists, blissfully unaware of the looming culinary catastrophe, would soon be arriving, sniffing the air for grilled sardines, fried courgettes, and the mythical *moussaka* of their dreams.

We had a problem.

A big one.

No cook.

No plan.

Claude, of course, saw this as destiny.

"I will cook," he announced grandly, striking a pose that implied he had been waiting for this moment his entire life.

"I studied gastronomy," he declared, "at the University of Life."

Alex kept her eyes on her coffee. "The last time you cooked," she said, "we had to scrape frogs off the patio and send the mayor's wife an apology card."

"That was *art*," Claude insisted, clutching his chest. "Frog confit with wild garlic foam!"

"It was pond sludge with butter," I reminded him.

"And you wore a cravat," Maria added. "That was the real crime."

Claude sniffed. "Genius is never appreciated in its time."

"Genius nearly gave three tourists salmonella," Alex said.

Before Claude could defend himself, inevitably, Stamos appeared.

Stamos – the local builder of things nobody wanted, and the reluctant builder of things you did.

Ask for a wall, and he'd give you a bread oven.

Ask for a bread oven, and he'd give you a gate.

Ask for a gate, and he'd start building a chicken coop, assuring you that "one day you'll thank me".

He had the unique ability to create entirely new structures out of thin air and spite – half the village didn't know where their patios came from until they woke up one morning and found Stamos sitting on their new paving, drinking coffee, and sending them a bill.

Today, he strode in ready to take his chance.

"I will do it," he announced.

He didn't specify what "it" was, which worried everyone immediately.

"I am the village BBQ king," he continued, puffing out his

chest as if expecting a cheer.

He said it loudly – perhaps too loudly – as though there might be rival BBQ monarchs lurking somewhere behind the lemon trees, waiting to challenge him for the title.

"I make fire," he said proudly, like Prometheus if Prometheus had slightly singed his eyebrows in the process.

Stamos wore an apron that read "License to Grill" and carried his own tongs, which he raised like a priest blessing the congregation.

Alex leaned towards me and whispered, "Every man believes he's a master of fire – right up until he tries to barbecue chicken. Then it's just a question of which will arrive first: food poisoning or the fire brigade."

And Stamos had form. There was the time he turned a lamb roast into what witnesses later described as "a pagan bonfire visible from the mainland". And, of course, there was the infamous incident when he somehow set fire to a salad. Not the plate. Not the tablecloth. The actual salad. It took three men, a bucket of seawater, and Maria fanning it with a copy of *Hello!* magazine to put it out.

"Miracle he didn't burn down the olive grove," Spiros said from his bench.

"Miracle he didn't burn down the island," Alex replied.

There was a pause – the kind of pause that suggested the gods were flipping drachmas to decide whether we lived or burned.

And then Dimitri appeared.

Dimitri – fisherman, philosopher, and the village's most enthusiastic supplier of aquatic chaos.

This was the man who once delivered an octopus the size of a coffee table to the taverna, insisting it was "perfectly normal for this season". The man who once arrived with a squid that still seemed to be negotiating the terms of its surrender. The man who once presented us with a fish so old it should have been collecting a pension and telling stories about the good old days before nets.

He was unpredictable, occasionally loud, and his rare grins usually meant one of two things:

1. Impending disaster.
2. An unsolicited philosophical lecture that would end with someone crying, someone swearing, and some-one agreeing to try salted jellyfish for breakfast.

That morning, he burst into the kitchen, smelling of salt, diesel, and misplaced confidence, and slapped one enormous, calloused hand flat on the counter.

With the solemnity of a man swearing in a new govern-ment, he announced: "I can cook."

Everything stopped.

Even the cat, who had previously been licking butter off a knife, paused mid-lick.

"You mean fish?" I asked carefully – because with Dimitri, *fish* was always the safest assumption.

"No," he declared, his moustache twitching like a small earthquake. "Everything."

He said it like a promise. Or a threat. And with Dimitri, it was usually both.

And then he held up a small crumpled paper bag.

"What's that?" Alex asked, narrowing her eyes.

"See, I've even got my own oregano," Dimitri said solemnly.

I sniffed cautiously.

"It smells... fruity."

"It's special," he said, as though this explained both the smell and the meaning of life.

Before anyone could mount a protest, Theodora appeared in the doorway, already dressed for departure – hat on, coat buttoned, bag in hand like a general leaving for war.

She froze at the sight of Dimitri in the kitchen, clutching his mysterious paper bag like it contained either dinner or doom.

Her eyes narrowed.

"Oh," she said, in the same tone she used for tax inspectors and overcooked lamb. "So *you* are cooking?"

Dimitri nodded. And just like that, the torch, or rather, the tongs, had passed.

Stamos stood there for a moment longer, apron sagging slightly, then muttered something about "checking the coals at home" and retreated to his shed, leaving Dimitri to claim the kitchen like a fisherman claiming a good spot on the jetty. Theodora crossed the room, took down the ceremonial ladle – polished once a year on Holy Thursday – kissed it like a relic, and placed it in his enormous hands.

"Use it wisely," she said. "If you burn the garlic, I burn you."

And then she swept out, leaving the smell of bay leaves and doom hanging in the air.

Claude immediately poured himself a glass of wine. "This is going to be magnificent," he said. "Or fatal. Either way, I'm staying."

Maria was already scribbling furiously, "Chef of Chaos Given Ladle of Power".

Alex sighed, rubbing her forehead. "Fine," she said. "But if the fryer explodes, you're repainting the ceiling."

By lunchtime, the taverna was full.

And Dimitri… was glorious.

He moved like a man possessed – chopping, frying, stirring, seasoning everything with great reverence and occasionally chanting to the beans as though summoning ancient spirits.

When he presented the first dish – sardines, grilled and dusted liberally with the "oregano" – Claude was appointed official taster (on the grounds that he was already halfway through his second glass of wine).

He took one bite. Chewed. Smiled. Then started giggling uncontrollably.

"This is… revolutionary," he said at last. "I can hear the sea talking to me."

"Is it saying anything useful?" Alex asked dryly.

"Yes," Claude said dreamily. "It's telling me to have another plate."

By the time the first wave of tourists had eaten, the entire taverna smelled like a suspiciously cheerful apothecary.

A couple from Bristol began dancing barefoot by the lemon tree.

An Italian pair lay on their backs, staring at the clouds and pointing out shapes that almost certainly weren't there.

A group of German hikers, previously stone-faced and orderly, began singing something that sounded suspiciously like Bavarian folk songs.

Maria declared herself the new Minister of Joy and began appointing a cabinet.

One Canadian man announced that he had discovered his "inner goat" and tried to climb the olive tree.

Claude started sketching a new mural for the back wall. "I am painting the spirit of the beans," he explained, which was concerning because there were no beans in front of him.

Spiros arrived halfway through the chaos, sat on his bench, and silently watched for a full ten minutes before delivering his verdict: "*Olokliri katastrofi.*" Complete disaster.

Then he ordered a plate of whatever everyone else was having.

By sunset, the taverna glowed.

Not from the lights – those had blown out hours earlier – but from the collective joy radiating from every table.

A couple got engaged by the bread basket.

Someone proposed a toast to Poseidon.

Even the cat looked sentimental.

And yes – by the end of the night, Katerina was painted.

Later that evening, Zorba returned from Kymi, smelling faintly of goat. He brought his chair.

He looked at the scene – the barefoot dancers, the painted goat, Maria writing manifestos by candlelight – and nodded. "I see you managed," he said.

"'Managed' might be a strong word," Alex replied.

He sniffed the air. "Is that oregano?"

"Yes," said Dimitri, polishing the ladle. "Dutch."

Zorba nodded again, as if this explained everything. "Shame I missed lunch."

We all laughed.

Tomorrow Theodora would return, order would be restored, menus reinstated.

But the recipes? Gone.

No one could remember exactly what Dimitri had done. Not even Dimitri. He just smiled, tapped his nose, and said, "The sea told me." And that was enough to make him a legend.

But just for this one day, the taverna cooked itself.

And it was glorious.

***

The next morning, the taverna was… quiet.

Suspiciously quiet.

The kind of quiet usually reserved for the day after a wedding, a storm, or an exorcism.

Claude was the first to appear, shuffling in barefoot, wearing sunglasses and what looked suspiciously like one of the tablecloths from last night.

"Morning," he croaked, as if words had suddenly become a luxury item.

"Why are you barefoot?" Alex asked.

Claude looked down at his feet, considered the question, then said, "I don't know. But I think I'm closer to the earth this way."

Maria arrived next, holding a notebook covered in scribbles that might have been recipes, poetry, or the first draft of a manifesto. "I wrote this at two a.m.," she said proudly. "It's either the next edition of *The Telios Tribune* or a love letter to a plate of sardines. Hard to tell."

Spiros shuffled past, still chewing.

"Are you eating leftovers?" I asked.

He grunted. "No. Breakfast."

By mid-morning, tourists began to wander back in – not for food, but to "feel the energy".

One asked if they could sit under the lemon tree and "absorb yesterday".

Another wanted to know what the beans were seasoned with, because she'd had "a spiritual breakthrough about her tax situation" halfway through the main course.

Dimitri sat at the corner table, calm as the sea at dawn, chewing a toothpick and staring into the middle distance like a man who had seen the divine and found it under a layer of breadcrumbs.

"You were amazing yesterday," Alex told him, pouring coffee.

Dimitri shrugged. "The food was ready to be cooked," he said, as though this explained everything.

Claude, still wrapped in his tablecloth, nodded solemnly. "I think we should let him cook more often. There was a… *vibe*."

"There was also a man playing the *bouzouki* on the roof," Alex pointed out.

Claude smiled dreamily. "Exactly."

Maria flopped into a chair, fanning herself with her notebook. "I think my chakras are still spinning."

"Is that good?" I asked.

She shrugged. "I don't know. But I'm writing an article about it."

Spiros stubbed out his cigarette, poured himself another coffee, and said, "Next time, double the portions."

And just like that, it was decided.

Dimitri would cook again.

Not because anyone fully understood what had happened,

but because the taverna hadn't felt this good in months, and we were willing to risk ceiling damage, fryer explosions, and possible municipal intervention to keep the feeling going.

Even Katerina seemed pleased. She was still painted.

And that was when Theodora came back.

She didn't just walk in, she *arrived*.

Hat still pinned, coat still buttoned, the very picture of a woman who had attended a christening, kissed a baby, judged everyone's shoes, and was now ready to restore order to the world.

She stopped dead in the doorway and took it all in.

The dreamy tourists swaying under the lemon tree.

Claude barefoot, draped in a tablecloth like some sort of Dionysian prophet.

Maria scribbling as if she were recording the fall of Rome.

And the goat, painted, clearly pleased with herself, sitting squarely in the middle of it all.

Theodora's eyes narrowed.

"What," she asked, with the calm menace of a woman who already knew she would not like the answer, "did you do to them?"

She didn't wait for a reply.

Into the kitchen she swept, opening cupboards, lifting lids, sniffing pots like a bloodhound, until she stopped.

And there it was. Dimitri's paper bag, sitting innocently on the counter.

She opened it, sniffed once, and her eyes went wide. "DIMITRI!"

The name cracked through the taverna like a church bell calling everyone to judgment.

Dimitri didn't so much wander in as manifest. One moment he wasn't there, the next he was standing by the stove, smelling faintly of seawater and moral ambiguity.

Theodora stood in the centre of the kitchen, apron flaring, holding the suspicious paper bag aloft like a relic at a procession.

"What," she demanded, each word sharp enough to cut feta, "is *this*?" She shook the bag for emphasis. Its contents gave a lazy rustle, which somehow sounded guilty.

Dimitri did not flinch.

"I found it yesterday," he said proudly, "on a table in the lemon grove. A tourist left it behind. Jasper, his name was. I think he was Dutch. Tall. Tie-dye vest. Man-bun. Talked about energy alignment. Called everyone 'man', including Katerina."

He puffed out his chest, as though this was all the justification required.

"It was a sign. A gift. I cooked with it."

Before Theodora could deliver the sentence, a voice rang out from the square. "Hey, wow!"

And there he was – Jasper, barefoot, tanned, wearing the same tie-dye vest, smiling like someone who'd never had a job in his life. "Did you guys, like, find my oregano?"

The taverna went silent.

Theodora turned slowly, clutching the bag like a weapon.

"This?" she said.

"Yeah, man!" Jasper beamed. "That's my *special blend*! Super-potent! You didn't, like, use it, did you?"

No one spoke.

Claude began laughing so hard he nearly toppled off his chair.

Maria scribbled "Divine Revelation Attracts Hippie" in her notebook.

Spiros lit another cigarette and suggested that next time we should sell tickets.

"Yes," Theodora said flatly. "He used it."

"All of it?" Jasper gasped.

"Yes," she said again, and tipped the last crumbs into the bin with the finality of a priest closing the gates of heaven.

Jasper stared at the bin as though he had witnessed the tragic end of a great love story.

"You *wasted* it!" he cried. "That was my best vibe batch!"

"No," Alex said, wiping down the counter, calm as a judge. "We served it with sardines. Now go tell the lemon tree."

Jasper looked at all of us, at Dimitri, still proud; at Claude, still barefoot; at the goat, still smiling like she had been to the mountaintop, and then grinned. "Cool," he said. "So when's lunch?"

Theodora raised the ladle like a sword. "When I say it's lunch," she said. "And next time, we just use salt."

She hung the ladle back on its hook with a clang that made even the cat jump.

And that was the end of it.

Or so we thought.

Because for weeks afterward, tourists came in asking for "the magic beans" or "the cloud sardines".

Some swore they had danced with the goat. Others claimed to have seen the Virgin Mary in the hummus.

We never served magic beans again.

Partly because no one could recreate them.

Partly because Theodora would have killed us.

And partly because, even by the end of the summer, we weren't entirely sure the goat had come back down yet.

CHAPTER FORTY-EIGHT

A Mayor's Manifesto
(of Doing Absolutely Nothing)

Sometimes, in the middle of the lunch rush, Mary would catch sight of Zorba at his table under the olive tree. Not cooking. Not shouting. Just… there. One elbow resting on the table, cigarette smouldering in the ashtray, eyes following the swirl of the taverna like a man keeping time with an orchestra only he could hear.

He no longer needed to be in the kitchen – not to prove anything, not to keep the chaos under control. His very presence was enough, like the old stone breakwater down by the harbour:

unmovable, reassuring, always there when the tide came crashing in.

He grumbled, of course. About the music. About the tourists. About the wine being too cold or too warm. But beneath the grumble was something softer, almost pleased, as though he had decided that the village, and the taverna, had passed whatever invisible test he had set them.

Every now and then, the light would catch him, and Mary would swear she saw the smallest flicker of a smile tug at the corner of his mouth. It was enough.

Zorba no longer had to cook to remind them who they were.

He was the weight in the centre of the table, the steady drumbeat beneath the laughter, the rock on the beach that never moved, no matter how wild the sea became.

Meanwhile, our other rock that never moved was – as usual – sitting on his bench by the sea. The problem, as Spiros saw it, was that people had completely misunderstood him.

He hadn't campaigned.

He hadn't promised reform.

He hadn't given a speech, printed a flyer, waved, smiled, or even remained upright for more than ten consecutive minutes the entire election season.

In fact, the only thing he had said with any conviction was, "I don't want the job."

And somehow, the village had taken that as a rousing manifesto. They decided that Spiros's refusal to leave his bench was not apathy but a *statement*. That his silence meant he was "listening". That his smoking breaks symbolised "a steady hand at the tiller".

Sitting, apparently, was his campaign. And sitting, Spiros could do better than anyone. And that, apparently, had been enough to win.

"Anti-ambition is the new ambition," Claude declared, designing a badge that read "Spiros 2025: Make Telios Sleep Again".

Maria drafted an editorial titled "The Power of Refusal: Why Silence Wins Hearts". It featured three quotes from Plato and one from Spiros that simply read, "Eh."

Still, a mayor, even a reluctant one, was expected to do something. Even if that something was nothing. And doing nothing, as it turned out, takes work.

Theodora arrived at the taverna with a to-do list, written on floral stationery and held together with a paperclip shaped like a harp.

"Here," she said cheerfully, placing it next to Spiros's glass of retsina. "Your first week as mayor!"

He stared at the list.

Then at her.

Then at the list again.

Then he went back to stirring his wine with the end of his moustache.

The list read:

1. Attend regional mayoral orientation via ferry
2. Approve two new recycling bins
3. Cut ribbon at the flower festival
4. Deliver welcoming speech at the Language School
5. Pose for portrait (Claude insists on charcoal)

"No," said Spiros.

"That's not how this works," said Eleni, who'd arrived with the village ledger and a sense of purpose that frightened animals.

"It is," said Spiros. "That's exactly how it works. I do nothing. You all voted for it."

"Doing nothing is not the same as refusing everything," Alex pointed out.

"Isn't it?" said Spiros.

He had a point.

After all, his entire platform, unofficial, unplanned, and largely misunderstood, had revolved around preserving exactly what we already had.

No innovation. No change. No budget meetings with people from Athens who say the word *synergy* without irony.

Just... life, as it was.

"His campaign promise," Claude added helpfully, "was 'leave me alone'. In all caps."

"Exactly," said Spiros. "I intend to keep it."

But there was trouble ahead.

The swearing-in ceremony was coming. He would have to attend. He would have to wear something other than his regular shirt, the one with the mysterious *tzatziki* stain shaped like Cyprus. More importantly, he might have to smile in a photograph. Spiros considered this the deepest betrayal of all.

"There must be a loophole," he pleaded.

"We could say you've already been sworn *at*," suggested Dimitri, "by several locals. That should count."

"It doesn't," said Father Evangelos, appearing like a moral shadow. "But I will allow him to wear sandals and sit down for the oath."

"Done," said Spiros immediately.

Still, the anxiety grew.

Zorba shook his head. "This is why I never stood. You give them one vote and suddenly they want speeches."

Even Katerina seemed concerned. She headbutted a pine bench that morning and bleated twice – a sign, perhaps, of political unrest.

So Spiros did the only thing he could.

He declared an emergency siesta. Signed no paperwork. Agreed to nothing. Approved no ribbons. Refused to enter any building that smelled of bureaucracy, or any other building for that matter. And thus, his term as mayor-elect began.

Not with a bang. Not with a plan. But with a nap.

And as the sun dipped over Telios and the shadows length-ened like long sighs across the terrace, Spiros sipped his drink and declared, to no one in particular, "I will lead this village the way a good chair leads your spine. By staying exactly where it is."

And we, the village, found that strangely comforting.

CHAPTER FORTY-NINE

The Quiet Approval

Z orba never said yes; he raised an eyebrow. The left one, the one he reserved for weather predictions and bad guitar playing. That was his way.

Zorba was a man carved from olive wood and rock. He believed in silence, tradition, and the kind of judgement you could only acquire by sitting in the same chair for twenty-seven years without blinking. Words were for people who didn't know how to communicate properly. Zorba could convey an entire philosophical argument with the right tilt of his head and a sigh that came from somewhere around the spine.

So when he had handed over the keys to the taverna, placed them in Alex's hand, we knew it hadn't been an invitation.

It had been a test.

And maybe, just maybe, a small, reluctant act of faith.

The taverna wasn't just a business. It was the heart of the village. It had been standing, squinting at the sea, for longer than any of us had been alive. It had survived storms, debts, goat invasions, and a brief but disastrous experiment with "fusion night" in 1993. Generations had passed through its tables: lovers, fishermen, tourists, politicians, liars, poets, and one very confused Australian who tried to pay in dried mango.

And Zorba had held it together.

Not because he loved it. Not any more. That part had drained away years ago, like wine spilt on a cracked floor. He had cooked until the joy turned to habit. He had stayed open long after his body told him to close. He had greeted customers like soldiers greet morning inspections – out of duty, not delight.

He didn't need it any more. But the village did.

So he stayed.

Until Alex arrived.

Now, let's be clear. Alex was an outsider. Not from another village – *from Athens*. Which, in Telios, made her roughly equivalent to a Venetian spy. Add in the fact that she was married to an Englishman who wrote things down and couldn't pronounce "*kolokithokeftedes*", and you had the perfect recipe for local suspicion.

But Zorba watched her.

He saw the way she listened, even when no one thought she understood. He noticed how she held steady when the old women corrected her, stayed silent when the neighbours gave advice, endured the leaking fridge, the groaning ceiling, and the bureaucracy baring its teeth.

She worked.

And more than that, she *cared*.

Not in the polite, tourist-brochure way. In the roll-up-your-sleeves, break-your-back, stay-up-late-because-the-menu's-wrong way.

So when she asked about the taverna – just quietly *asked* – Zorba looked at her for a long time.

He said nothing.

But something in his shoulders shifted. He stood a little straighter. As if a weight had moved.

That's when he gave her the keys.

It wasn't a gift. It was a gamble.

And he waited.

He didn't help. Not once. He sat in his chair, his chair, the one no one else dared touch, and watched. Once, he raised both eyebrows at the same time, which we all agreed was a sign of either mild respect or an approaching thunderstorm.

But slowly, quietly, things changed.

The lights worked. The menus made sense. The goat was given limited access.

The tourists came, not for slogans, but for stories. The locals returned, not for discounts, but because the music sounded like memory. Plates were served with laughter instead of stress. Wine was poured with ceremony instead of sighs.

Zorba didn't praise. That wasn't his way.

But one evening, late, after the rush, when the candles had burned low and the cats had stopped begging, he came to the threshold of the kitchen.

Alex was scrubbing a pan the size of a satellite dish. I was stacking glasses. Theodora was arguing with a sponge.

Zorba watched for a moment.

Then, without a word, he walked to his chair, sat down, and, after a long pause, said, to no one in particular, "It's good again."

In Zorba-speak, that was a standing ovation.

That was an opera.

That was everything.

And that's the moment I understood this wasn't just about a taverna. It was about honour. About letting go of something you loved before it crushed you. About trusting that someone else might carry it forward, not the same way, not perfectly, but with love and stubbornness and the right amount of garlic.

That night, Zorba stayed longer than usual. Words were scarce, but none were needed. But before leaving, he nodded at Alex. And she, warrior, leader, Athenian-invader-turned-village-anchor, nodded back. Just two keepers of a legacy, passing it quietly from one hand to the next.

And outside, the sea kept whispering. As if it, too, approved.

CHAPTER FIFTY

THE SWEARING-IN

The day of the swearing-in ceremony began, as most disasters in Telios do, with good intentions, bad planning, and Claude wielding a staple gun.

The pergola in the square had been decorated with olive branches tied into knots of "symbolism", which Claude described as "aesthetic democracy". There were fairy lights. There was bunting. There was an old disco ball someone had borrowed from the *kafenio* and never returned. A table had been laid with *koulourakia* shaped like gavros fish, and a hand-lettered sign that read: "Telios Welcomes a New Era!" The sign had glitter.

No one took responsibility.

Maria wore her serious blazer, carried three pens, and had already assigned headlines in her notebook. Eleni had a folder of paperwork thick enough to cause a small landslide, while Father Evangelos stood beneath the pergola, adjusting his cassock with the expression of a man who'd rather be exorcising pigeons.

Alex stood with her arms folded, radiating suspicion and volcanic energy. She wasn't dressed for politics. She was dressed for an argument. And she was waiting for the first excuse to start one.

Spiros, naturally, was late.

Not theatrically late – that would imply he had planned his arrival at all. No, he shuffled in just before noon, coffee in hand, same shirt as usual, now bearing a new stain shaped like the island of Naxos. He looked up, saw the crowd, the lights, the goat in a rosette, and frowned like someone being offered alcohol-free beer.

The square hushed.

Father Evangelos opened a weathered book of oaths, cleared his throat, and began the ritual.

"Do you, Spiros Papadopoulos, swear to–"

"Wait," said Spiros, raising a hand.

And everything paused.

"Do I get an assistant mayor?" Spiros asked.

Eleni, who had clearly prepared for this moment in a way

that suggested previous incidents involving livestock and loopholes, flipped through her notes with the precision of a civil servant and the flair of a magician.

Page seventeen. Section three. Subclause (c): "In the case of incapacity, madness, or divine intervention, a mayor may appoint a deputy."

She looked up. "Yes."

The crowd shifted. A communal murmur rolled across the square – not quite a breeze, but something that made the old men lean forwards and the cats flee in quiet dread.

Spiros, who had until now shown the same emotional range as a granite wall, suddenly moved with purpose.

He turned to the crowd, and then to Alex.

"Then I appoint Alexandra."

Time froze.

A fly changed direction mid-air. Somewhere in the distance, a cat stopped mid-wash. Katerina stopped chewing on the microphone cable. Even the sea seemed to hold its breath.

Alex stood bolt upright, wine bottle in one hand, her dignity in the other.

"What?" she said, not loudly, but with the kind of quiet precision that could curdle milk and make goats reconsider their life choices.

Her eyes swept the square, looking for backup.

George became fascinated by his own shoes.

Dimitri stabbed patterns in the dust with his trident.

Claude polished his glasses as if solving the Middle East crisis.

Maria scribbled furiously in her notebook, documenting history as fast as she could write.

Spiros didn't wait. "She already runs the taverna," he said with a shrug. "She runs everything, really."

There were nods from the crowd.

"She's terrifying," offered Dimitri. "But in a helpful way."

"She knows everyone's name and isn't afraid to use it," Spiros continued.

"She has wine," added Claude, as though this clinched the argument.

"She once got the water board to back down with nothing but a look."

"And she is probably the most sensible person here," whispered Maria.

Spiros, who rarely strung more than two sentences together, cleared his throat, raised a crumpled piece of paper like a magician revealing the final card, and said flatly, "And with that... I resign."

Silence.

Then chaos.

Maria gasped so hard she inhaled an olive. Claude immediately declared it was performance art. Theodora crossed herself, then again, just to be sure. Father Evangelos stared at the resignation as though it had personally insulted the Apostles.

"But you're being sworn in," the priest protested.

"No," said Spiros, stretching his back like a man shedding ten years and a municipal planning commission. "I'm being freed."

He handed the resignation to Eleni, who nodded solemnly, then produced a stamp the size of a small goat and slammed it down with holy finality.

Alex still hadn't moved. "You… manipulated the entire village to avoid going to a committee meeting?" she said.

"Yes."

"And now I'm in charge?"

"Yes."

"I will kill you."

Spiros sipped his coffee. "I accept my fate."

The crowd waited, holding its collective breath.

Alex stared at the sky, as though waiting for divine lightning or a passing helicopter to lift her out of this reality.

"But if I say no," she whispered, half to herself, "we would have to re-run the election. Nichos could win."

A collective shudder passed through the square.

"Or worse," Alex added darkly, "the goat."

The crowd turned to Katerina, who was now chewing on a tourism brochure titled "Your Quiet Greek Escape".

"I can't believe this," Alex said, pacing. "I moved here for a slower life. I run a taverna. I write menus. I'm not–"

"A mayor," said Zorba.

She glared at him.

He shrugged. "Neither was he."

Alex paused and looked around – at the villagers, at Katerina, who was hopefully eyeing the ballot box again, and finally, at the resignation still in Eleni's hands.

"I want an assistant," she said.

"You get one," Eleni replied.

"I want a salary."

"That's extra paperwork."

"I want immunity from tourists asking where the beach is while standing on it, from the water company, the wine shortage, and anyone named Nichos."

"No one has that kind of power."

Alex sighed.

"Fine," she said at last. "But if the roof blows off, it's not my fault."

Applause broke out, hesitant at first, then louder.

Spiros sat down and smiled, the satisfied grin of a man who had passed the buck, the budget, and the responsibility for every broken streetlight and pothole in the village.

And Alex?

She accepted the position the way one accepts a slightly cursed heirloom: reluctantly, but knowing full well that if she didn't, someone worse would.

Possibly someone with a spreadsheet.

Or hooves.

And so, as the paperwork was amended, the goat was coaxed away from the ballot box, and Maria began frantically revising her headline to "Alex the Unwilling: A New Dawn for Telios", the mood shifted. Beneath the shock and the shouting, something settled.

Alex didn't smile. But she stepped forward. Took the oath. Refused the flower crown someone tried to sneak onto her head. And said, simply, "Fine. But I'm cancelling all future meetings that include the word vision." When asked about her platform, she said, "Chaos with dignity."

The crowd roared.

As for Spiros, he lit a cigarette and, with the contentment of a man who had threaded the needle between obligation and genius, said, "I told you. I'm not the mayor type."

No one argued.

Because true leadership isn't always about stepping up.

Sometimes, it's about sitting back down, and making sure the right person stands in your place.

CHAPTER FIFTY-ONE

One Last Night at the Taverna

The posters had been torn down.

Nichos had gone quiet, which was either an act of grace or the onset of a slow political sulk.

Alex was now mayor, by technicality and trickery, and Zorba had whispered "finally" under his breath before ordering a round of sardines.

So we did the only thing we knew how to do: we cooked.

That evening, the taverna wasn't just full; it spilled. Tables stretched into the road and the lemon grove. The sea glimmered like it approved. The grill was lit. The wine was open.

Katerina was wearing a sash that said, "Deputy of Snacks".

Claude had hung fairy lights that immediately blew a fuse.

Maria declared it symbolic.

Father Evangelos brought two bottles of something unlabelled and possibly sacramental. He said a blessing over the moussaka and then joined the queue for meatballs.

Spiros refused the head table. He sat in his usual spot, smoking and pretending not to enjoy himself.

Zorba cooked. Not because he had to, but because he wanted to. Just for tonight. He barked. He judged. He charred things on purpose. And the village loved him for it.

Alex ran the night like a conductor possessed. She shouted over music. She redirected the smoke. She scheduled a spontaneous speech. She accepted three cakes, rejected four kisses, and delegated seven tasks with the efficiency of a dictator with excellent cheekbones.

And somehow, through the noise and the plates and the people… it worked.

It was messy.

It was loud.

It was home.

Midway through the evening, Maria stood on a crate. "I would like to make a toast," she said, holding up a wine glass already half-spilled. "To the village."

"To madness," someone shouted.

"To our new mayor," Maria added, gesturing to Alex, who tried to duck and ended up caught in a garland made of an olive branch. "And to the goat," she finished, as Katerina claimed a chair near the grill.

Everyone cheered.

And then, of course – the dancing began.

Alex led the first round.

Arms around shoulders. Sandal to sandal. The old dance, the good one, that beautiful slow spiral that speeds into chaos, joy, surrender.

Even Zorba got up.

Even Claude joined in, although no one was quite sure what rhythm he thought he was following.

Theodora wiped her hands on her apron and danced with George. They didn't smile, not really – they moved in that quiet way people do when they've survived a hundred storms together.

The goat knocked over the wine again. We didn't mind.

Then it happened.

Mary had had the night off again. Which in itself was suspicious considering Andonis had left, and she no longer needed to keep away. She was the kind of woman who danced through fever, flirted through food poisoning, and once worked a double shift with a broken sandal and a riot unfolding after a tourist asked Theodora if she had a vegan menu.

So when she wasn't here by sunset, people noticed.

Zorba raised an eyebrow. The second one joined in when she still hadn't arrived by dessert.

That's when they came in.

Paulo first. Still in his soft linen, his tan darker now from weeks of fixing boats and lifting barrels and disappearing for hours at a time with no clear destination. He arrived through the lemon grove.

Then Mary stepped through. Hair slightly curled. Eyes brighter than usual. Dressed not for serving, but for something else. Something unmistakably… significant.

They walked in together.

Not one behind the other. Not accidentally aligned.

Together.

It was like watching a lightning strike in slow motion. Faces froze mid-forkful. Eleni's pen hovered mid-air. Zorba exhaled so slowly I thought he'd forgotten how.

They crossed the floor and sat at the best table, the corner one, slightly secluded, overlooking the sea. Claude had placed a single candle there earlier, "for ambience", he'd claimed. Now it flickered like a herald.

No one spoke, but the sound of forks stopping was deafening.

It was the kind of silence that makes you wonder if the world has ended, or if everyone just collectively decided to stop breathing.

Mary didn't flinch. She smiled – calm as a saint – and

reached for the wine jug like she had every right to, poured two glasses, and clinked hers gently against Paulo's.

Theodora emerged from the kitchen.

And everything – if possible – went even more still.

Not just quiet. *Pinned-to-the-wall* still.

Claude stopped mid-bite, fork halfway to his mouth.

Dimitri crossed himself, twice, to be safe.

Eleni suddenly found the floor fascinating and bent to re-trieve an imaginary crumb.

Alex began polishing cutlery with exaggerated focus, as though her life depended on the shine.

Even Katerina, who rarely respected moments of human tension, stopped chewing and stared.

Theodora stood there, framed by the kitchen door, and delivered a full, unblinking Theodora stare – the kind usually reserved for overcooked lamb, government inspectors, or people who said they preferred their feta "mild".

Then she spoke. "Who is this?"

Her voice wasn't loud, but it landed in the room like a stone in a well – deep, certain, and rippling outward.

Paulo swallowed, straightened in his chair, and opened his mouth to answer. "The boy has manners," someone whispered.

"His shirt's too clean," someone else added.

"Mary brought him in. On her own. On a day off," said Maria, who had already opened a new notebook titled "Breaking: Romance at Zorba's".

"Is he a cousin?" asked Father Evangelos, grasping for a respectable explanation.

"He's not *that* Greek," Zorba said, finally.

Paulo, to his credit, smiled. "Paulo. Nice to meet you."

Theodora smiled.

And then, the unimaginable: she laughed. It was low, a chuckle more than anything. But then it built into a proper laugh – the kind that fills kitchens and knocks dust off old shelves.

"Well," she said, folding her arms. "At last."

And just like that, the taverna breathed again. Tension, like steam, rose and vanished.

Mary was *dating someone*. Mary, who dodged proposals like olive pits. Mary, who once told a handsome waiter from Thessaloniki that she had an allergy to compliments. Mary, who had – until now – shown more affection to the bread basket than any living man.

And here she was.

Sharing olives. Laughing quietly. Letting Paulo pour her wine without biting his hand.

Love, apparently, had entered the taverna. Or at the very least, heavy flirtation with a dessert course.

I'd seen Mary do a hundred things with elegance: carry plates, dismiss advances, silence a room. But I'd never seen her sit through a whole meal with someone, not fidgeting, not performing, just… there. Content.

People buzzed. Chairs creaked as people leaned in. The whispers began.

Zorba said, "About time."

Eleni crossed out three lines on her spreadsheet and replaced them with a heart.

The goat trotted up, sniffed Paulo's sandal, and (approvingly, we assume) left it unchewed.

By the time dessert arrived, Mary and Paulo were an institution. Just like that.

A candle, a shared plate of *loukoumades*, and the kind of silence that said something important had already happened, long before they walked through the door.

Later, as we cleaned up, Claude leaned over to me and whispered, "Think it'll last?"

I looked towards their table, still full of laughter and crumbs. Still warm with something gentle and real.

"I don't know," I said. "But it started with olives. That's usually a good sign."

And then Mary winked at us.

Which either meant "thank you", "mind your business", or "we'll talk later".

Knowing Mary, it was probably all three.

The night ended as all good nights should. With too many empty glasses, not enough chairs, and a goat sleeping on a table.

Alex raised a toast.

"To all of us," she said. "Especially the stubborn ones."

And we drank.

Because if there's one thing we know in Telios, it's that when everything else falls apart, you feed the people, you dance with the chaos, and you let the goat do whatever she wants.

That's the law.

And we wrote it ourselves.

CHAPTER FIFTY-TWO

ZORBA'S AT MIDNIGHT:
OR "HOW WE ACCIDENTALLY BECAME A METAPHOR"

By the end, we weren't the same.

Zorba's Taverna – the scruffy, sunburned little miracle we'd built from wine crates and stubbornness – had changed. Or rather, the world had changed around it. We were still us. A bit louder, a bit older, but still here. Still standing. Slightly tilted, yes, but still. The pergola now had a permanent lean to the left. The chairs had stories. The tables had scars. The menu was unintelligible by design.

Somehow, we had become *fashionable* – and we had survived. Depressing, really. Because we only opened Zorba's to give it back to the village. A place to eat, laugh, argue, dance, cry quietly behind the olive jars, and shout at a plate of fish.

Still, some things hadn't changed.

Claude still wore mismatched sandals and was halfway through a mural of Spiros made entirely of chickpeas. Maria still took notes at inappropriate moments. Katerina had achieved minor celebrity status and was rumoured to be negotiating a cookbook deal.

And Alex?

Well, Alex was the new mayor.

Alex never really won the election; she was ambushed by it. Spiros played her like a seasoned fisherman teasing a sleepy octopus out of its cave.

She celebrated by announcing no more forms, no more speeches, and free wine on Wednesdays.

Spiros, of course, never stood for office again. He claimed victory by sitting. People still came to him for advice, cigarettes, and something from whatever mysterious jar he kept under the bench.

And Mary? She was still unmarried. Which was fine. Mostly. Probably. But something had shifted. A certain gleam had returned to her eye. She had been seen walking with Paulo along the beach, book in hand, smiling for no reason, and once laughing at one of Claude's jokes. (It wasn't funny. That's how we knew this was serious.)

Theodora was watching. Closely. The kind of maternal stare that could break glassware.

"Maybe," the village whispered, "it's time."

And this time, no one disagreed.

Because in Telios, time wasn't linear. It moved in spirals, like the dance, like the vines, like the gossip.

And we had other things to worry about.

Our fame, such as it was, had consequences. Bloggers had come and gone. The health inspector had returned, taken one look around, and left trembling – again.

For now, we were safe. But if the fame came back? Next time, we would need to be ready. Prepared. With a plan.

"A second taverna," Alex suggested. "Somewhere that'll be a decoy. Preferably uphill so they get tired before they arrive."

"A travelling food truck," said Claude, already sketching the logo. "Serving existential gyros – lamb, onion, and one deep personal question per plate."

"Pop-up dining on the ferry," offered Dimitri. "They eat, they leave the island, problem solved."

"No chairs," said Maria, not looking up from her notebook. "If they can't sit, they can't post."

"An underground taverna," Zorba added. "Literally underground. Password required."

"A rogue cooking school for emotionally unstable tourists," Alex said again, now warming to the idea. "Let them chop onions until they cry out their feelings."

No one knew which plan was best.

But we could feel it.

Change was coming.

Waiting just beyond the hills – like thunder in the olives.

But for tonight, we sat together beneath a crooked sky of stars and pergola beams, drinking *tsipouro* and sharing leftovers that tasted better because they'd been argued over.

Claude played the *bouzouki* badly.

Father Evangelos said a slow, slurred blessing involving Homer, cinnamon, and possibly a chicken.

Alex danced with a stranger and corrected his footwork.

And Mary looked happy. Really happy. And that, honestly, was terrifying.

***

The season had settled. The tourists had thinned, like *tzatziki* on the last day of a wedding. The sky softened, the sea exhaled, and somewhere, behind the taverna, past the lemon trees, the goat was chewing on the municipal newsletter again.

We sat around one long table, not out of necessity, but habit. Claude had brought his own wine. Zorba was peeling pistachios with the slow precision of a retired titan. Maria scribbled quotes onto napkins "just in case". Theodora muttered about stock levels. Alex smiled – it was small, but it was there.

Spiros was exactly where he always was, which had now

made him a symbol rather than a mystery. Eleni had already begun tracking his bench time like it was a civic duty.

And then, as if summoned by fate or fish guts, Dimitri arrived wearing his best hat, the one with fewer fish scales stuck to it.

He burst through the garden gate as if he'd just solved both love and the secrets of anchovy fermentation. He held aloft a wine glass – half full, mostly of olive pits.

"Friends!" he declared, "And enemies I haven't met yet!"

We braced. So did the goat.

"I would like to propose a toast," he continued, standing on a rickety flower crate that once housed tomatoes and, briefly, Claude. "To chaos! To stubbornness! To fish that never arrive and plans that never survive!"

"To your hat falling in the soup," said Alex, dryly.

He raised the glass anyway. "To us. A village that functions like a broken *bouzouki*: badly, loudly, but somehow still producing music."

The table laughed. Even Zorba managed not to roll his eyes.

"And to Peter!" Dimitri added, pointing a grape-stained finger at me. "Our chronicler, our spy with a notebook, the man who came for peace and accidentally became Greek."

I opened my mouth to object. But… he wasn't wrong.

"But would you go back?" asked Claude.

I looked at them, this constellation of beautiful disasters. The artists and bakers, the gossipers and guardians. The woman

I loved, the goat I'd sort of adopted, the village that had somehow made me one of its own.

I raised my glass.

"I came for peace and quiet," I said. "I got goats, politics, bureaucracy, health inspectors, three accidental engagements, a nervous breakdown about oregano, and a family."

Pause.

"And I wouldn't trade it."

There was a brief moment. Not long. Not sentimental. Just… right.

Dimitri nodded solemnly, then promptly fell off the crate. The goat tried to eat his shoelace.

Zorba, almost smiling, muttered that phrase again: "It's good again."

And it was.

The sun dipped behind the sea.

A cat knocked over a wine glass.

And Telios – glorious, unpredictable, absolutely imperfect Telios – exhaled.

So from all of us, from Claude, from Katerina, from Zorba in his chair and Theodora at her stove, from Alex with her hair wild and her soul louder still, from Mary with a secret revealed and a future, from a village that somehow made it through another summer with only minor property damage… From Zorba's, we wish you a good night.

And we hope to see you soon.

But not *too* soon.

We're trying to keep things under control. Sort of.

END OF BOOK TWO

(Book Three? Let's just say the goat has plans.)

BONUS CHAPTER FROM

ZORBA'S EMBRACE
LOVE, LIES AND LEMON GROVES

THE THIRD BOOK IN THE ZORBA SERIES

ZORBA'S EMBRACE

LOVE, LIES & LEMON GROVES

PETER BARBER

CHAPTER TWO

The Warmth You Can't Order Off the Menu

When I was a child in England, winter mornings arrived quietly, like they were sneaking in before you could protest. You'd wake under a fortress of blankets, exhale, and watch your breath rise in pale clouds, each one a reminder that the fire downstairs hadn't yet been coaxed back to life.

The frost on the *inside* of the window was a gallery all of its own: ferns, feathers, and the faint tracery of autumn leaves, painted by an invisible hand in the night. It made the glass opaque, as if winter was determined to keep its own secrets.

I'd press my palm against it. It was always shocking, that first contact. Not quite cold, not quite hot, just that strange, biting burn that made your fingers recoil before you could decide which it was.

Downstairs, the ritual of morning began with the clatter of the coal scuttle, the scrape of the poker, and the reluctant roar of the fire. You learned quickly that "warming your hands" didn't mean holding them too close, unless you wanted to smell like singed wool for the rest of the day.

And then, years later, I found myself in Greece.

Winter here doesn't creep in. It sweeps down from the mountains, rattles the shutters, and flings rain against the windows sideways to see if you're paying attention. The air smells of woodsmoke, oregano, and the occasional whiff of a neighbour's sheep.

The cold has a different face here. You feel it in the marble floors, in the way the stove breathes unevenly, in the draught that somehow finds its way under the door no matter how many rugs you pile up against it.

But in Greece, winter mornings don't start with silence. They start with a knock at the back door, or sometimes no knock at all, a neighbour coming in to see if you've lit the fire yet, bringing with them gossip, olives, or unsolicited advice about your chimney.

And that's the difference, really.

In England, winter was something to endure until the

spring bulbs pushed through the frost. Here in Greece, winter is something to share, with friends, with the village, with anyone who happens to wander in and claim a seat by the stove.

And the windows? They stay clear. No frost to block the view. Lemon trees swaying in the wind and the sea beyond, reminding you that spring isn't a promise here, it's only the next chapter.

It was winter in the taverna, and the weather outside had developed a personal grudge against everyone.

The sea was throwing tantrums at the shore. The wind had teeth. And the rain had moved beyond falling – it now came in diagonals, sneak attacks, and occasional sideways slaps that felt like regional insults.

And yet… we were full.

Packed.

The pergola groaned under its plastic walls, puffing in and out like a stubborn lung. Every table was claimed, layered in coats, elbowed by wine glasses, scattered with olives and theories. Inside, we had people at the bar, behind the bar, and one particularly flexible man *on* the bar, who insisted it was warmer up there and wouldn't come down unless promised soup.

There were two stools in the kitchen and someone in a hat asking Theodora if the oregano was seasonal. She gave him a look that suggested he might become seasonal himself, depending on his next sentence.

The storeroom, technically reserved for broken furniture and Alex's mayoral desk, had been converted into an impromptu backgammon arena. There were five players, which is two too many, and a very old cat serving as referee.

Spiros was out on his bench, as usual. He wore three coats, two scarves, and the distant expression of a man pondering the fall of empires. A large glass of *tsipouro* steamed gently in his hand. He refused to come in.

"If I give in to the cold," he said, "it wins."

We were not sure what "it" was. Possibly the government. Possibly pneumonia.

And then… it happened.

Someone brought a *bouzouki*.

He arrived like fog: quiet, unexpected, and already part of the evening before anyone realised. He huddled himself against the plastic wall of the pergola, sat down on a wooden box that may once have held aubergines, and strummed a single note.

Just one.

And the whole taverna went still.

It was beautiful – the kind of sound that doesn't ask for attention but simply collects it. It slipped through the steam and the wine and the arguing, and it settled into the bones of the place like it belonged there all along.

Even Theodora paused.

Even the goat went quiet.

And slowly, as if the weather had been bribed, the cold

outside seemed to retreat – not because the stove was working better (it wasn't), but because something warmer had taken its place.

Someone clapped. Someone else sang half a verse of a song no one remembered learning. Claude added a harmony that was legally questionable but enthusiastic.

Plates clinked. Feet tapped. And for a few glorious minutes, the taverna wasn't just warmer, it was *alive*, in that particular Greek winter way where the walls sweat before the people do.

Zorba came in halfway through a *rebetiko* tune, looked at the chaos, people dancing with spoons, someone cutting cheese with a wood chisel, a pair of pensioners arguing about onions, and nodded.

"Too much joy," he said. "I'll eat later."

And with that, he turned around and went to the *kafenio*, muttering something about needing peace and the dignity of a proper chair.

Inside, we kept going. The *bouzouki* player never said his name. He didn't need to. He just played.

And we – the crowd of villagers, romantics, cynics, accidental dancers, soup thieves, and wine philosophers – we followed. Because that's what a winter night in Telios is for.

Not tourists.

Not schedules.

Warmth. Music. Nothing more, nothing less.

Just the kind of night that leaves no photos, only stories.

ACKNOWLEDGEMENTS

I would like to thank **Debbie Chapman** – editor, truth-teller, and literary locksmith.

Somehow, she managed to prise open the cluttered cupboards of my manuscript, identify the half-eaten storylines, the forgotten metaphors, and the plot points still wobbling on dodgy legs, then calmly, surgically, and with a frightening level of glee, dismantled the lot.

And then – miracle of miracles – she helped me rebuild something I'm proud to offer my readers.

Thank you for your sharp eyes, your sharper notes, and your infinite patience with both the text and the man behind it.

(And for not once calling me a goat. At least not in writing.)

For my wife Alex

Who makes chaos look like choreography.

Who makes every Greek morning worth writing about, and every Greek evening worth surviving.

Without you, none of this would exist.

Not the story. Not the food. Not the life we somehow built, and certainly not the books.

You are the reason we stayed, the reason we laughed, and the reason the village still believes in small miracles.

You remind me why we started this, and why we never stopped.

This book, like all the best parts of my life, has your fingerprints all over it.

Even if you insist you're "not really in it".

(You are on every page. And always will be.)

You carry this whole adventure, and occasionally me, with strength, humour, and a bottomless handbag of solutions.

You find joy in madness. You order chaos. You make it all work.

This book is yours in every way but name.

Also: you were right about the aubergine. And the electrician. And the sign.

And – fine – the goat.

And finally, to the cast.

Please lift your glasses to the to the ones who stayed, the ones who left and returned, and the ones who never quite left in the first place.

And to Katerina the goat.

She knows what she did.

About the Author

Peter Barber is the award-winning author of the *Parthenon and Zorba's Taverna* series, humorous, heartfelt explorations of Greek village life that have delighted readers around the world.

A British native who traded drizzle for sunlight, Peter swapped the grey skies of England for the blue horizons of Greece, and in doing so, found not only a new home but a new voice. His books capture the irresistible mix of beauty, chaos, and humanity that defines Greek life, told with the dry wit of an Englishman trying (and mostly failing) to stay sensible in a country where nothing ever goes to plan, and somehow that's the charm.

The *Parthenon trilogy, A Parthenon on Our Roof, A Parthenon in Pefki,* and *The Parthenon Paradox,* introduced readers to Peter's world: a British outsider lovingly absorbed into a village that runs on rumour, tsipouro, and eternal optimism. At the heart of it all stands Alex, his fiery, fiercely Greek wife, part muse, part hurricane, whose influence has turned his quiet English logic into something far more entertaining.

Now, in his new *Zorba's* series, Peter returns to the same world, a fictionalised village inspired by real life in North Evia, to tell a broader story of community, hope, and the absurd heroism of everyday people. *Zorba's Parthenon: A Taverna by the Sea* follows the fight to save a beloved taverna from red tape, developers, and fate itself. It's a tale of laughter, loyalty, and the unbreakable bond between a village and the sea, a (mostly) true story about stubborn love and comic resistance.

Blending memoir and fiction, Barber's writing has been praised for its warmth, vivid characters, and the ease with which it finds humour in the tragic and meaning in the ridiculous. His books are a tribute to Greece, its food, its spirit, its contradictions, and to the people who remind us that paradise is rarely perfect, but always worth fighting for.

When he's not writing, Peter divides his time between Greece and the UK, where he claims to be working but is often found in a village café "researching dialogue." He continues to find inspiration in the laughter, gossip, and good chaos of his adopted home.

Whether you've lived in Greece, fallen in love there, or simply dream of escaping to a sunlit terrace overlooking the sea, Peter's books will make you laugh, sigh, and perhaps understand a little more about the stubborn joy of living.

The Zorba's Taverna series celebrates what Peter does best, finding comedy in catastrophe, poetry in everyday life, and humanity in all its noisy, glorious imperfection.

www.ingramcontent.com/pod-product-compliance
Lightning Source LLC
Chambersburg PA
CBHW071433190726

48292CB00001B/219